CHANEY'S CHOICE

A
FIRST NOVEL

by

Chris Parker

The Malvern Publishing Company Limited

Published by
Malvern Publishing Company Limited
P.O. Box 16
Malvern
Worcs. WR14 1UH
England

ISBN No. 0-947993-26-6

Printed and bound in Great Britain by
Paradigm Print, Gateshead, Tyne and Wear

For Chrissie ... of course.

'Life's business being just
The terrible choice'

Robert Browning

ONE

The audience filed in; hushed, expectant. Some talking in quiet whispers, others looking with obvious excitement at their surroundings. It was one of the larger studios in the Television Centre, seating five hundred people. The seats, low-backed and covered in soft green velvet, were in stark contrast to the expensive high-tech equipment on and around the apron of the stage and hanging from the ceiling. This mattered little to the people who were finding their allocated seats and preparing themselves for the programme that was due to begin in forty minutes. They did not expect a comfortable evening. It was the last thing they wanted...

Brian Chambers, floor manager of the 'Living Today' programme for the last five years, interrupted his conversation with a cameraman to watch the people filling the studio. They were always the same ...with the same excitement, the same feigned nonchalance and the same desire ...but they never ceased to fascinate him.

'The fascination of the horrible,' Brian murmured.

'Say again?' The cameraman frowned; followed Brian's gaze.

'I can't help but wonder about all - this.' Brian gestured vaguely in the direction of the audience, more than half of whom were now seated.

'It's an atmosphere thing, isn't it?' the cameraman queried. 'I'd always believed that they were invited solely for the 'One to One' spot. For Chaney's benefit.'

'Yeah,' Brian nodded, 'they are. They wouldn't come for any other reason, certainly not to watch the filmed reports.'

'They're not needed for those, are they?'

'What I can't get used to is the demand for seats,' Brian continued, ignoring the question. 'People are desperate to come here to watch, what - a fifteen, twenty minute interview? - when they don't even know beforehand who Chaney's guest will be.'

'More like a victim than a guest,' the cameraman smirked. 'They're not interested in the characters though, are they? Only in the result.'

Brian nodded a second time. 'They want to see someone hurt, ruined maybe, and they are prepared to travel hundreds of miles for that. They wait months for tickets, just hoping they'll see someone publicly humiliated. It all seems a bit sick to me.'

'I didn't realise you were so sensitive,' the cameraman grinned. 'You'd have been no good at the time of the Romans, with the gladiators and all that. Caesar, those about to die...'

'Fuck them,' Brian said and walked backstage. The audience were in position.

* * * * *

Chaney came into the sink; staring silently at his reflection as if at an enemy.

When he felt the warmth of the fluid on his fingers, he cleaned himself, needing five paper tissues. Man size. The reflection grimaced but he ignored it, intent on his preparation. He pulled his shirt straight, fastened his trousers, put on a tie; he took a large swig from the bottle of Black Label, swilled it round in his mouth before spitting it into the sink. Saliva mixed with the whisky; he put on his jacket. Looked for a second time into the mirror.

Chaney was ready.

He had watched the same video three times in as many days, but he needed to watch it again.

-To be sure, to be sure.-

He removed the film from its plain, black casing, dropped to his knees in front of the machine.

-For what we are about to receive.-

He slotted it into place and retired to an armchair, the remote control in his hands. It bore the brand name and symbol, Blauplunkt, blue spot. The machine itself was remarkable. It had a twenty-eight day memory, rapid picture search, five programme record, an unusual slowing facility that allowed you to record four hours' viewing on a three-hour tape, and he hated it. Hated his dependancy on machines. He pressed the play button. The machine whirred into action and the screen fuzzed with a million snowflakes on a dark night.

He took a drink from the heavy crystal tumbler and curled his lip in a silent snarl as the whisky burnt him: his first of the morning. Andrew suddenly appeared on the screen and he put the glass down and straightened in his chair. Andrew smiled; he was wearing a plain grey suit and, as ever, a shirt and tie that did not match. The 'Living Today' logo behind him, lost its shape and meaning as the camera closed in. Andrew began his introduction. 'Bastard!' - Someone had switched the volume off; he pressed the appropriate button. Felt the sweat under his arms '... an intriguing prospect, with, dare I say, two old campaigners together? Sorry Jon'. The audience laughed. 'Now over to you, for this week's 'One to One'.

The audience clapped spontaneously and Chaney watched them, studying individuals: they were his now.

'Facing me tonight is Mr. David Bryant M.P.' His words silenced them.

-Be still my beating heart.-

'One of the most successful of the so-called 'new breed' of politician, he has agreed to...'

- commit ritual suicide -

'... openly discuss any aspect of his professional or private life in front of our live studio audience'

- camera two -

'and before you, the viewers.'

- Face him; move the body; assume the position. Smile.-

'Mr. Bryant, welcome to the programme.'

'Thank you. It's a pleasure to be here.'

-Bullshit. You don't come for pleasure.-

'Your success as a businessman has been well documented. The youngest ever chairman of one of Britain's largest companies...'

- A bruise below the left ear -

'To what extent was your success determined by your social background?'

- It's a pleasure coming.-

'There are I believe two great forces that influence people. The external forces: family, education...'

- Fuck you. There's only one.-

'...and so on, and the internal forces. Erm...'

- Desire.-

'To question only the significance of the external forces, is to negate the importance of the internal ones.' Bryant smiled, scratched his neck. 'Obviously, I was greatly influenced by my father,'

-Say what you like. You won't finish.-

'who was, as you know, a successful businessman in his own right. Although of course...'

'You do accept that the'

- one, two, slowly -

'external forces determined at least the direction your life took?'

'It would be naive to do otherwise.'

'Then a change in your original circumstances could well have prevented you from reaching your present position?'

'I have been known to speculate about many things, Mr. Chaney, but never the past.'

- You will.-

* * * * *

Anthony Hyndman, sitting at home, watched the Bryant interview and wondered. He wondered why his colleague had agreed to appear without first consulting him - particularly with the election so close at hand. He wondered if the Right Honourable member for Malvern fully appreciated the danger he was exposing himself to; but most of all, he wondered what Chaney knew. 'After all, everyone's got a skeleton. Or two.' He mused. 'And that bastard makes a living opening other people's cupboards.'

Had it not been last November when Chaney had taken the then Bishop of Durham and opened him up to the public, revealing a drunken, rambling old man, with a fondness for children that he had not, perhaps, always controlled as he should? And the subsequent resignation, inferring guilt rather than martyrdom, caused a scandal that had only just subsided, and left Chaney's television ratings as grotesquely high as they had been for God knows how many years now? Hyndman shook his head; gave himself up to the memory. He had watched that interview and been sickened by it. Not by the wasting of a prominent Church leader: that was part of the game, and besides, he privately cared little for the organized Church. No, he had been sickened by the manner of the wasting; glimpsing beyond the clinical, callous approach, a feverish excitement and intensity that repulsed him in the way sexual depravity repulsed him. Seeing not only the professional do-or-be-done-by approach of the gladiator, but the Emperor beyond: dry-mouthed, panting, sweating - controlling. Anthony Hyndman watched the interview now, and was, ever so slightly, worried.

'Five years ago you announced your intention to enter politics.'

'Yes.'

'And then you resigned from your post as chairman.'

'That's right.'

'So that's where he's going.' Hyndman spoke out loud, relieved that he had at last determined what would be at the heart of their conversation. The Thornecliffe trophy.

'Who's going where?' Michelle Hyndman entered the room. A dark-haired, elegant woman, whose recently opened fashion boutique had already established a reputation for attracting a very high class clientele. Being the wife of one of the country's leading statesmen - a possible future Prime Minister - had certainly helped, but no one who knew her doubted her own ability or business acumen. She sat down beside her husband. 'Who's going where?' she repeated.

'He is.' Hyndman nodded towards the screen.

Michelle followed his gaze.

'Do you mean David, and if so, where is he going?'

'Doesn't matter.'

Michelle heard the note of impatience and smiled.

'Shall I go?' She stood up, smiling because of her love for her husband and because she knew him better than anyone else alive. He was not the hard man the tabloids loved to pretend he was.

'No, no of course not.' He took her hand. 'Sit down, please.'

She smiled again and obliged. 'It's just that we could have done without this right now. It isn't a good time for David to be taking chances.'

'Has he something to hide?' Michelle frowned, she had met David Bryant on several occasions and been impressed. In her experience, it was unusual for one so young to display any level of selfless commitment, but his work for industry, particularly his creation of the Thornecliffe trophy, reflected just such a quality.

'I don't know,' Hyndman shrugged. 'But you tell me someone who hasn't.'

'Have you?'

He smiled. 'Not from you, sweetheart.' He kissed her lightly on her forehead. 'But I really do need to concentrate on this. Just in case.'

'O.K.' Michelle feigned sorrow. 'I lose again.'

'You've never lost in your life,' he laughed.

'Neither have you.'

'No,' he said, the humour leaving him. 'Neither have I.'

* * * * *

Chaney sensed the change in the audience: expectation turning to impatience; well, it never had been for them.

'You don't regret your decision to become an M.P.?'

'Most certainly not. Even at that time the economy was in a somewhat shaky position, and I hoped that, as an M.P., I could make some contribution to help steady it.'

'So you created the Thornecliffe trophy?'

'Yes. The competition was devised and companies were invited to enter.'

'Tell me about it.' And Chaney moved; the first time since the interview began.

At home, Hyndman saw it and cursed, reaching into his briefcase to take out the small blue book that he had hoped he wouldn't need.

In the studio, people began to fidget, to look around at the cameramen, the sound technicians, at the preparations for the next part of the programme being made silently on another part of the floor; this was a well-known topic.

'The idea behind the competition is quite simple. Companies compete at a variety of levels, until eventually there are only six left.'

- Is it a love bite? -

'These are our finalists and from this group our specially selected committee choose the winner.'

- Can't be from a fall, can't land on your neck -

'The company who will receive the Thornecliffe trophy and the accolade of being Britain's outstanding company of the year.'

- Could have something wrong inside, haemorrhage. -

'You had over two hundred companies enter the competition last year.'

'We did.' Bryant nodded and felt himself straighten in his chair.

- Thinks he's on parade. This isn't a game, boy. -

'And this year we expect even more.'

'Tell me, with such large numbers involved, can you really assess the worth of each company?'

'Yes indeed. It is vital that we do.'

'Can you explain, please?'

'What the fuck is he doing?'

Randal shook his head and lit another cigarette. 'I don't know.'

'What does that mean? You're supposed to be in charge round here.'

'Do you want to tell him that?' Randal snorted with disbelief. 'That's not the way you handle Jon, you've got to give him space.'

'And look what he's doing with it!' The man's voice lowered, emphasising his anger. 'You're talking about giving him his own series and now he starts to screw up! I think he's past it. Have you considered that?'

'No I haven't. And I'll tell you why.' Randal blew the cigarette smoke out hard, aiming for the ceiling.

'You mention Jon Chaney to anyone out there,' he gestured wildly. 'Anyone at all, and they'll all tell you the same thing. He's the biggest bastard they've ever seen in their lives. He does to the rich and famous what most of them would love to do to the rich and famous, but he does it in such a way that they hate him for it. Maybe, they hope, just maybe, someone will sit in that chair one day and screw him, and they'll keep watching until it happens. Year after year, just like they always have. And until it happens, I won't ever think that he's past it!'

The man calmed. 'But there's not much time left.'

'No.'

'He does know something - about Bryant, I mean?'

'Of course he does.'

'He told you?' The man leaned forward; interrogating.

'Yes.' Randal met his gaze, the lie filling the space between them like a cloud.

Bryant came to the end of his explanation and stopped. One of the first things his father had taught him: when there is nothing left to say, say nothing. He waited. The silence grew. He heard some movement in the audience and he glanced towards it. Chaney's voice took him by surprise; it seemed surprisingly loud.

'What does the winning company receive?'

'Oh yes, the-er-first prize. It's really quite outstanding.' Thinking: "Why am I suddenly so nervous? We're nearly through." 'The winning company receives a cheque for £250,000 and, of course, the trophy itself. As you know, the competition has only been in existence for three years, but its prestige is such that the previous winning companies all recorded an increase in sales and profits of over 50% during the year following the award.' Bryant felt the sweat on the palm of his hands and he wiped them surreptitiously on his trousers. Chaney watched.

'I believe this year the competition was particularly close?'

'That's right, it's a well - worn cliche but...'

'What the hell is going on?' The man hit the desk with the palm of his hand. 'He's got sixty seconds left! What the hell can he do in sixty seconds?' Randal said nothing.

Hyndman frowned and closed the book. Perhaps he had been wrong after all.

Chaney nodded calmly. 'In fact, as chairman your vote was needed to determine the outcome?'

Bryant was more aware of the pounding of his heart than any other sensation in his life, but he had to answer.

'Indeed it was.'

'And the winning company?'

'Elmhurst Computers.'

'Of course.' Chaney stopped abruptly, staring, as if hypnotized, at a spot above Bryant's left shoulder. The audience murmured their bewilderment; Bryant thought his heart would burst.

'Thank you,' the voice boomed again, 'Mr. Bryant, for being my guest on tonight's programme.'

'Th - thank you.' Bryant smiled with relief. He had made it. He watched Chaney turn to face a camera, and decided that the reputation was not deserved.

'Facing me tonight has been Mr. David Bryant M.P., the founder and chairman of the Thornecliffe trophy awards. A man of exceptional talent and immense personal integrity, no doubt modesty has prevented him from mentioning the substantial retainer he is paid yearly by Elmhurst Computers for his services as a commercial consultant. I'll be back on Thursday.'

- Fuck you. -

TWO

The old soldier felt no fear. In his time he had faced men who wanted to kill him, and he had sent men, good men, to their deaths. He had appeared many times on television in the past, and although he understood the nature of their meeting, he firmly believed the children's rhyme ... words could never hurt him.

He was a frail-looking man, the veins on the back of his hands were pronounced and his eyes appeared to have sunk into his skull. He was wearing a navy-blue three-piece suit, and his heavy black shoes were spotlessly clean. Because he was waiting, he took the gold pocket watch from his waistcoat and looked at the time. He noticed his hands; they trembled slightly. It had been that way for, oh, over a year now. He smiled: time marching on. He knew of no army that could stop it.

* * * * *

There was a stunned silence: Chaney felt the adrenalin coursing through him; to his left, Bryant moved in his seat; to his right, Andrew frowned and coughed nervously, raising his fist in front of his mouth.

The applause broke like a giant wave.

Anthony Hyndman was furious. The revelation of Bryant's misconduct would cause the party untold harm in the lead up to the forthcoming election; it would mean the end of one man's promising political career; and it had taken Hyndman as much by surprise as it would everyone else. Damn that man!

Hyndman opened the blue book, found the number he was looking for and dialled it. The phone barely rang before it was picked up.

'Hello?'

Hyndman noted the anxiety in the other's voice - he had seen the interview.

'Hello George'.

'Oh.'

'Yes, I'm delighted to speak to you too.' Hyndman paused deliberately, but the offer was ignored. 'I want you to do something for me.'

'I thought you would.'

'I need confirmation, George. You have been watching television I take it? Good. Then you will understand my ... shall we say, my concern?' His voice hardened. 'I don't like finding things out from the television. Particularly about my colleagues. You get me absolute proof George. And do it tonight.' Hyndman hung up. The responsibility for salvaging the party would be his, he had very little time and he could not afford to fail. He stared at the T.V. screen, seeing the final moments of the 'Living Today' programme, his face hardening into an emotionless mask - the tabloids would have loved it.

'Are you ready for dinner, love?' Michelle appeared in the doorway.

'Any time you say.' He smiled, his eyes shining with affection, and Michelle felt the same warm glow inside that she had the first time he had smiled at her, some twenty years before.

'Two minutes then'. Michelle went back into the kitchen; he switched off the television.

'For God's sake Richard, grow up!' 'The shout, coming from the study, rang through the house and Hyndman padded towards it, his movements surprisingly fluid for so big a man.

His two children, Sarah, aged sixteen, and Richard, some two years younger, were engaged in one of their frequent disputes. Hyndman opened the study door to see his son standing in one of the red leather archair holding a magazine above his head, just out of his sister's reach.

'What's going on here?'

The shouting stopped, the magazine lowered, the boy stepped down.

'It's my pop magazine, Dad. He won't give me it back.' Sarah smiled apologetically, her large brown eyes appealing for help, so much like her mother.

'That's not true, it's mine Dad.' Richard stood in front of the armchair, hoping his father would not see the indentations his feet had left in the soft leather.

Hyndman nodded thoughtfully and controlled his urge to smile. 'I see. It seems that we have a serious situation here.'

'I'm prepared to let her borrow it.' Richard moved forward a pace, realised his mistake and shuffled back. Hyndman wondered, not for the first time, if the boy would grow up to be a politician. He hoped not.

'I'll tell you what we'll do,' Hyndman pronounced judgement. 'You give me the magazine, I'll tear it in two and give you half each. O.K.?'

'Right.'

'I'll agree to anything as long as he doesn't get his own way.'

Hyndman frowned in disbelief; wondered why it was so much easier in the House. 'Haven't you two ever heard of Solomon?'

'Which group does he play for?' Richard asked, with wide-eyed innocence. Their laughter was interrupted by a call from the kitchen.

'Come and get it!'

Hyndman paused briefly as his children moved past him. 'Yes, that's what I'll have to do,' he thought, closing the door behind him.

* * * * *

Chaney picked up the bottle of Black Label from its place beside the sink and hurled it against the dressing-room wall. A myriad pieces of glass showered the room, but the liquid clung to the wall, staining it, racing to the floor. Orgasm, bloody useless dribbling... Chaney smashed his fist into the mirror above the sink. It cracked, a spider's web, and the reflection smirked and shrugged and dared him to the fray.

He used his right fist and his full body weight, smashing it into the face, breaking it. And he didn't feel the pain. But the reflection moved again, mending, smiling and he snarled at it and struck again, taking the skin off his knuckles.

Aaaah! He hit and hit and spat, blinding the enemy to his blows and through the rage came the clarity that always served him so well before the cameras. Chaney backed off a pace, picked up the chair and drove it against the glass, the legs striking face and stomach and then it left him. The chair felt real and solid, and he gripped it, squeezing life out of it, and as he held on the frustration gave way to fear, and it slipped from his grasp. Chaney fell to his knees, his hands clutched at the dressing table and he slumped forward, his forehead resting against the back of his hands: a position of prayer. His face hidden, Chaney felt tears well up in his eyes and then they swept across his face like wind across a barren desert.

* * * * *

The pheasant was superb: a large bird, quartered and casseroled in port. 'Faisan en Casserole,' Michelle told the children, but Hyndman suspected they would forget. They were at that age when it was almost obligatory to forget. Potatoes seasoned with garlic and a fresh, crisp salad completed the meal. Michelle was an excellent cook, particularly of French cuisine, and Hyndman ate slowly, savouring the food and the conversation.

'There was a new boy at school today.' Richard hurriedly finished his glass of wine, and spoke directly to his father.

'Oh yes.' Hyndman ignored the hint - one glass was sufficient.

'Yes, he-er-he asked me what it was like, having a politician for a father.'

'What did you say, Richard?'

Hyndman sipped thoughtfully at his own drink; had there been a faint note of concern in his wife's voice?

'I told him it was marvellous.'

'I'm pleased.' Michelle visibly relaxed.

'I told him you earned pots of money and spent most of your time at home.' Richard beamed in delight.

'I don't think that's funny!'

'It's alright dear.' Hyndman leaned forward. 'It's only school-boy humour.'

'That's not the point.'

'Yes it is.' Hyndman smiled reassuringly. This was so unlike Michelle; he made a mental note to question her about it later. 'What did the boy say, Richard?'

'Oh, nothing much.' Richard blushed, the joke had clearly misfired.

'Most of my friends think we're really lucky, having a famous father.' Sarah came to his rescue and he cast her a thankful glance. 'They say they'd love to see their fathers in the newspapers.'

'I think they would soon change their minds.' Michelle looked to her husband for confirmation. 'It can be very upsetting sometimes.'

'Here,' Hyndman pretended not to notice and poured his son another drink.

'Gosh, thanks Dad.' The colour left Richard's face, his embarrassment forgotten.

'I thought the children were only allowed one drink with their meal?' Michelle's face was stern.

'They are, normally, but tonight we are celebrating,' he said, pouring wine first into Sarah's and then into Michelle's glass.

'What are we celebrating?' Sarah picked up her glass, excited by the sudden announcement. Her father followed suit.

'Us,' he said, smiling at his wife.

Hyndman was drinking his second cup of coffee, the children had returned to the study and he and Michelle were alone, when the phone rang.

'It's for me.' He rose quickly and easily, and Michelle wondered if the subtle change she noticed was real, or existedonly in her imagination. She knew that he could not have survived for so long politically without a certain, well, toughness, but that was a reflection of his professionalism, not his character. Surely?

Hyndman closed the lounge door behind him, and when he picked up the phone his voice was cold and remote.

'That took you a very long time George.'

'Sorry Mr. Hyndman, but I had to be sure.' How could he have known? The man was uncanny, frightening. The sort of man you would never cross.

'Oh yes George, I agree. We have to be sure. The question is, what do we have to be sure about?'

'It's as he said. Bryant has been paid by Elmhurst for the past sixteen months.'

'There is documentation?'

'Yes. You'll have copies in the morning.'

'And the competition?'

'It's a little more difficult -'

'I'm not interested in the degree of difficulty.' Hyndman struggled to control his impatience.

'No, of course not.' The man paused, licked his lips.

'Given the time restriction, it is impossible to prove that he influenced the competition, other than when he made the casting vote. In that situation though, it was always obvious who he would vote for.'

'I see.'

'If you give me a little more time, I'm sure I could come up with something. There are so many people involved in the competition -'

'That won't be necessary George. I'm afraid as it is our friend has rather shot his lot. Besides, I'm sure that, given a day or two, the press will unearth all the gory details. There is one thing you could do for me though.'

'Anything you say, Mr. Hyndman.'

'I need to know who Chaney has lined up for the programme on Thursday.'

'That's easy. It's Carol Hampson, the Alliance candidate for Brentford.'

'I know who she is.'

'Yes, of course.'

'You are sure, aren't you George?'

'Absolutely. Is there something I can do?'

'No George, you have done everything you could. Now it's my turn to handle things.' Hyndman replaced the receiver; a smile spread across his face. In the kitchen his wife began the washing-up.

* * * * *

'Jon?'

Chaney walked past him as if he did not exist, and Randal fell into step behind.

'Jon?'

Chaney stopped.

'I've been looking for you.'

'Found me.'

'Are you alright?'

Chaney began walking again.

'Jon, I'm concerned.'

'I'm alright.'

'I'm concerned about the interview.'

Chaney stopped dead.

'What about the interview?'

'Jon, we go back a long time in this business.' Randal felt the tension, spoke placatingly, gestured with open hands. 'We're used to working together.'

'I work on my own'.

'Sometimes there are problems. We make mistakes. We all do. We're only human, for God's sake.'

'What about the interview?' The words came out of a vacuum. See the man, the corridor, the wall, feel nothing, let things come out.

'It wasn't your best, Jon.'

-You are the best, Jon. There's been no other man like you.-

'The bottom line is, you handled it badly.'

-When you touch me Jon, it feels oh.-

'By your standards that is. In terms of what we've come to expect.'

The man came suddenly into focus, pushed himself to the fore. An insignificant man.

'You must have felt it yourself Jon'.

-Crush him like an insect.-

'Didn't you?'

'I crushed him.'

'But you left it so late.' Randal heard the words, distant and menacing, the sound of far-off thunder, but he had no choice. He had to risk the storm.

'It's never too late.'

'For God's sake Jon, it was a cheap thrill and the programme doesn't need them anymore!' Randal shouted, saw the realization flash into Chaney's eyes, noticed for the first time how red his face was, and the spell was broken.

'Cheap! Listen, I did what I've always done. What you expect me to do. And don't give me any crap about what the programme needs. Our figures are good because of me. The people out there -'

'For Christ's sake, you deliberately held back!'

Randal took the initiative, no longer afraid; the storm would not break. 'You set him up half-a-dozen times and each time you let him go! Playing games that no-one else understood. And I had to say, "Don't worry, he knows what he's doing." Shit.' Randal turned away, stuffed his hands in his pockets.

Chaney watched this man, his producer, behaving like a love-sick schoolboy.

'What's your problem?' He was calm now, and controlled, as he always was. A professional. 'Bryant will be headline news in the morning, and that sort of publicity guarantees top ratings.'

'I know.' Randal smiled, considering what he should say next. 'Listen Jon, I'm not in a position to go into details right now, but there are certain possibilities - exciting possibilities - open to us - to you - right now. It's important you show people you're as good as...' He stopped himself.

-Michael is breathing down your neck.-

'It's important you show some class, Jon.'

Chaney looked at his watch.

'I have to go.' He walked to the lift with Randal beside him and said nothing. He pressed the button.

'What possibilities?'

Randal shrugged apologetically.

'Just give me some time, huh? Just a couple of weeks.'

Chaney pressed the button a second time; stared at the wall. Randal changed the subject.

'Bryant is going to have a very rough ride in the house.'

'Yeah.' The lift was coming.

'How did you find out that he hadn't declared his connection with Elmhurst?'

'I haven't.' The lift arrived.

'Oh shit.' The door opened. 'What if you're wrong?'

'I'm not.' Chaney stepped inside. 'Serve the bastard right.'

'What if you are?'

Chaney shrugged. 'I'll invite him back.' The door closed; the lift descended.

Chaney stepped out into the gloom of the underground car park and reached in his pocket for his car keys. His hand was sore, but he refused to look at it; it was only a superficial wound. Nothing inside.

The car park was less than half full; steel columns, shadows, the orange haze of the lights. The silence.

-I will find out.-

Chaney walked towards the car, a black Jaguar, parked some twenty yards to his right. A shadow moved behind it. His heartbeat quickened, his fist clenched, the keys protruding from between his fingers. He was almost at the car, head bowed slightly; fighting the desire to scream for joy.

'Good evenin' sir.'

He saw the movement first and his hand was on its way, wanting to thrust the keys into neck, cheek, eye.

'Nooo!'

The security man jerked backwards, eyes wide with fright; Chaney regained control as quickly as he had surrendered it. He felt the blood pounding in his head. 'I'm...I'm sorry, Mr. Chaney, I didn't mean to frighten you'. The old man moved closer. 'I saw you get out of the lift; thought I'd say goodnight. What's so funny, sir?'

Chaney opened the car door and got inside.

'I watched the interview.'

Chaney stopped.

'Did you?'

'Yes sir. I've got a little portable in my office.'

'What did you think?'

'I thought you set 'im up lovely, sir. Mind you, I always knew you would. Told the wife as soon as I 'eard 'e was on. E'll be no match for Mr. Chaney I said.'

'How did you know?'

'Age and experience, that's what it's all about. He might sound good talkin' in the House of Commons, but he's still shittin' yella. He's too young to deal with you, Mr. Chaney.'

Chaney pulled the door to and turned the ignition.

-God, how I envy him his age.-

The Jaguar roared off into the night.

The roads were busy. It was raining heavily.

-Don't talk to me about class. I've been at the top for too long. Since the beginning....In the beginning was the Word....Blue lights flashing, police car... But you shouldn't keep secrets. There are always secrets. Too many secrets. Secrets from yourself.-

Chaney realised almost too late that the car in front of him had stopped. The Jaguar skidded on the wet surface, the seat belt tightened automatically against his chest; he stopped with only inches to spare. The driver in front got out. A beard and glasses and Chaney noticed a sticker in the car's rear window.

'When times are busy - remember God '

He wound down his window, the rain refreshed him.

'Didn't you see this line of cars?'

Chaney looked ahead, saw the traffic jam and two police cars; there had been an accident.

'No.'

'Then you shouldn't be driving.'

'I'm not.' Chaney turned his face into the rain, licking the moisture from his lips.

'Do you need something?'

-Arrogant bastard.-

'Yes.'

'What do you need?'

-To stone a Samaritan.-

'To know what sort of driver God would be.'

'Do you think that's funny?'

'You're getting wet.' The rain bounced on the bonnet of the car,

'Yes.'

'Do you think it's worth it?' Chaney closed the window, his right shoulder and upper arm were wet. The man returned to his car. Chaney switched the radio on. He couldn't win tonight, no matter how fast he drove.

Some time later an ambulance drove by on the other side of the road, and a little time after that the line of cars began inching its way forwards. Chaney could see the accident now: a bright red - or was it distorted by the light and the rain, or was it blood? - Cortina had run up onto the pavement and smashed into a lamp-post. The concrete had sliced through the bonnet almost reaching the windscreen.

Glass sparkled on the ground.

-Didn't you see that line of lamp-posts?-

A policeman was walking down the centre of the road, stopping at each car in turn. When he reached Chaney he opened the door a couple of inches and peered inside.

'You'll have to make a detour. We are turning all traffic off to the left, about thirty yards ahead, until we've cleared the road.' He walked on, without closing the door.

Chaney released the seat belt and got out. Half a dozen paces and he reached his target un-noticed. He opened the door forcefully.

'I've got it!'

-Jump you bastard jump.-

'What do you want now?'

'I know the answer to my question.'

'Well?'

'He'd be a traffic cop.'

* * * * *

It was Anne Chaney's birthday party. Six guests had been invited, they were all present; a buffet spread covered the dining room table - the drinks cabinet was open; crumpled, brightly coloured wrapping paper could be seen in a wicker basket in one corner of the lounge; the house was warm and bright and Anne was enjoying herself more than she had expected to.

'It really is excellent.' Russell Tobin said, returning the painting to his hostess. 'Do you sell many?'

'Oh heavens no. I only paint for my own pleasure.'

Kay joined them, bringing Anne another glass of punch - her third of the evening. 'I've never tried to sell one.'

'You should. I think you would do very well.'

Anne blushed at the compliment, blaming the punch for her girlish reaction.

'Oh I don't think so. I only -'

'Don't be so silly.' Kay's voice was firm and sure. 'You are a talented artist and people with talent should share it with the rest of us.'

'You know you are welcome to have any picture you choose.'

'That's not what I mean. What I'm saying is -'

'Do you have many other pictures, Anne?' Tobin did not want to be drawn into the debate.

'Stacks of them. Most are wrapped up upstairs, but there are some down here in the study, if you want to see them.'

'Perhaps another time.' Tobin glanced at his empty glass and smiled.

'Please let me get you another drink, Mr. Tobin. I'm afraid I...I'm not a very good hostess.'

'Not at all, you are most charming. And please, call me Russell.' Tobin offered his glass and Anne remembered the painting.

'How silly of me. I'll have to put this away first, but if you let me take your glass I will pour you another as soon as I've finished.' She glanced at Kay. 'Would you ask Paul to help me?' Holding the painting in both arms, across her chest, and Tobin's glass between the thumb and forefinger of her right hand, Anne manoeuvred her way past the other guests, towards the study.

Kay watched her mother-in-law struggle out of the room and thanked God that she wasn't like her. It was due in part to her generation, her education, and to the fact that she was not married to a bastard like Jon Chaney, but mostly it was because she had cultivated a character that did not allow itself to be bruised, physically or mentally. Her husband was talking to the Swifts and she went over to him, placed a hand on his shoulder.

'Your mother wants you to help her with the drinks.' He was tall and slim, with a writer's hands. So unlike his father.

'O.K.' And to the Swifts : 'There's no need to rush. I'll see to the others first and by then you should be ready.'

'What about me, darling?' Kay cocked her head slightly to one side. 'After all, you are driving tonight aren't you?'

'So it seems.'

'Good. Then I'll have another vodka.' She waited until he turned to go. 'And Paul?' He stopped, twisted his top half to face her, his eyebrows raised, but with no sign of anger on his face. So unlike his father. 'Not too heavy on the tonic. There's a dear.'

They had first met at university. Paul was in his third year, studying philosophy and sociology, she was just beginning a three-year course in business studies. Their first encounter had been a disaster. It had taken place in the canteen. Paul had tripped, lost control of his food tray and spilt most of his salad and iced water in Kay's hair and onto the pink mohair sweater her boyfriend had bought only two days before.

'Oh my God, I'm sorry. I mean I just lost my balance and it just went everywhere...Here, let me help you get the bits off your jumper...I'm sorry! I didn't mean to touch you there...'

Her scorn and anger changed to interest and bewilderment when she discovered who his father was. Two weeks later she was invited to the family home for dinner.

After the meal she was left alone with Jon Chaney for the first time, while Paul helped his mother in the kitchen. He walked behind her, as she sat at the table, sipping brandy.

'As you imagined?' He asked, his hand reaching down to envelop her left breast.

'Yes.'

His hand slipped underneath, forcing the breast upwards slightly. 'Had you imagined?'

'I'm not scared of you.' His hand moved lower and inwards, pressing over her heart.

'Does that matter?'

'I'm going to marry your son.'

'Here's your vodka.'

'Oh. Thank you darling.' The Swifts had moved away.

Kay saw them on the far side of the room, talking to Russell Tobin.

'I thought we agreed you were driving tonight?' Paul leant closer as he spoke and lowered his voice.

'We did.'

'Then why are you drinking vodka?'

'I changed my mind.' Kay smiled and tossed her head, feeling her hair swing behind her. 'Now do stop fretting and look after the guests like a good boy. You know your mother can't cope.'

Paul didn't move. 'Why do you do it, Kay?'

'Because it's fun.'

'That isn't an answer.'

'But do you know what is?' She hissed, feeling like a student at one of his lectures. 'Do you know what an answer really is professor? Do you know what it feels like?' Paul stepped back, surprised at her ferocity, but she pursued him. 'I'll give you an answer if that's what you want.'

'There's no need for ...'

'Remember the first time we met, the first time you touched my breast?'

'For God's sake Kay -'

'Don't you think it's going well?' Anne joined them, beaming. The alcohol had reddened her cheeks and her eyes shone with a voracity they rarely displayed. 'I must confess, I'm enjoying myself.'

'I think it will be sensational,' Kay emptied her glass. 'When I've had another drink.'

'I didn't expect the party to stop, just to watch him on television.' DavidSwift was a thickset man of medium height, with curly black hair and a beard that was just beginning to show patches of grey.

'Then you hadn't thought it through very carefully.' His wife, Jane, regarded herself as Anne Chaney's only true friend. A friendship that first developed some seven years ago, when they met in the village supermarket and Anne discovered she had left her purse at home. Jane believed in first impressions, and her first impression of Anne was of a gentle woman, possessed of a nervousness that was rarely seen in one so well-dressed. Jane had introduced herself, lent her the money and invited Anne home for coffee. By lunchtime Jane had realised the wisdom of her observation, and the nature of its cause, and in the ensuing years she had come to love Anne as a sister, albeit a younger one.

Jane smiled at her husband and slipped her hand into his, feeling the power of it. He had carried her home once, when their car had skidded off a wintry road and into a ditch. Jane had sprained her ankle, crying in pain and fear. He had lifted her out of the car; talking quietly, calming her, soothing her, and then he walked, with her in his arms, for over two miles to the local surgery. It was a memory Jane treasured.

'She always watches him on television.'

'What, twice a week?' David's voice was deep and resonant, even when surprised.

'Of course, he's her husband.'

'That sounds like an apology to me.'

'Don't criticize Anne in that way. It's not fair.' Jane withdrew her hand.

'That's not what I meant.'

'I know.' She pursed her lips in thought. 'It can't be the same for everyone, you know.'

'Can't it?'

'No. Different people have to find different ways.'

'But it must always be good.' David put his arm round Jane's shoulders and pulled her close. His presence threatened to convince her.

'Are you sure?'

He kissed her forehead. 'What other reason is there?'

* * * * *

'So Paddy says to Mick 'Hey Mick, you know every time I make love to the wife, I wear two contraceptives.' and Mick says to Paddy 'Why is it you wear two?' And Paddy says 'To be -'

-Piss off.-

Chaney switched the car radio off.

-If it's not new don't bother. If you're not new don't bother.-

Chaney swung the car round a bend. Fifty miles an hour; he felt the back end straying, straightened it.

-Michael is new isn't he?

So what? Newness is beginning; weakness. Newness is handfeeding and nappies. Newness is shit.

They say he's better than you when you started.

Who does? Tell me one. Tell me.

Randal might.

Not Randal. Not to my face.

They think it.

How do you know?

Michael has the potential. He's the only one.

How do you know?

They could replace you with Michael. Think about it.-

The cat was hunting, not for food, but for the joy of killing. It had killed once already that evening, a small field mouse it had found near a bale of hay, but that was not enough. Now it padded through the grass by the roadside, alert for any indication of prey nearby. There was none and so it moved cautiously onto the tarmac. The cat heard the roar, sank down instinctively, its claws desperately seeking a grip. Shut its eyes against the power of the lights.

The Jaguar's near-side wheel crushed its head.

Chaney saw the shape, felt the bump, and eased the car to a halt. He climbed out, aware of the tension in his lower back, and walked slowly to the front of the car. He squatted beside it and checked for damage, using his hands more than his eyes. The car was unmarked, apart from the mess on the tyre. Chaney straightened, pausing for a second with his hand resting on the near-side wing, then he walked back, towards the cat.

* * * * *

For Sylvester Harris the party held no surprises. He had known Anne for almost as long as he had known, and worked with, her husband. He did not condemn her for staying with a man who treated her the way Chaney did, but neither did he condemn Chaney's behaviour. 'Fate,' he mused, noticing that the ice had melted in his glass. 'We are what we are. We do what we do. We never know why.' Russell Tobin approached him. It was the first time the two had met, and they had not yet had a chance to talk privately.

'A strange night.' Tobin looked at the others as he spoke.

'What makes you think that?' Sly swilled the liquid round in his glass; it had lost its appeal.

'A party without a host. A hostess who is clearly not used to drinking so much; and a live television programme that is compulsory viewing. It's all a little...' Tobin searched for the right word, 'childish, wouldn't you say?'

'You're very quick to criticize.'

Tobin smiled disarmingly. 'Not at all. Purely an observation.'

'Surely not.'

'I'm sorry?'

'Observation and interpretation.' Sly looked directly at the publisher. 'Do you think they can be twins?'

'Aah, I see. A man of words.'

'Not at all. Quite the opposite in fact.'

'Oh?' Tobin's head, the chin jutting forward, moved from side to side with quick, inquisitive movements. Rat-like, Sly thought. 'Then what is your interest?'

'Pictures. I began taking black and whites and finished up in a television studio, directing.'

'Making moving pictures.'

'Something like that.'

'And which do you prefer?'

Sly shrugged. 'They both have their moments.'

'And are they both more powerful than words?'

'Absolutely.'

'Then you really believe a picture paints a thousand words?'

'No. A picture, a good picture, tells the entire story. There is no limit to it.'

'How can you be so sure?' Tobin sensed that he had reached the core of the man, and he wondered why it had been so willingly revealed. 'Perhaps it's the drink', he thought. 'He has drunk an awful lot tonight. More than anyone else.'

Sly put his glass on the coffee table and straightened to his full height. Tobin noticed the way his chest swelled proudly as he spoke, the words slow and considered.

'Every man understands one thing. It isn't something he learns, it's something he knows, something he's born with. Some people - most people - never take the trouble to find out what it is, and of those who do, many refuse the challenge of it.' Sly rocked on his heels and Tobin readied to catch him.

'I accepted the challenge, surrendered my life to it. I understand pictures.'

'That's a very romantic scenario.'

Sly came out of his reverie. 'Besides, the man who first said "a picture paints a thousand words.." '

'Yes?'

'...he was a writer.'

'Are you talking about my father?' Paul smiled inquisitively.

Tobin shook his head. 'No, we were just...'

'Making generalizations.' Sly retrieved his glass.

'And generally speaking, I usually have a drink about now.'

He left them.

'Does he usually drink this much?'

Paul shrugged. 'More, when he's not driving.'

'You've known him a long time, I take it?'

'Oh yes. My father and Sly have worked together for years now. He's a good family friend.'

Tobin raised his eyebrows; cocked his head.

'Truly. When my father first began, Sly took the risks, gave him the chances he needed. Without Sly, who knows, he might never have made it.'

'You don't believe that?'

Paul smiled. 'Perhaps not.'

Anne Chaney was getting worried; that queasy feeling in her stomach was getting worse. She was sure she was going to be sick. She sought Kay's assistance. 'What shall I do? I can't afford to be ill, not tonight, not with all the guests here.'

'Why not? Men do it all the time.' Kay was impatient to continue her conversation with Jane. 'They go out every week, get pissed, throw up, and say they're just being macho. Don't worry about it. If you have to, just puke up on the carpet. It's your house.'

'Why not go into the kitchen and drink a glass of water?' Jane saw the desperation in her friend's eyes. 'Or just sit quietly for a while. I'm sure it will pass.' She smiled reassuringly.

'Yes, I think you are right. I'll sit quietly.' Anne disappeared into the kitchen, unaware that her departure was being watched.

'So we really are past the point of no return?'

Kay nodded. 'The date is set; there's no going back now.'

Jane folded her arms in front of her chest, hugging herself.

'Aren't you scared?'

'Why should I be? It's for her own good.'

'Yes, I know but... When are you going to tell her?'

'It needs to be soon, we don't have much time to play with.'

'When exactly?'

'Some time this week. Only I'm going to be away on business until Saturday.

'What?'

'So I thought you could tell her.'

Sly was the first to see the Jaguar's headlights coming up the drive. 'He's back!' He looked at his watch. 'And he's lost convincingly.'

Tobin did not understand. 'What has he lost?'

'The race, from the studio to here.'

'I'm afraid I'm confused.' Tobin frowned. 'Who does he race?'

Kay walked forward, watching the lights as they neared the house, hearing the purr of the engine. 'Don't apologize. You couldn't be expected to understand.' The car stopped, the lights vanished, night returned. 'He races himself.'

Chaney sat in the Jaguar; smelt the leather.

-Home sweet home.-

He got out, walked round to the front passenger door, opened it, picked up a green, stained plastic bag from the floor of the car, closed the door and walked into the house.

-Happy birthday to you.-

They were all in the lounge, some pretending not to have noticed his arrival.

-Happy birthday to you.-

The Swifts standing alone, together, their shoulders almost touching; Sly, Tobin and Kay, nearest the windows, an unusual grouping; Paul by the drinks cabinet, such a good little boy; and Anne - just come in from the kitchen? - watching his every move.

-Happy birthday dear Anne.-

'I hope you don't mind, but I've brought another guest; a fellow traveller.'

Chaney reached into the bag: threw the cat on the floor; heard Jane scream; saw Tobin involuntarily step back a pace; saw Kay flinch and then steel herself; caught the fire in David Swift's eyes; watched Anne struggle for breath, eyes opening wide, and then pass out, falling to the floor, her head thudding into the tangled mess of blood and fur.

-Happy birthday to you.-

THREE

Chaney had insisted they all stay and David Swift had had no choice. Jane was upstairs, caring for her friend.

She had been the first to recover from her shock, no, that was not true, she had been the first to go to Anne's aid. Sylvester Harris had remained unmoved through it all, calmly sipping his drink as if distanced from the event. Kay had actually been the first to recover, but then she had watched Chaney. Studying him with an intensity David felt, but could not define. Jane dropped to her knees beside Anne's head, touched her but then pulled away, looked up at her husband. He saw that the colour had drained from Jane's face, realised that his fists were clenched.

'Help me.' Jane's hands opened wide, begging. 'Pick her up.'

'No.' David moved towards her. 'She must remain still.'

'Then get rid of...that!'

David knelt beside Anne, so close that his knees were touching her shoulder and upper arm. He slid his left hand underneath Anne's forehead, aware of the clammy feel of her flesh, of the bits sticking to it. The matted fur, the blood, and the way the cat's body moved beneath the pressure of his hand. He reached across, took hold of Anne's right shoulder and eased her body upwards. As he did so she moaned and her eyes fluttered.

'It's alright.'

He moved her only a few inches, laying her on her side, with her left cheek resting on her outstretched left arm. Anne moaned again and stirred, like a child caught up in a bad dream. David glanced at his wife, forced a smile, and said.

'You'll need some water.'

'Yes.'

He heard the tremble in Jane's voice and realised that, for the first time, she could see Anne's face.

'Fetch it now.' David's voice was low, soothing. He was carrying her again. Jane left the room and David waited until the door closed behind her. Then he picked up the cat by its back legs, and came to his feet. The body hung loosely in his grasp, the mis-shapen end touching his trouser leg once, twice.

'Now what shall we do?'

David looked at Jon Chaney, thought he saw a half-smile and wondered at his sudden fury.

'We must make sure it doesn't ruin the evening, Anne wouldn't want that.'

David saw apparent concern on Chaney's face: an appeal to reason.

"It's a game. He's just playing a sick, bloody game!"

'I think you have already accomplished that.'

David took a step towards the door.

'Do you?'

The smile was full now, revealing the upper teeth, and David had stopped and returned the stare before he realised his mistake. "Damn! It's what he wanted me to do." Their eyes locked. David clenched his lower jaw and willed the other man to look away. He saw the smile flicker and felt a moment of triumph, "I've got him!'" And then it returned, the upper lip curling until the smile became as threatening as the eyes. "A wolf." David felt his resolve weaken. "No, no just a man. Just a man playing games." He worked some saliva into his mouth. "Then why can't I look away?"

Kay watched the struggle - understanding it better than the others - and felt an almost sexual excitement. Her heartbeat quickened.

'Will this do?' Jane returned, a glass of water in her hand.

'Yes.' Paul moved forward, towards his mother.

'David?'

'Yes, yes that will be fine.' David blinked, turned away. 'I'll need somewhere to put this.'

Paul nodded.

'There's a dustbin outside the back door, to your left. Near the garage. I'll take it, if you want.'

'No. That's O.K. It won't take a minute.' David moved towards the door. Chaney stepped to one side.

'Take this.' He was still holding the green plastic bag. 'You will need something to wrap it in.'

David lowered his eyes, nodded.

'Good. Let me help you.' Chaney opened the bag. 'Pop him in.'

On the floor, Anne Chaney opened her eyes and rolled onto her back. 'My head hurts.'

David left the room.

Paul had still not recovered from the shock. His father had never done anything quite as bizarre in the past, and Paul's mind filled with questions. One of which was answered when Jane Swift appeared briefly in the doorway to announce that Anne would be rejoining the party, once she had washed and changed. He sought out his wife and found her standing alone in Anne's study.

'What are you doing?'

Kay looked over her shoulder and raised her hand guiltily from the desk as he approached her. Paul thought he saw a trace of disappointment in her face.

'I wanted to be alone.'

'Yes, I can understand that.' Paul stood by her side. Kay smiled, hiding her face in the shadows. "No, my fine young professor, you don't understand at all."

'Why did he do it?' It seemed right to ask his wife. Paul often thought that she understood his father better than he.

'Are you asking me why he threw it down, or why he brought it home in the first place?'

'Either. Both.'

Kay thought about the first time she had been alone with Jon Chaney. Why did he do it? 'Why don't you ask him? He is your father. Your creator.'

'That doesn't mean that I can -'

Kay whirled to face him, the suddenness of her movement shocking him into silence. She held his face in the palm of her hands, stroking the lobes of his ears between thumb and forefinger.

'That doesn't mean that you can what, my love?' Kay studied his features as if for the first time, slid her thigh between his legs, pushing gently into the groin. Paul felt her warmth, saw the hunger in her eyes. 'I want you to take me now.' Kay bit his chin playfully, felt him wince. 'Only I think you are too afraid.'

Paul closed his eyes, felt the hardening in his groin and knew that she was right.

'You're drunk.'

'Of course.' Sly took the offered drink, gin with a dash of lime. 'But then, have you ever known me when I'm not?'

'When you're working.'

'That's a separate part of my life.' Sly lowered his voice, looked directly at Chaney. 'You understand that.'

'I understand your fear.'

Sly scowled. 'What do you mean?'

'You're afraid to give yourself to it fully. You might pretend that you have, but we both know that's a lie. Sometimes I can smell your fear.'

'You are different tonight. Even in the interview.'

'You need to conquer your fear, extend your talent.'

'And be taken over by it?'

'Never.'

Russell Tobin changed his mind. It had been a mistake to come to the party. He would say what he had to and then leave.

Jon Chaney was on the far side of the room, talking quietly to Sylvester Harris. Tobin approached him, a forced smile on his face.

'Jon! I really enjoyed the show tonight.'

'Which one?'

'Well, the-er, the interview. I thought it made terrific viewing.'

-Am I supposed to be pleased?-

'Didn't you, Sly?'

Sly sipped at his drink and silently cursed Tobin; it was a topic he had not wanted to discuss.

-Why take so long?-

'Yes.'

-Unless you know something too.-

'Anyway Jon, there is something else that I really want to talk to you about.' Tobin pressed on, keen now to make his departure. 'It concerns the publication date. There is a possibility that we will have to change it. Put it back a little.'

-He's lying.-

'We're both aware that a book like yours has enormous sales potential. It's imperative that we don't make any mistakes now.'

-He's already changed it.-

'Perhaps we could meet in my office sometime next week ?'

-On your home ground.-

'Why don't we discuss it now?'

'Come now Jon, I don't really think this is an appropriate time or place.' Tobin smiled, willing Chaney to concede.

Sly thought "He smiles like a politician."

'Why not?'

-A bestseller. We both know it will be. And then a second.-

'Well...Because...well...' Tobin ran his hand through his hair, glanced down at the floor. 'This is a social occasion. People are here to enjoy themselves.' He remembered Anne, the way she had cried hysterically when she saw her face, tattooed with blood and fur, in the mirror above the fireplace. What possessed the man?

'Is that so?'

-It's my book. About my life. You only gave me the title.-

'Of course it is.' Tobin tried to force the image from his mind. 'I've certainly enjoyed myself.'

-Haven't we all?-

'But I don't have time to stay and discuss business now.' Tobin looked at his watch, emphasising the point. 'I've a busy day planned for tomorrow, and a couple of phone calls still to make when I get home.' He paused. 'Can we agree to meet in my office next week?"

'Why not? I'll phone you in the morning. Make an appointment.'

The sudden change made Sly blink; Tobin struggled to hide his delight.

'Then you can tell me the new publication date.'

'Right, I'll -' Tobin realised his mistake. 'I'll look forward to your call. Now, if you will excuse me, I really must go.'

Chaney nodded.

-So easy.-

'Please give my...my thanks, to Anne.'

Chaney waited until Tobin had reached the door.

'Russell!' Saw the fear in the publisher's eyes. 'I'm delighted you were able to make it tonight.'

'Yes.'

Kay entered the room, brushing past Tobin as she did so. He felt her breasts against his upper arm.

'Goodnight, Kay.'

'Are you leaving so soon?'

'I'm afraid I've still got some work to do.' He could see her nipples through the pure white of her blouse, and he blushed when he realised she had seen him look.

'Have a safe journey.' Kay took his hand, squeezed it gently.

'I will.' Tobin closed the door behind him.

'She's taking a long time.' Chaney was suddenly beside her. Kay smiled. She had never heard him refer to Anne by name.

'Any woman would. It's not often we get the chance to make two entrances in one evening.'

'Have you been with her?'

'Of course not. I was in the study.'

'Alone?'

'For a time.' He was very close to her; Kay made sure they did not touch.

-So you think you are going to marry my son?

I know I will.

You know nothing.

I know many things.

I have no reason to believe that.

How can I prove it to you?

Leave your brandy. Walk with me into the study-

Paul had no desire to follow Kay back to the party. Instead, he opened the patio doors and walked out, into the garden. The fruit trees made a clicking noise as the wind moved among their branches, the grass, frost covered, crunched beneath his feet and the night air chilled him. Paul breathed in deeply, held his breath until he could feel his heart pounding and then exhaled. He watched his breath turn into mist.

"Why can't I hate? God knows, there are so many reasons why I should."

Paul turned to face the house. The light in his mother's bedroom was still on. Through the curtains he could see two shadows: one low and still - his mother, perhaps, sitting on the bed - the second moving freely around the room, its movements always centring on the other. That will be Jane, he decided. Helping.

"God, why can't I hate?"

- Because you are scared.-

The first shadow stood up and moved; the light in the bedroom went out.

"She's ready! She's going back to the party!"

Paul's feet slipped on the grass as he raced into the house.

'Where's mother?'

Kay spun round, startled, and moved half a pace away from his father.

'Where have you been?'

'Outside.'

Kay noticed the moisture on his shoes.

'Where's mother?'

'Upstairs.'

'No, she isn't.' Jane Swift entered the room, smiling in triumph. Her eyes revealed her fear. 'Ladies and gentlemen. The birthday girl!'

Jon Chaney led the applause; Kay the last to join in. Anne stopped barely two paces inside the room, her hands raised protectively in front of her chest.

'I would just like to say ...' Chaney stepped forward, walking towards Anne with his hands open, reaching for hers. The applause stopped abruptly.

'...that on this very special night, it is my pleasure to see my wife looking so well. ' Chaney led Anne into the centre of the room.

David Swift saw the fear grow in his wife's face, realised that she was looking at him and hoped that his own fear did not show.

'And she is looking so very well.' Chaney continued, 'Don't you agree?'

The silence was not complete: Paul shuffled nervously; Sly picked up his glass from the coffee table, the crystal clinked against his heavy, gold bracelet.

'Well. Don't you?' Chaney's voice hardened. 'Paul?' Chaney raised his left hand, pointing the forefinger at his son. 'Isn't it true to say that your mother hasn't changed in the last decade?'

Paul glanced at Kay, realised that she had moved away and was watching him.

"She is observing him," Sly thought.

'No, I don't think she's changed.' Paul said at last. Anne returned his smile.

'Of course you don't - and you'd be right. She hasn't changed for years, and you - our dearest friends - can see her now looking as she has for what seems like an eternity. Not a day over sixty.'

Jane saw her husband's knuckles whiten as he gripped his glass; saw Anne's face pale behind the recently applied make-up. "Please God, not again!"

Jon Chaney felt the silence this time. It entered the room with an almost physical presence, and he welcomed it, encouraged it, until he knew it had touched them all, and then he laughed.

'Jon?' It was the first time Anne had spoken since her reappearance. 'What have you done to your hand?' Chaney's laughter stopped. Anne lifted his hand so that she could see it more clearly. The skin was torn in places, but more noticeable than that, what had first caught her attention, was the bruise, jet black in colour, running down the back of the hand from the middle knuckle to the wrist.

'There's nothing wrong with it.' Chaney pulled away and flexed his fingers.

'My hand has nothing wrong with it.'

David Swift saw the ugly bruise, following the line of the bone. "It's broken," he thought.

'But look at it.' Anne followed Chaney, trying to take the hand again. 'It's in a terrible state. What have you done to it?'

'Nothing.' Chaney brushed past her, moving towards the door. 'Forget it..'

'But it could be serious. I think you should ...'

But he was already gone, slamming the door behind him. They heard his footsteps going up the stairs, and then a sudden pause.

Chaney stopped, stared at his hand, smashed it down onto the bannister.

'It doesn't hurt!' he shouted, his voice echoing around the house.

Later that night Jon Chaney woke from his nightmare and felt the pain in his hand. He sat bolt upright in the bed, forced the images from his mind.

Slowly Chaney regained control of his breathing. Beside him Anne snored gently. He got out of bed, put on his dressing-gown and went downstairs. The lounge stank of alcohol. He could see two wine bottles standing by the fireplace. The drinks cabinet was still open.

'God, it's cold!'

Chaney thought he saw the curtains moving in Anne's study and moved forward to investigate. Someone had left a glass on the floor and Chaney kicked it over.

'Shit!'

The French doors were open and Chaney pulled them to, fastened both locks and drew the curtains. Someone, probably Paul, had forgotten to close them earlier in the evening.

-Shall I close the doors?

No.

Then what shall I do?

There are rules.

You disappoint me.

My rules.

I understand.

Look to your left. Can you see into the dining-room?

Yes.

Clearly?

Yes.

Can you hear them in the kitchen?

Yes.

Then show me what you know.-

She knelt down before him and undid his trousers. He was hard before she touched him.

FOUR

The old soldier took his seat on the dais and poured himself half a glass of water. He raised it to his lips and drank. His hands stopped trembling.

Peter Randal arrived at his office early that morning to find the day's newspapers waiting for him in a neat pile on his desk. He poured himself a coffee, black, no sugar, and scoured the papers, interested in only one item. He found it in every edition, and one tabloid even led with the story.

"They are jumping the gun," Randal thought, but the paper's enthusiasm relaxed him, increased his own confidence.

"Chaney's got them looking, and with a bit of luck it will turn into a race. The first to the kill."

He eased back into his chair, loosened his tie, undid the top button of his shirt.

"Unless of course they are given something else to distract them."

Randal considered again the phone call that had woken him some two hours earlier.

'Mr. Randal?'

'Yes.'

'This is Anthony Hyndman speaking.'

'I'm sorry?' Randal stifled a yawn and looked at his alarm clock: 6.05.

'Anthony Hyndman.'

'Oh. Yes Mr. Hyndman. I'm sorry.'

'There is a matter of some urgency I wish to discuss with you.'

'When?' Randal sat upright in his bed, like a soldier coming to attention.

'Now.'

'I see.'

'Good.'

Randal shivered. The voice was no more than a gentle caress, but it contained a quality that reminded him of a surgeon's knife. 'It concerns your programme 'Living Today'.'

'Yes, Mr. Hyndman.'

'I would like to take part in that programme. Specifically in the section you call 'One to One'.'

Randal felt his heart leap. 'I'm sure that could be arranged Mr. Hyndman. We would be delighted to have you on the programme. Could you give me some indication when you would be available?'

'Tomorrow.'

'What?' Randal swung his legs over the side of the bed, ran his hand through his hair.

'There is, as they say, no time like the present.'

'But I'm afraid that would be quite impossible, Mr. Hyndman. You see, we have already arranged for ...'

'...Carol Hampson to appear. I know.'

'Then you must see why...'

'...last night she agreed to step down. To let me take her place.'

'Why the hell would she do that?' Randal stood up, realised that he was shouting at one of the country's most illustrious politicians and didn't care. It was his programme.

'Let's just say it was an act of noblesse oblige.'

'You can't expect me to believe that. She isn't even in your party!'

'Frankly Mr. Randal, I don't care what you believe. The point is, you have a vacancy to fill and I am offering to fill it. Now, do you really want to turn me down?'

Randal resisted the urge to hang up. Hyndman was right. And it would make terrific television.

'As I said Mr. Hyndman, we would be delighted. It has just come as something of a ...'

'...Shock? Yes, I can understand that.' The voice was almost a whisper. Randal strained to hear it. 'And who knows? It might not be the last.'

The line went dead, left a buzzing in his ear that struggled to break into his consciousness.

The orange light on his intercom was flashing; Randal pressed the appropriate switch.

'Yes Tracey?'

'Mr. Chaney is here. Shall I send him in?'

'Yes.'

Chaney opened the office door and walked into the room. Randal rose to greet him.

'How are you this morning?'

Chaney shrugged and sat down. Randal followed suit. He saw the bruise that dominated the back of Chaney's right hand and remembered the broken mirror in the dressing room. Still, today there were more important things to consider.

'Have you seen the papers?'

'No.'

-Of course I've seen the papers. I gambled on the papers.-

'It's just what we needed, they went for it in a big way. But they were cautious Jon.'

-Not all of them.-

'They talked about implications, possibilities. Nobody wanted to commit themselves on this one.'

-Yet-

'But I'm sure when they start digging, they'll come up with something.'

-He isn't scared of it anymore. He's scared of something else.-

Randal steepled his fingers and leant forwards onto the desk, taking his weight on his forearms. He smiled at Chaney.

-He doesn't want to tell me, but he's got to. It's something urgent.-

'Tell me something Jon.'

'What?'

'About Carol Hampson.'

'What do you want to know?'

'What have you found out about her?'

-He never asks.-

'Why?'

Randal placed the palms of his hands against the desk top and eased himself back. He rolled his head slowly round his shoulders, heard the uppermost part of his spine clicking as he did so.

-You can run, but you can't hide. -

'Let me put it another way Jon. How easy was it to find out about Carol Hampson? I mean, could someone else come into possession of the same information. If they had the right contacts?'

Chaney's eyes narrowed.

-What the fuck is happening here?-

'It's possible.'

'That's what I thought.'

-Someone's blown it.-

Randal stood up, rapped the desk with his knuckles and walked behind Chaney.

-Keep looking straight ahead boy.-

'I had a phone call this morning Jon. Very early this morning.'

'There's no law against it.'

'From Anthony Hyndman.'

-Bryant!-

'Although he didn't say it outright, the nature of our conversation inferred that you were right about Bryant. His days are numbered.'

'Why would he let you know that?'

Randal stopped walking, rested his hands on the back of Chaney's chair.

-You're not my fuckin' barber.-

'Why does any politician do something for nothing?'

'What does he want?'

'He wants you Jon.' Randal moved again, to the far side of the room, and poured himself another coffee. Chaney barely noticed.

-Push your shoulders down. Relax your hands, your feet. That's it. Now control your breathing, slow the heartbeat, that's the most important thing. That's it. That's it. Stay in control.-

'He wants to be in Thursday's programme, Jon.'

Chaney spun in his chair, faced his producer.

'That's impossible. We can't cancel.' And then he understood.

-Of course. Hyndman's found out too. Used it to scare her off.-

'You agreed?'

Randal nodded, looked away. 'Yes. To be honest with you Jon, I wouldn't have refused even if I'd wanted to. For years now the press have painted him as the party hard man.' Randal chuckled. 'He is probably the only man in the country who is as unpopular as you. It will make compulsive viewing. Think about it.'

The orange light on the intercom flashed and the machine buzzed like an angry wasp. Randal crossed to his desk, sat down and flicked the switch, his movements sharp and impatient. 'Tracey, I don't want to be disturbed. I'm busy.' He looked across his desk at Chaney and forced himself to continue. 'He's taking a terrific gamble, Jon. If you can find something that will take him out, the damage it will cause to the party will be enormous.'

'And if I can't?'

Randal stared into his coffee. 'You have no choice Jon. As I said yesterday, this is an important time for you.'

-That again! So many bloody questions.-

'Then postpone it. Give me some time.'

'I can't do that.'

Chaney slammed the desk with his hand. Randal saw him pale slightly. 'What the hell do you expect me to do? I'm not a bloody magician!'

'But that's just what you are! To the people out there, you're the man who pulls the truth out of some invisible hat and shows it to the nation.'

Chaney pushed himself away from the desk and stood up. 'You're really going through with it?'

'All the way.'

'What if I screw up?'

'You can't.'

'If I do?'

'You have no choice, Jon.'

'Bullshit.' Chaney stormed out of the door, slamming it behind him.

-There's always a choice.-

* * * * *

Anthony Hyndman was aware of the risk he was taking, but it did not worry him unduly. "After all," he told himself as he drank his first cup of tea of the morning, "I have the initiative. I arranged the encounter, to put him on the defensive. He has so little time to work in, that is a key factor. The element of surprise is mine." He glanced at his watch. "I wonder if he knows yet?" Michelle joined him at the table, placing the laden toast rack between them.

'What happened last night? I saw so little of you after dinner, I forgot to ask.'

'About what?' Hyndman selected a piece of toast.

'David. On television.'

'Oh, that. I take it you haven't seen the papers yet this morning?'

'Oh dear. That sounds ominous.'

'Mmm.' He chose the orange marmalade.

'What will happen to him?'

'I'm sure he will do the honourable thing.'

'And the party?'

'Aah.' Hyndman spread the marmalade carefully, evenly, paying it too much attention. 'Now that is a little more worrying.'

'What will you do?' Michelle never doubted that it would be her husband's job.

'I already have.' He smiled at her and took his first bite of toast.

'Can you tell me?'

'Of course.' And he did. Emphasising the need for a swift response, the lack of public credibility the disclosure would cause the party and the fact that Chaney had barely thirty six hours to prepare for a new interview. He was careful not to mention the telephone conversation he had had with Carol Hampson.

'But...but that's blackmail!'

'You can hardly call it that. Why not look on it instead as one professional's attempt to save the career of a colleague?'

'Suppose I tell you to piss off?'

'You could always take that risk.'

'Besides, you could be bluffing. You can't know for sure that Chaney has that information.'

'That's true, but I can be sure that he will have the information by Thursday night.'

'You bastard!'

'Please, that's no way to talk to someone who, after all, is only trying to do you a favour...'

Michelle frowned. Despite his matter-of-fact approach she knew that he was taking a gamble. And for very high stakes. Michelle felt a small knot of fear in her stomach. "That's to be expected," she told herself."I'm afraid for my husband, in case he loses."She picked up her knife and chose her first piece of toast, the unwanted doubt still nagging in her mind.

'You are very quiet all of a sudden.' Hyndman poured himself a second cup of tea.

'What do you expect? I worry about you.' Michelle smiled weakly.

'You don't need to.' Hyndman slid his hand reassuringly over hers. 'I can handle Chaney.'

"But I'm scared of what will happen if you don't."

Michelle put down her knife and raised her napkin to her mouth, trying to hide her fear. "I'm scared of what I might find out."

When Anne Chaney woke up that morning, her husband had already gone. He had slept alone in the second bedroom and after she had made her own bed, she tidied that. The shirt he had been wearing sat in a crumpled heap on the chair, his socks and underpants were on the floor. With both rooms tidy, Anne went into the bathroom, washed, combed her hair, and went downstairs.

Within an hour she had hoovered, washed the glasses and plates, and put the empty bottles outside by the dustbin. With that done, she poured herself a glass of orange juice and took it with her into the study. Today she would begin a new work. A charcoal sketch of a stray dog she had photographed some weeks earlier. All Anne's pictures were of animals, but this one was different.

"My first character study." Anne reminded herself, clipping the photo to the board, above the left-hand corner of the paper. "All these pictures, and this is the first time I have ever tried anything even a little bit different." Anne smiled, a sad, wistful smile; she was willing to admit the fear to herself, but she was still ashamed by it. "Drawing and painting animals now for all those years. Ever since ..."

The memory made her stop her preparations and added to her mood of melancholy. Anne could see it still, as clearly as the photo on the board before her: the colour, the movement, the expressions. And because she felt herself being pulled into it, Anne closed her eyes, squeezing them tightly shut, until the picture dissolved into blackness and she could no longer see it.

"Concentrate," she told herself. 'You must learn to concentrate.' And with that Anne picked up a charcoal pencil and began her first, preliminary sketch.

* * * * *

Anthony Hyndman arrived at his office at 9.30. He had been there for a little over one hour when his secretary told him about the call.

'Thank you, Pauline.'

Hyndman picked up the phone.

'Hello George. I had just about given you up for dead.'

'I'm sorry Mr. Hyndman. I couldn't contact you any sooner, you see -'

'I'm not terribly interested George.' There was a polite knock on the door, and Hyndman's secretary entered the office, placing a buff-coloured folder on the desk in front of him. Hyndman's raised eyebrows signalled his thanks. He watched the sway of her bottom as she left the room. 'What I am interested in, are the results of the recent Marplan poll concerning the presence of nuclear arms in this country.' Hyndman opened the folder, left the receiver snuggled between his left ear and shoulder. It contained the information he needed for this afternoon's meeting. He began to digest it, storing it in the compartment he had already mentally reserved for it.

'Yes George, I realise the figures are not due for official release until the 30th. Unfortunately I can't afford to wait that long.'

It was the way he always worked, the reason why he was so efficient: keeping his mind as orderly and organized as a filing cabinet. It was an ability Hyndman had first developed during his teens. As an enthusiastic chess champion with his sights set on national selection, he challenged his friends to play him, three or four at the same time, while he, the aspiring master, turned his back to the boards; relied solely on his memory to beat them. By the time he left school, he had been able to play six opponents at once in this fashion, could see six grey cabinets in his mind, could make a move and then lock it away until its turn came again.

'I need them on my desk by mid-day tomorrow, at the latest.'

During his years at university, Hyndman lost his desire to become a chess champion, realising instead that there was a greater game of strategy he could enjoy. A game in which the principles were the same, but the rewards infinitely greater. So he turned again to the grey cabinets in his mind, and they had remained with him over the years, growing steadily in number as his responsibilities increased, until now he could open and close any number of them at will, without ever letting one spill over into another. It was the way he organized his life.

'Thank you George. I'm sure you will.'

Hyndman replaced the receiver and closed the folder. He drummed his fingers on the top of the desk and smiled, feeling the smile spread across his face until his cheeks touced the lower rim of his glasses. He was ready now. George would get him the information he required - would not dare do otherwise - and Chaney could not expect that; could not prepare for it. Yes, he was ready now. The cabinet closed.

Hyndman leant forward, spoke into the intercom.

'Pauline. Will you come through.'

The office door opened.

'Yes, Mr. Hyndman?'

'Two things Pauline. I would like you to make sure that a dozen red roses reach home before I do.'

She made a note on her pad.

'Then I want you to send a telegram saying ...er...'

Hyndman leant back in his chair, looked up at the ceiling. '...Appreciate your willingness to oblige. Looking forward to our meeting. Yours etc.' He brought his weight forward, looked again at his secretary. She had already finished writing. 'That is to go to the television studios. To Mr. Jon Chaney. O.K.?'

'Yes sir.' Pauline turned to go.

'And Pauline?'

'Yes Mr. Hyndman?'

'Don't forget the roses.'

He waited until the door had closed behind her and then turned his attention to the blue, heavy folder on the right of his desk. Opened another cabinet.

* * * * *

Chaney poured himself another whisky, sat down in the armchair, found the silence in the room oppressive. He had left Randal's office that morning, walked down the stairs, out of the building and into the car park. Michael had just arrived. His Rover was parked next to the Jaguar and he greeted Chaney with a cheerful smile.

'How's it going, Jon?'

Michael was a good looking man, with short blond hair, the body of an athlete and a manner that reminded Chaney of himself some twenty years before.

'Who's on the programme tomorrow?'

'I am'.

Chaney's first instinct had been to drive to Katherine's house, but he changed his mind before he was half-way there.

'Hello Jon. What a surprise to see you. You don't normally come round on a Wednesday.'

"No. I've got some free time today.'

'Are you alright Jon?'

-Piercing brown eyes.

They can see inside you.

Almost.-

'Of course I am.'

'Are you sure?'

'God no, I'm scared.'

-Hold her tight. Lose control of the fears.-

'You don't know how scared...'

So he had driven aimlessly, out of the city. Travelling much too fast, using motorways and side roads. Overtaking other traffic, taking far too many chances and trying to lose himself in the power of the car. When that failed, Chaney stopped on a grass verge on a quiet country road and tried to sleep. Ordered himself to centre on the darkness before his eyes, but he could not, feeling instead the memories growing inside, and he squeezed his eyes together to shut them out. The darkness sparkled with light and the pictures appeared.

A small boy, smartly dressed in the black and gold of his school uniform, reaching up to hold his mother's hand as they walked between the rows of beds. Their reflections shimmering in the floor, her footsteps crisp, echoing.

'Why is it so quiet, mother?'

'Because the people here are poorly, dear.'

'Why don't they all have visitors, mother?'

'Because some people don't have a family.'

'Don't they have friends?'

'Some don't.'

Walking past. Being watched. Holding your hand tightly.

'That means Daddy is one of the lucky ones?'

'Yes dear.'

Here he is now. Sitting up. Wearing the red pyjamas we bought him specially for this visit.

'Hello, Daddy.'

Chaney swirled the whisky round in the glass and stared into it.

-They give you so little time.-

The liquid settled.

-And expect you to use it-

The clock in the hallway chimed four.

-You've got two days Jon, and you can't afford to lose. Find something. In two days.-

The front doorbell rang.

-But that isn't true, is it? They didn't give you two days.-
'No, less than two days.'

The front doorbell rang.

-He has only the same amount of time, but he made the decision. That has never happened before. It has always been my decision.

Before.-I can't afford to lose...-'

'It's open!'

Paul entered the room. He was wearing a navy blue Adidas sweatsuit and white training shoes.

'Aren't you ready?'

'No.' Chaney finished his drink.

'Are we still playing?'

'Why?'

'You are normally ready to go.' Paul gestured towards the glass in Chaney's hand. 'Do you think it's a good idea?'

'It won't affect me. I'll still be able to grip the racket. Hard enough to beat you.'

Paul frowned. 'How many have you had?'

'What are you talking about?'

'The drink.'

'The drink makes no difference.' Chaney stood up.

'Then what were you ...' Paul realised his mistake...'Of course, your hand. I'd forgotten about that.'

-So had I.-

Chaney walked over to the drinks cabinet, unscrewed the top off the whisky bottle, felt a twinge of pain. 'Do you want one?'

Paul shook his head. 'The court is booked for half past.'

Chaney poured himself a measure. 'Just a small one then.'

'At least it should deaden the pain,' Paul said.

'From what?'

Chaney stood by the cabinet, applying pressure to the glass with each finger in turn, found the weakness.

'There is always a weakness.'

'How do you know, Jon?' Sly scratched his head in bewilderment. The light reflected off the heavy, gold bracelet.

'It's the law of nature. I can prove it to you.'

'How?'

'Put me in front of the cameras. Let me choose my guests. I will show you their weaknesses...'-

'Your hand. It must be sore.'

'Do you think it will give you an advantage?'

-There is no pain-.

'I hope not. I would prefer to beat you when you are at your best.' Paul perched himself on the chair arm, and noticed the way his father's fingers were working on the glass. "I feel nothing," he thought."If he died in front of me now, I would feel only that I had been robbed. Of my chance to hate."

'You will never beat me.' Chaney put the glass on the cabinet. The drink was untouched. 'If I was blind and crippled, you would never beat me.'

'Why is that?' Paul had been playing squash for over three years now, his father less than half that time. Although they played together at least once every week, Paul had never beaten him.

'Because you only want to win.'

'And?'

'And I need to.' Chaney strode out, into the hall, in search of his sports bag. 'That's the difference between us. Why I'm a success and you will never be.'

Paul followed him. 'I don't think I would ever want to be what you would regard as a success, father.'

'Oh. And why is that?' The bag was under the stairs, his plimsolls beside it.

'Because it involves too much pain.'

Chaney opened the bag. His white shorts and shirt were neatly folded inside. Anne had remembered.

'As a psychologist, I thought you would have understood.' He put his plimsolls in the bag, on top of the shorts.

'Understood what?'

'About the importance of pain.' Chaney straightened.

'How it makes you strong and keeps things in perspective. You take a look at the real world sometime. You will see that the weak all have one thing in common.'

'What is that?'

'They are the people who spend all their time trying to avoid pain.'

'Is that a fact?'

'Yes. They are the people who have forgotten that, for a human being, development involves pain. Birth involves pain. Pain is growth!'

Paul silently cursed himself for being drawn into the argument. 'Very profound, father. You sound just like a professor.'

-Growth is pain.-

'But I'm afraid a lecture will only serve to make us late. So why don't you save it for another time, huh?'

'Right. Let's go.' Chaney made for the door.

-Today, you won't score a point.-

* * * * *

Anne Chaney struggled for over three hours to get the sketch right. She found that she could copy the dog's features, but somehow that was insufficient.

"It looks like him," she told herself, "but mine is ...boring. Just a picture of a scruffy dog, not at all like a survivor."

That was the title she had chosen for the piece, even though she was unsure that she would ever be able to finish it.

"It is so difficult. Still..."

Anne renewed her effort, becoming totally engrossed in the problem she had set for herself. By the time the hall clock struck two, the character she had hastily photographed as it passed her in a country lane, was beginning to appear on paper.

"Oh my God! Is that the time?"

Anne had promised to be at Jane's house by two, and it was a good ten minutes' walk. She moved the easel away and stood up, dropping the pencil onto the stool she had just vacated.

"I will carry on with you tomorrow," she said, wagging her finger at the photo. The phone rang.

'Jane!' Anne hurried out of the study and picked up the receiver in the dining-room.

'Hello, Jane?'

The line crackled with life.

'Hello? Who is this? Hello?' There was no reply and Anne reached down, grabbed the book that was by the phone and began searching frantically for Jane's phone number. In her hurry she turned the page twice before she realised where it was. 'That's it. Of course.' She ran her nail underneath the number, backwards and forwards, scoring lines on the page. 'I'll hang up. Phone Jane. Go round in a taxi.'

'Anne.'

'Oh! Anne jerked the receiver away from her ear as if it had burnt her. She had not expected a voice - and not that voice. She gingerly returned the phone to her ear, prepared to discover that she had made a mistake. 'Jon?'

'Yes.'

'What do you want?' His voice was hoarse.

'Nothing.'

'Then why did you call?' Strained, in a way she had not heard before.

'What are you doing?'

'I was just going out.' It was almost a whisper now. 'Jon? Jon, are you still there?' The noise on the line seemed to be fading with the voice.

'What is the matter, Jon?' The line went dead. Anne lowered the phone, held it in both hands for a moment and then replaced it. She waited for twenty minutes and then phoned a taxi. When she arrived at Jane's she was almost an hour late.

But he did score. More points than he ever had before, and Chaney knew that it was only the rage inside him that had carried him to victory.

After the game, Chaney ran his shower water until it was almost unbearably hot, feeling it strike against his body like a thousand burning needles, turning his skin pink with the intensity of their effort. He closed his eyes, submitted to the power of the water. It gushed and hissed above him, trickling off his body into puddles round his feet like rain dripping from a roof.

- He cannot beat me. Because I need to win. I have to win. But then, so does he...-

Chaney raised his head, felt the water sting against his eyes, the soft part of his throat.

-Only twenty-four hours.-

'Are you coming out now?'

'What?' Chaney opened his eyes. Paul was standing next to him.

'Only I forget to tell you, I've got a book at home that I promised to give you. It's for Mum.'

'What's it about?'

'Portrait painting.'

Chaney reversed the dial on the shower. The cold water seemed to freeze his insides.

'Ready now.'

* * * * *

Kay lay in the bath and watched the steam rise lazily into the air. Her hair was tied in a bun, and only her head, shoulders and the uppermost slopes of her breasts protruded from the water. She raised her left leg, lifting it until the pink of her toenails emerged from the floating mountain of soap suds. Kay smiled at the way they clung to her skin, and then relaxed the tension, heard the plop as her leg submerged again. She stretched out slowly, her feet reaching for the other end of the bath. She felt the heat clean her.

"Most people never learn how to relax," she told herself. "Perhaps that's a good thing." Kay eased herself up, until her top half was almost clear of the water. She wiped the suds from her breasts, noticed how they glistened with moisture, and reached for the soap.

"Jane was seeing Anne today," Kay remembered. "I wonder if she told her?' "She ran the soap gently over her chest, from the collar bone down to the ribcage. "No, she can't have done. She would have phoned me. I'll give her a few days yet. Now that she believes that the responsibility is hers, she won't back down. I'm sure of that." Kay sank down, washing the soap from her skin. "I wonder what Anne will say when she finds out?" Kay smiled. "Not that it really matters. She'll go through with it whatever she says, I'll see to that."

The front door opened and Kay tensed slightly.

'Paul?'

'Yes.'

'What are you doing home so early?' Kay replaced the soap and left her arm resting along the top of the bath.

'I forgot that book that you bought for my mother. We've just popped in to get it.'

'Why don't you stay for a drink?' Kay pushed herself upright. 'I'll be down in a minute.'

'Actually we are in a bit of a rush.'

'There's always time for a drink.' Chaney walked into the lounge. 'I'll have a Scotch to celebrate my win.' Paul followed him. The book was on the floor by an armchair. Paul picked it up. 'Here. Better not forget this.' He threw it to his father. 'It's a good book. I was looking at it this morning.'

'Had you nothing better to do?' Chaney sat down on the settee, placed the book beside him.

'I'll get you your drink.'

-Good boy.-

'Make it a large one.'

'And mine.' Kay was wearing a red silk house-coat, tied loosely at the waist, so that Chaney could see the droplets of water clinging to the skin above her breasts, and the redness of her inner thigh as she moved past him.

-You bitch.-

'Where is the book?' Kay stood in the centre of the room.

-Parading.-

'It's here.' Chaney patted the cover.

'Haven't you got something more appropriate to wear?"

Paul walked towards them, carrying a drink in each hand.

'Oh don't be silly Paul, I've just had a bath. And, after all, this is my father-in-law.' Kay moved the book and sat down next to Chaney.

-Did you think I'd be too scared?

No.

Then, did you expect me to do that?

I hadn't considered it.

Will I be expected to do it again?

Perhaps.

Don't you know?

I don't plan.

Even when you are my father-in-law?-

'What does that mean?' Paul handed them their drinks.

'It means that we are family.' Kay shrugged. 'We have no secrets.'

'You don't expect me to believe that?'

Kay laughed. 'Darling, you know that I wouldn't lie to you.'

Paul glanced at his father, looked down at the floor. Chaney took a large drink of his whisky, rinsing his mouth with it, before allowing himself the pleasure of its warmth in his stomach.

-I saw it in his eyes. It was almost as if... I wonder if he'll turn? Or is he too much like his mother?-

Kay picked up the book and flicked through the pages so quickly that the paper made a continuous purring sound as it escaped the pressure of her thumb.

'I hope Anne will be pleased with this. I'm sure it will be of some use.' The purring stopped. 'You know it surprises me that she has never tried to sell any of her work. She has such a natural talent, she could do very well. I'm sure if she just sold one or two pictures she would realise that for herself and treat the whole thing a bit more seriously. After all, nothing succeeds like success. Isn't that right Jon?'

-Twenty-four hours.-

Chaney finished his drink. 'Paul told you, we're in a hurry.' He stood up, saw the surprise in Paul's eyes and the anger in Kay's. 'Are you ready?'

'Sure.' Paul took the car keys from his pocket, tossed them casually in the air and caught them again. 'It will suit me to be home early. I've a lecture to prepare for tomorrow.' He paused, bent down and kissed Kay on the cheek. 'I won't be long,'

Kay listened to the sounds of their departure, and then emptied her glass. 'Things are going to change,' she promised herself. 'Let's see how you cope with that, mister television man.' Kay shivered, pulled the house-coat more tightly around her, saw the cover out of the corner of her eye. 'Damn it!' Paul had forgotten the book.

-I'm so tired. It's the game, exhausted me.

You know that's not true. The game never tires you. He's not good enough for that.

Then what is it?

It's the adrenalin kick.

No.

Feel it! If you won't listen, feel it inside yourself.

It's there now because ...

It's been there all day. Ever since you found out...

You're wasting it!

No.

Listen to me! This is what Hyndman wanted. To make you think you are out of control, to make you waste your energy. You have done the same thing yourself. Remember?

Yes.

Good. When you are calm you can prepare yourself.

Yes. But now I'm tired. So tired...

Then sleep. You have the time.

Yes.

Sleep.-

* * * * *

Anne Chaney was a silver-haired woman in her late forties, with corns on both feet and a face that had never been beautiful, but was now beginning to reflect a lifetime of insecurity and worry.

She had first met Jon Chaney at a party that a friend had persuaded her to attend, and she had been shocked, firstly by his absolute confidence in himself and his ability to succeed, and secondly by his interest in her. When he asked to see her again, she agreed, and three weeks later, when he told her they were going to bed together, she was pleased. They went to his flat and used a rather dirty single bed, that creaked and groaned and made Anne think that the whole thing was rather silly. Although she subsequently shared his bed on many occasions, Anne was unable to ignore the sound of the springs, and whenever she left the flat, she did so hurriedly, with her chin held tight against her chest and her eyes downcast, dreading a chance meeting with one of the other tenants, and a knowing smile or comment.

As the months passed and their relationship continued, Anne's need for John Chaney became almost unbearable. He represented the security, the confidence, the will, that was missing in her life. He became a rock for her to shelter behind, the protection she had longed for, and so she clung to him in desperation and fear, because she was certain that one day he would leave her. He never did and Anne Chaney learnt too late in life that those things a person needs most, and those they fear, are exactly the same. They just differ in size.

Anne opened the front door of her house and paused on the step. The house was dark and cold; deserted. So different from her arrival at Jane's.

'Anne! Where have you been? I was worried sick. I phoned you twice. The first time it was engaged, the second time there was no answer. Are you alright...?'

They sat and talked, drank tea and looked at several articles about spring fashion in a number of women's manazines. But mostly they talked. About Anne's art work. She was embarrassed at first, but then, as her confidence grew and she relaxed, Anne seized the opportunity to talk at some length. It was unusual even for Jane to show so much interest.

'It was Sly who was responsible - well, indirectly, - for my becoming an... for my interest in drawing and painting.'

'Oh?'

'Yes, he bought me a camera, years ago now, as an anniversary present. He spent hours showing me how to use it, but I just couldn't get the hang of it. It was far too complicated.' Anne paused, remembering her struggle. 'It was really frustrating, taking all those photos of animals and birds, and not one of them came out right. I was always using the wrong exposure, the wrong light setting, or something. In the end, I hid it in a wardrobe, waited six months and then sold it. I bought an easel and my first set of paints with the money. You see, it had given me something... An interest in pictures.'

'And you went from strength to strength.'

'Oh, I wouldn't say that. The new picture I've just started is causing me all sorts of problems.'

'Why is that?'

'Because I decided it was time to try something a little more adventurous.'

'Mmm. Sounds exciting.'

'Not really.'

'Perhaps I could come round and take a look?'

'Of course. I'd be delighted...'

Anne stepped into the hall and closed the door behind her. The cold made her shiver through her coat and she hurried into the lounge.

'Oh God!'

The figure of her husband was sprawled out on the floor.

'He's dead!' Anne's hand clawed at the wall and found the light switch. Chaney's eyes were shut; she could see no sign of breathing.

'Phone Paul!' Anne backed away from the still form, felt herself shaking with terror. 'I must phone -' A snore of gargantuan proportions reverberated through the room. Anne screamed in fright; Chaney grumbled quietly to himself and turned on his side.

'He's asleep.' Anne leant against the wall, welcomed its support, and calmed herself. Chaney snored again and Anne realised the new problem she faced. After a moment's deliberation, she removed her coat and laid it over Chaney. Satisfied that he had at least some protection from the cold, Anne switched off the light and went to bed.

FIVE

The old soldier smiled and watched Chaney study the audience as they applauded. "They are his spur," he thought. He took a final drink of the water and settled into a more comfortable position in the chair. They were about to begin.

'Facing me tonight is Sir Henry Seymour-Jones, V.C. Although he is now retired he has been one of the country's most popular military leaders. He has agreed to openly discuss...'

The old soldier listened carefully to the introduction, enjoying the formality of it, and when Chaney turned to face him, he saw the challenge in his eyes.

'As I said Sir Henry, you have had a most distinguished military career, so tell me, when you look back at that career, do you do so with regret?'

The old soldier laughed, a gentle, honest laugh, without any trace of fear. 'If I may say Mr. Chaney, that really is a most interesting ...and dangerous ...question.'

'Dangerous, Sir Henry?'

'Please, your strategy is a fine one, don't sully it by pretending it was not intended. We both know that I cannot answer your question without condemning myself.' He paused briefly, ran his tongue round his lips. 'An admission of regret would be seen by many as an admission of failure. Yet if I do otherwise, you will no doubt remind me ...and your viewers ...of some of my more obvious mistakes, and ask me why I don't regret them. Yes, an excellent manoeuvre Mr. Chaney, I congratulate you.'

'I require only your answer Sir Henry...'

* * * * *

Anthony Hyndman woke feeling alert and refreshed. Last night had been a family night; he had taken the children to see the latest Spielberg film, and then on to meet their mother for dinner, in their favourite Italian restaurant.

'I must admit, I'd have preferred it if you had been an actor.' Sarah confessed, as they walked down the cinema steps. 'It would have been really something having an actor for a father.'

'But he is, in his own way.' Richard replied before his father could. 'All politicians are.' Hyndman silently thanked God that Michelle was not with them, and changed the topic of conversation. The meal was a great success.

'What time is it?' Michelle rolled sleepily onto her back.

'About ten minutes before breakfast.'

Michelle's eyes opened. 'You mean we're late?'

'Just a little.'

'What about the alarm, why didn't it wake us?'

Michelle eased herself up onto her elbows.

'I didn't set it.'

'Why not?'

'Didn't need to. I knew I would wake up this morning.'

'And did you?'

'Yes.'

'Then why didn't you wake me?'

'There's no rush.' Hyndman straightened his arm across Michelle's pillow and she lowered herself onto it, rolling onto her side, her head resting against his shoulder. 'I've just been lying here thinking.'

'Oh?' Michelle remembered and her fear returned.

'About tonight?'

'What? No, no, about last night.'

'Doesn't it scare you?'

Hyndman smiled, wanting to reassure her. 'No, he doesn't scare me.'

'How can you be so sure?' Michelle felt his warmth, was comforted by it.

'Because I'm an actor.' He kissed the top of her head. 'And because I don't make mistakes.'

* * * * *

The mirror had been replaced. No questions asked. Chaney stared into it now, aware of the lines on his face, the bags under his eyes.

-You look like death.-

Chaney had woken in the middle of the night, his body cold and stiff. He lay still beneath the flimsy covering for some time, listening to the sounds of the house. The arm he had been sleeping on tingled with life and he wriggled the fingers. The other hand felt worse than it ever had. Twice, playing squash, he had almost cried out with the pain of holding the racket. He raised the injured hand above his chest. The skin was white, ghostly. The bruise was spreading, or was that shadow?

-You look like death.-

Chaney heard footsteps approaching, a cursory knock on the door, and Randal appeared.

'Are you ready?'

'What does that mean?'

Randal closed the door. 'Look Jon, I know we are asking the impossible but,' he shrugged,'there really was no alternative. Sometimes force of circumstance takes over. You know that as well as I do.'

'I'll manage.'

'I'm sure you will.'

-For the first time you don't believe it.-

'Is that all?'

'No, there is one other thing. Hyndman is due to arrive in the next fifteen minutes. Do you want to have a word with him before you go on the set?'

'No. Make him wait.'

-You're clutching at straws.-

'O .K.' Randal reached behind him, opened the door.

'Right then, I'll leave you to it.'

-You do that.-

Because he was beginning to concentrate on the pain in his hand Chaney stood up, walked the length of the lounge, into the dining-room and the study beyond. He pulled back the curtains; the moonlight painted the room grey and blue, giving it a character he had never noticed before. Chaney moved slowly in a tight circle, observing the room, studying the detail of it and searching for its essence as if it were a living thing. Shadows, shapes ...the smell. An artist's room. Chaney had never thought of it as that before. A board was in position on the easel and

Chaney picked it up, holding it at an angle, using the moonlight for the greatest effect. In the centre of the paper was the outline of a dog's head; only its eyes were drawn in detail. Chaney found himself staring into them.

-A tough little bastard.-

The first thing Randal noticed were the eyes. "He's not wearing his glasses," he realised as the distance between them closed.

'Mr Hyndman.' They shook hands. Randal noticed the politician's pudgy fingers, "He's more overweight than I thought," and was unprepared for the power of his grip. Hyndman smiled.

'You seem surprised.'

'Sorry?' Randal resisted the temptation to massage his hand.

'When you first saw me, you seemed surprised.'

'Oh yes, I apologise Mr Hyndman. I expected you to be wearing glasses. I thought for a moment I was welcoming the wrong man.'

'Contact lenses.' Hyndman beamed.

'Of course.'

'In fact I will let you in on a secret, Peter... I may call you Peter?'

'Please...'

'..Splendid.' Hyndman's arm snaked round Randal's shoulders as they walked. He felt the weight of it. 'Between you and me, I hate wearing the damn things. So bloody uncomfortable.'

'Then why..?'

'A disguise.' Hyndman tapped the side of his nose with his forefinger. 'Blinds the public you know.'

'From what?'

'The real me.'

'I don't understand.'

'Simple really.' Hyndman's pace slowed. Thinking : "I'm not going to let you off the hook yet." ' I am a public figure. I need some way of distracting those around me. An image if you like. Pop stars hide behind their clothing, their hair style, actors behind their characters, I use my glasses.'

'I still don't see how they help you. Everyone expects you to be wearing glasses.'

'Exactly.' Hyndman stopped. 'So all I have to do is take them off, put in my contact lenses, and I can walk round un-noticed. Ingenious, eh? Wear the disguise so frequently that no-one recognises the real you without it.'

'I understand now,' Randal said, moving away from the pressure of the arm. "And Chaney will too. He's stripped ready for battle." He smiled at the politician. 'I trust you are, er, suitably prepared for tonight? Appearing at such short notice as you are.'

'Mr Hyndman?'

'Yes, Pauline?'

'A gentleman has just delivered a package for you. He says it contains some information that you urgently require. What do you want me to do with it?'

'Bring it in, Pauline. Bring it in.'

Hyndman returned the smile. 'No need to worry on my account, Peter. Ex-boy scout, you know. Ready to go the distance, if it's required.'

'Come now, Mr Hyndman.' Randal glanced at his watch, wondered what Chaney was doing now. 'You make it sound like a competition....'

Chaney spat the whisky into the sink; his final act of preparation.

-We start equal. That's the only thing I can know for sure. I have nothing and neither does he. Equal.-

He switched off the light.

-He believes he is better than me.-

* * * * *

Sylvester Harris had escaped most of the bombing. He had been moved to a country home, a farm, before the worst of the Blitz began. The farmer and his wife were surprised when their new charge showed no sign of sorrow or fear at his sudden change of circumstance. They decided, sitting at the large, oak kitchen table on the third night after his arrival, that the boy had come from an unloving home.

'The lad shows no emotion.'

'He's subdued, that's all.'

'No, he's not holding it back. I've watched him. I don't think he feels anything.'

'You're being too harsh. He must be under a terrible strain.'

'He gives no sign of it.'

'We can't expect anything from him. We haven't raised him.'

'No.'

'Just give him time, he'll prove you wrong. Besides, even the animals have feelings.'

'Yes. Perhaps they'll teach him...'

For three months they saw no change in him. He performed the simple tasks he was given without complaint. He was always polite. He spent most of his free time alone, walking round the farmland. One day the farmer questioned him about it.

'Do you miss your home?'

'This is my home.'

The farmer raised his eyebrows in surprise. 'Do you feel that?'

The boy shrugged. 'This is where I am.'

'Are you happy here?'

'I enjoy the country. I hadn't realised it was so beautiful.'

'Do you want to stay here, to become a part of it?'

'That's impossible.'

'Then what?'

'I want to capture it.'

The farmer thought about that a great deal, and then discussed it with his wife.

'There is a way,' she said. 'Give him Peter's camera. Show him how to use it.' Peter was the son they had not seen for two years. He was at war. The farmer followed her advice. The photographs the boy took surprised them both.

'You see,' his wife said, with a triumphant smile. 'He does have feelings.'

* * * * *

Sylvester Harris arrived at the television studios only ten minutes after Anthony Hyndman. He had been the third person

Randal had told about the change in the 'Living Today' programme. The second person was talking quietly to Randal when Sly entered the room. Both men looked up at the interruption. Randal nodded a greeting.

'Ah, Sly.' The other man moved away from Randal, gestured towards a chair. 'I'm pleased you are here. Come in. Sit down. Now I won't have to repeat myself.'

Sly did as he was asked, saw Randal grimace and understood the warning. Something was wrong. The man glanced over his shoulder. 'Peter?'

Randal sat down and lit a cigarette.

"It's going to be a lecture." Sly thought. The man rubbed his hands together.

'I will be brutally honest with you both.' The man's eyes flickered from one to the other. 'I feel that this sudden alteration has come at a most opportune time. After Chaney's - how shall I say - undisciplined performance on Tuesday, I have come to doubt the wisdom of your original idea. The Bryant interview was ruined by unnecessary selfish indulgence. Verbal masturbation, gentlemen, not something I wish to promote.' The man smiled at his analogy. 'Indeed, the way he has conducted a number of his most recent interviews has raised certain questions in my mind. It is, I believe, quite possible that the man is past his best. In which case there will be no point in you pursuing the creation of his own series.'

'But the newspapers all carried the Bryant story.'

Ash fell from Randal's cigarette.

'I accept that. Unfortunately, I am not in the business of publishing newspapers.' The man smiled again. "He's a humourless bastard," Sly thought.

'How do you intend to reach a decision?' he asked.

The man bowed his head, acknowledging the question.

'I was rather hoping Mr Hyndman would do that for me,' he said.

The audience murmured their surprise when Hyndman took his seat next to Chaney. Andrew said the usual things and finished: 'With a change from his advertised guest, here's Jon, with Thursday's edition of 'One to One'.

The applause was restrained. Chaney saw people pointing at Hyndman; nodding their heads vigorously at those sitting next to them.

-I don't need a plan. I can beat him without. The way he moves. The way he sits. He's over-confident. That's his weakness. He'll make a mistake because of it. I know he will. God, my hand is so sore...-

Chaney saw the movement out of the corner of his eye. Andrew was signalling to him. The applause had stopped; he did not know for how long. There was some movement in the audience. Sweat on his back, soaking his shirt. Chaney began.

'Facing me tonight is Andrew Hyndman M.P. Seen by many as a future leader of the country, he is a man of immense political experience, whose direct, forthright approach has enabled him to stay firmly in the political spotlight for many years. Tonight he has agreed to openly discuss any aspect of his professional or personal life in front of our live studio audience and before you, the viewers.'

His face dominated the screen and Michelle Hyndman hated him. "Please God, let Tony be alright. No secrets, please." The camera moved back and Michelle could see her husband now. Sitting with his legs crossed, his hands clasped, resting on his lap, watching Chaney perform the introduction with a confident half-smile on his face.

'Mr Hyndman, welcome to the programme.'

'Thank you, Jon. I was pleased to be invited.'

Hyndman paused and stared into Chaney's eyes, letting the smile spread slowly across his face. "I will finish your career. Remove your sting."

He continued: 'Although, I must say, that with a general election only weeks away, I do hope you are not going to concentrate on my past. That has, if anything, been too well documented. Unless of course you have found something new that has been overlooked?' Hyndman looked at the audience. 'I do believe that is your speciality.'

The laughter was quiet, appreciative. They were on his side. Chaney felt himself blush.

'No...No, like so many others I share your concern with the present.'

The man turned to Randal. 'Does that mean he doesn't know anything? Or are we playing stupid games again?'

Randal shrugged. 'I don't know.'

'Sly?'

'I haven't spoken to him for a couple of days. So your guess is as good as mine.'

The man nodded, looked again at the screen. His face an expressionless mask.

Hyndman recognised the ploy; negated it with ease.

'No, Jon. Not my concern for the present. My enthusiasm. And come election time, I believe the voters will show quite categorically that they share my enthusiasm for the work this government has done.'

'We can take that as a prediction?'

'It is what I see in my crystal ball, yes.' More laughter.

-Go screw yourself.-

'We are not here to play games, Mr Hyndman.'

'Indeed not.'

Michelle saw it again. So clearly this time that she knew it was not a figment of her imagination. A toughness that frightened her. "How can he be like that?" she asked herself. "He's never like that at home. Not once in nearly twenty years. He has always been so gentle." Michelle picked up the remote control, realised that her hand was shaking. "So which do I believe in?" Michelle pressed a button, switched the television off. It was a question she did not want to answer.

'There has been a great deal of discussion in the House recently about the role armed police should play in maintaining law and order in our city's streets. Mr Hyndman, should our police carry firearms?'

-I'll make you squirm, you bastard. They'll be on my side. By the end.-

'Let me say to you Jon ...and to the audience and the viewers at home ...the same as I said to my colleagues in the House.' Hyndman leant forward slightly in his chair, punctuated his comments with gentle movements of his hands. 'I believe in giving professional people the responsibility we pay them to accept. I would never dream of telling a surgeon how to perform an operation, or indeed, a refuse collector how to collect refuse. It follows therefore that we should allow a Chief Constable to instruct and arm his men as he sees fit.'

'You're saying that it's not your problem?'

'Not at all. I am saying that I have faith in professional people to do the job that they have been trained to do.'

'Despite the fact that in the last twelve months two innocent people have been shot and killed by armed police officers?'

-The people's spokesman, that's it! I'll isolate him.-

'Yes. They were, of course, two unfortunate incidents, and I was as saddened by them as everyone else. But the fact of the matter is, that in any profession accidents occur with a regrettable inevitability. That you can only cite two such examples is, in fact, a reflection of the exceptionally high standards our police maintain.'

-Don't look at me as if I don't understand. You don't care any more than I do.-

'Regrettable inevitability?' Chaney raised his voice, his face showing his outrage. 'An innocent man is shot through the head by people who are actually paid to protect him, and you calmly sit there and refer to it as a regrettable inevitability?'

'Unpleasant though it might be, it is an apt phrase, Mr Chaney. I suspect it suits most circumstances.'

Chaney saw the flash of anger and felt a thrill of excitement.

-That's it, let the people see. I'm getting to you, aren't I? You don't scare me.-

'In that case, let's move on to another topic that the government seems to regard in the same vein. Unemployment, Mr Hyndman. There are now more people out of work in this country than ever before, and all the evidence suggests that if the government pursues its present policies it cannot expect to reduce those figures by very much. ...Unless of course it is your intention to put more armed police on the streets.'

They laughed with him now and Chaney felt his heart-beat quicken.

-Listen to them. I told you what I would do. Listen!-

Hyndman noticed the change in their reaction, realised how close he had been to losing his temper. "Don't become so involved," he told himself. "Remember, this is only a game. He'll give me a way in sooner or later ... and then I'll finish it. Finish him."

'This government certainly does not see unemployment as being inevitable, and it is quite clearly not, as you would suggest, a by-product of government policy. However, it is true to say that unemployment, like any other ill, can only be cured gradually...'

'How much time do you want?'

'How serious is the illness?' Hyndman paused briefly, emphasising his point. 'Those members of other political parties who offer instant guaranteed solutions are, I feel, being somewhat over-optimistic. Remember...'

Hyndman looked directly into the camera and Katherine Durham studied his face with interest.

'...When we talk about millions of people unemployed, we are actually talking about a problem that no working politician has ever faced before. It is a problem unique to our time, so how can anyone be certain what the remedy is?'

"A powerful man," Katherine decided. "It's not an image. It would be easy to misjudge him."

Katherine switched the television off and called out softly. 'Soul?'

Her tortoise-shell cat miaowed its answer and walked sleepily from behind the settee, pausing once to stretch, arching its back until it seemed the spine must snap.

'There you are, sweetheart. Let Mummy give you some milk.' Katherine picked up the cat and disappeared into the kitchen.

'But the fact of the matter is, unemployment has risen enormously since you came to power.'

'Due to factors beyond our control, as I said. And yet, despite this, we have still been able to...'

Randal reached for another cigarette. The packet was empty. Damn! 'I think we need to remember that Jon is under a great deal of pressure.' Randal struggled to keep his voice dispassionate. 'He has had very little time to prepare.'

'Through no fault of his own.' Sly stood up, turned his back on the screen.

'You would have done the same, Sly.' Randal was suddenly very tired; he rubbed his hands over his face. 'I had no alternative.'

'That is not strictly true.' The other man spoke, without turning his attention from the screen. 'There was an alternative, but you would have been ill-advised to consider it.'

Randal massaged his forehead with his fingertips. 'It's an obvious contest. A kind of public challenge match. I suppose it had to happen one day.'

The man nodded. His smile was thin and hard; the slightest crack in winter ice. 'I agree. A most fortunate inevitability....'

Chaney had changed the subject, moved on to the question of nuclear arms.

'Are you personally in favour of the deployment of this kind of weapon in our country?'

Hyndman shifted in his seat, straightened his tie.

-Something's wrong! It's as if he's been waiting for this.-

'My own views are an irrelevancy here. As a member of parliament my job is first of all to assess the mood of the nation, and then to argue in favour of whatever action satisfies the majority. That is the democratic procedure.'

-Lead him away from this. Find something else.-

'Do you seriously believe that you can do that without holding a referendum? - Another democratic procedure, which many people argue is required when a government is in the process of making the most important decisions.'

-Let him answer and then move again.-

'As I am sure you are aware, Jon, there are other ways of assessing public opinion. As you know, Marplan recently carried out a most detailed survey of this issue, the results of which are not officially due out for several days. However...' Hyndman smiled, paused, gave the fear chance to grow. '...I am now in a position to give you just some of the figures the poll will offer.' Hyndman removed a folded sheet of paper from his inside jacket pocket. 'I believe this will represent yet another 'first' for your programme.'

Chaney saw Hyndman's look of triumph, thought of Randal, watching, in another part of the building, and realised he had lost.

'That looks like a winning move.' Sly's face was emotionless.

Randal crushed the empty cigarette packet and hurled it against the screen. 'Shit!'

The man turned away from the screen, the first time he had since the interview began, and looked at the other two. 'Mr Hyndman has been as unpredictable as ever. The question now is, can Chaney pull something out of the bag at the eleventh hour?'

Randal snorted. 'It's a hat.'

'I beg your pardon?'

Randal shook his head, turned to Sly. 'You're a gambling man, Sly. What odds would you offer?'

Hyndman finished reading, tapped the sheet of paper in conclusion. 'So there you are, Jon. Some indication of how the public feels on this matter, and those figures at least show that the government's approach has considerable support.' Hyndman folded the sheet and returned it to his pocket. 'And your reaction?'

-I'm finished.-

'It's, er, interesting to hear that the majority of those questioned are in favour of a dual key system.'

'Isn't it?' Hyndman smiled.

-For God's sake, speak!

I can't.

He's using the silence against you!

He doesn't need to.

Speak!-

'Tell me, what other topics would you like to discuss, Jon?'

-What other topics are there?

Don't lie down to him now!

I didn't have time to prepare.

Think!

About what?

The answer. You have the answer!

Where?-

The old soldier smiled, unaffected. 'You can rest assured, Mr Chaney, that I will answer your questions with complete honesty,' he said. 'After all, that is the only way to stop chaps like you taking the offensive. Tactics, you see, giving the enemy what he least expects. Damn good thing, too...'

'Jon?' Hyndman frowned, glanced at Andrew on the other side of the set. Chaney came out of his reverie.

'Communication. Let's talk about communication.'

-It's not over yet.-

'Obviously as a politician, Mr Hyndman, you are primarily concerned with communication on a variety of levels.'

'Obviously.'

'It would also be true to say, would it not, that a politician's success reflects their effectiveness as a communicator?'

'Yes.' Hyndman felt Chaney's new enthusiasm; his first slight sense of doubt.

'Then why is it that effective communication is so rarely achieved?'

Hyndman straightened suddenly as if stung, his eyes narrowing. 'What?'

Sly felt it too. He turned to Randal, saw the new-found hope in his face. 'I'd give you even money!'

'Even now, Mr Hyndman,' Chaney continued, 'with the eyes of the nation upon us, we confine ourselves to playing those trivial word games expected of us by our peers. The type of game you have learnt so well during your career as a politician. The type of game you are so capable of winning.'

-The type of game you are about to lose.-

'What are you talking about?'

'Honesty, Mr Hyndman...'

-Smile. Pause. Make sure they are with you.-

'...We could call it the forgotten factor.'

-Don't let him finish.-

'Really, this is not meant to be a philosophical debate.' The audience was suddenly very quiet. 'It is a political discussion ...'

-Now!-

'You separate the two?'

-Eye contact. He's going to reply.-

'Let me put this question to you, bearing in mind that my audience and I require an honest answer...'

-They are mine.-

'...You described yourself earlier as a, well, as a public servant. One who determines the nation's requirements and then acts accordingly. Tell me, how will you react if your party is not returned to power in the forth-coming election? Will you accept ...as a public servant should ...that the voters have made the correct decision and that your policies are not what they desire, or will you quietly assume that a mistake has been made and their choice is a poor one? Which will it be, Mr Hyndman?'

-Like a fish out of water.-

'There's no need to rush. There's plenty of time.'

'Well!' The man stood up and turned his back on the screen. He had seen enough. 'A most ingenious manoeuvre. Poor Mr Hyndman daren't say that he would agree with the decision...'

'And can't say that he wouldn't.' Randal felt the tension leave him.

'Exactly.' The man nodded. 'They have bloodied each other, and with so little time left,' he glanced at his watch, 'it means the only possible result is an honourable draw.'

'And the champion remains?' Randal raised one eyebrow questioningly.

'Yes. And he needs to be informed that he is to have his own series.'

Sylvester Harris looked up at the ceiling and allowed himself a satisfied smile. Mercury and Saturn were in conjunction, exerting a powerful influence; he had never doubted that Chaney would survive. 'He will want to know why he wasn't consulted earlier. Jon doesn't like being kept in the dark.'

'I appreciate that.' The man put his hand on Sly's shoulder, patted it as he spoke. 'Which is why I thought that you, his most trusted colleague, should be the person to tell him.'

* * * * *

'There is something that I want to talk to you about.' Paul switched off the television, he hadn't wanted to watch his father anyway, but Kay had insisted.

'Oh?' Kay stretched out on the settee. Paul remained standing.

'I think we are both in need of a change. I think it would do us good.'

'Really?' Kay studied her fingernails. The paint was slightly chipped on two of them. 'What did you have in mind - a spring holiday? Somewhere warm I hope.'

'No, something a bit more permanent than that.'

'Such as?'

Paul breathed in deeply. 'I have been offered a new job. A promotion.'

Kay looked up. 'Then take it. It needn't affect my work.'

'I think it will.'

'Why?'

'It's in Sydney, Australia.'

Chaney was exhausted. He lay down on the bed in his dressing-room and closed his eyes.

-You beat him. He did everything he could and you beat him. Who cares?-

Chaney turned on his side.

-You will. In the morning.-

'Jon?' Sly, his head poking round the door. 'Are you asleep?'

'No.' Chaney sat up. 'What do you want?'

'It was good.'

'It always is.'

'We need to talk.'

-There are exciting possibilities open to you.-

Chaney blinked, came alive. 'Give me five minutes. Then I'll see you upstairs, in the bar.'

'Why the hell didn't you tell me of this earlier?'

'There seemed to be no point.' Paul spoke calmly, pleased that his news had so annoyed his wife. 'Until I was officially offered the post, there was nothing to discuss. Besides,' he couldn't resist this, 'you were so busy arranging my mother's....little surprise, that I didn't want to distract you.'

'But you hadn't even told me that you were looking for a new job!'

'I wasn't. This one was, sort of, thrust under my nose.'

'Huh.' Kay snorted with contempt. 'That's the only way you get anything.'

Paul smiled. 'Including you, dear.'

Sly placed the two glasses on the table and sat down. 'Well, what do you think about it?'

'My own series?' Chaney pursed his lips, tapped his thumbnail against his teeth, as he considered it again. 'Sounds good. Very good. But what about the work I'm doing now?'

"Living Today'? You'll stay with it. It will make you one of the most watched men on television.'

'Yeah...'

'You make it sound like there's a problem.'

'Randal knew.' Chaney's face was stern.

Sly sighed, the moment could not be avoided any longer.

'Yes.'

'For how long?'

'Oh,' Sly gestured vaguely, 'about a couple of months.'

'A couple of months...' Chaney nodded thoughtfully. 'And what about you?'

'It was my idea, Jon.'

'Shit!' Chaney turned away.

'There were a few problems.' Sly spoke quickly. 'It was decided that you needn't be told unless the go-ahead was given.'

'What problems?'

'The ratings.'

'We've topped the ratings every week since the series began!'

'That is the problem. You've been at the top for so long, some people argued that you had got to start going downhill soon. That if the slide came before the series, there was no way it could succeed.'

'What changed their minds?'

Sly shrugged. 'This week. Bryant, Hyndman, Randal, me.' He pointed a finger. 'You. Everything came together at the right time.'

'One big happy family.' Chaney bared his teeth. Sly clapped him on the shoulder. 'So, when are we going to start celebrating?'

'As soon as you have told me what the series will be called.'

"Chaney's Choice',' Sly said, raising his glass.

-My series!-

SIX

Katherine Durham's house had mirrors in every room. She collected them in the way she collected all things that intrigued her.

Katherine had just hung the latest addition to her collection in the hall. It was a rectangular mirror, some three feet in length, with a shining silver rim and a design in the centre that hampered its efficiency as a looking-glass. The design was circular in shape, split into two by an "S" shaped line running the length of its diameter. The uppermost half had been coloured black, but both halves contained an additional smaller circle, drawn parallel to each other in the centre of the whole.

Katherine stepped back from the wall, studied the mirror and adjusted it; repeating the procedure several times until she was sure it was straight. The mirror had only arrived that morning, sent to her by a friend from the States, and Katherine had been delighted to receive it, understood its significance. The Yin and Yang symbol, an expression of Taoist belief, representing the rhythm, the energy, of nature. It was a belief first expressed in the Book of Chuang Tzu, written some three hundred years before Christ: the universe is governed by the twin forces of Yin and Yang. Katherine could remember so clearly the first time it had been explained to her.

'Within the Yin and Yang symbol we have perhaps the most obvious expression of the Chinese understanding of reality.' The lecturer had paused, pushed his glasses more firmly in position. 'The universe is filled with energy, a living, flowing energy, that can be seen to take two forms. The first we call Yin, the quiet energy. Yin is winter, Yin is feminine. It is what we might call the more passive of the two energies. Yang, on the other hand, is summer. It is masculine, the more obviously creative force in nature.' Katherine had sat spellbound, forgetting not for the first time to make notes.'The Yin and Yang symbol show us that these two forces overlap. They are connected by their very existence one to the other. As man is but a microcosm of the universe, it can be seen that he too is a mixture. Of positive and negative, of masculine and feminine, of good and bad. Taoists aim to achieve harmony within their lives, by attempting to balance the forces of Yin and Yang within themselves. When this has been accomplished, it can be said that man is truly at one with himself..'

'What happens when a person does not achieve this balance?' Katherine had raised her hand, asked the question, almost without realising it.

The lecturer, a small, balding Chinese, had smiled at her as if at a child. 'Consider for yourself...' He paused and for a fearful moment Katherine thought she would have to answer her own question, but no. Sooner or later, that which is not balanced topples over. Of course...

Katherine made her final adjustment to the mirror and smiled into it, amused that the symbol should create an unfinished reflection - no harmony there. She stepped back, heard a car slowing outside and glanced at her watch, a puzzled frown on her face. He always arrived at the same time; he was never early. The car appeared to have pulled up outside, the engine idling. Katherine remained still, her head cocked to one side as she listened. The mirror caught the essence of her posture: an almost feline awareness; caught her straightening slightly as the car drove away; caught a half-smile as she realised she had worried needlessly. Chaney was nothing if not predictable.

-I knew all the time!

Of course you did.

They thought they could hide it from me.

Let them think that.

Worms.

The early bird..

They thought they could hide it from me!

Secrets.

Ha! There are no secrets. They only think that.

Secrets...are a figment of other people's imagination.-

The traffic lights turned red and Chaney eased the car to a halt. It was another cold night. The car heater warmed him. His hand no longer hurt.

-'Chaney's Choice'-

Traffic began to cross in front of him. A silver-blue Mazda pulled up on the inside lane.

-Fuckin' shark.-

Chaney twisted in his seat, studied the driver. In his early thirties, with styled brown hair and a moustache. Wearing a suit of indistinguishable colour...

-Salesman.-

...tapping out a rhythm against the steering wheel with one hand, picking his nose with the other. Chaney laughed.

The lights changed, caught the other driver unprepared; the Jaguar was first away.

* * * * *

Jane Swift poured herself another sherry. "I'll have to go in a minute," she told herself for the second time. "I said I'd be there at eight and it's past that now." Jane sipped at her sherry. "Still, I shouldn't feel guilty, Anne was late arriving here yesterday."

Anne...

Her husband had not believed it either, but he still felt that Jane should go through with it. 'Kay won't be away on business - and if she is, she will have arranged it deliberately. No, she just wants you to be the one to tell Anne, to face the possible explosion. ' He shrugged. 'And all things considered, I think it would be best if you told her. You will bring a calming influence to bear, I'm sure.'

David smiled, put his arms round Jane's waist.

'You do think we are doing the right thing?'

'I think it is too late to worry about that now.'

'But you didn't say anything in the beginning, when I first told you.'

'Who knows how another person will react? I can't say for sure that it's right, or wrong.'

Jane pulled away, her mind filling once again with doubts. David followed her, put his hands on her shoulders.

'I would have just been happier about the whole thing if it hadn't been Kay's idea, that's all.'

'So would I.' Jane finished her sherry. The alcohol seemed to have no effect on her at all, she was more nervous now than she had been all day. "If only I knew what her reaction would be," she thought as she walked into the hall and put on her coat. "Whatever else happens, I must make sure it doesn't ruin our friendship."

'I thought you'd have gone by now.' David closed the front door behind him. He had been working late at the office, his plans for the the proposed sports complex had to be finished in the next two weeks, and he was still behind schedule.

'I'm just on my way.' Jane accepted his kiss on the cheek.

'How do you feel?' David took off his scarf, began to unbutton his coat.

'Well,' Jane raised her eyebrows, nodding her head stoically. 'I suppose there are times when I've felt better.' David put his coat on the hanger and turned to face her again. 'Like the time we crashed the car. And when I'm sitting in the dentist's waiting-room. Times like that.'

David smiled. 'I'm sure it will all work out just fine. I have every confidence in you.'

'What about Anne? How much confidence do you have in her?'

It was David's turn to raise his eyebrows as he searched the ceiling for an answer. 'Sufficient,' he said, 'to think that she will get by with your support.'

'You certainly know how to fill a girl with confidence.'

'I'm just being realistic.'

'Mmm.' Jane voiced her other worry. 'What do you think he will say when he finds out?'

'Chaney?'

Jane nodded.

'I would think he will be too busy to even notice, and if he isn't I don't think he will give a damn.'

'Yes, I suppose you are right.' Jane turned the latch, pulled the door open a couple of inches.

'Although, in some respects it would be nice if he got involved. I'm sure Anne would be pleased.'

David's face clouded. 'I think it would be best if he stayed well away.'

'How far would you like?' Jane's tone was deliberately flippant, not wanting her husband to be seized by the melancholy that had engulfed him after the party.

David grinned. 'Somewhere the other side of the Styx.'

'I'll ask Anne if he has any swimming trunks.' Jane stepped outside to the sound of his laughter. The cold night air made her shiver. "I knew I should have had another sherry," she told herself as she began the walk to Anne's.

* * * * *

Katherine Durham sat on the edge of her bed, a towel beside her, and brushed her hair for the third time that evening. As she did so she stared into the gilt-edged mirror, her largest, fastened to the wall, running almost from floor to ceiling and enjoyed her reflection. She was a beautiful woman. Her lithe, supple body developed and maintained by regular Nautilus workouts and by the daily practice of Tai Chi had, she knew, an elegance even in repose. Her brown eyes sparkled. 'As precious as diamonds,' Ralph had said after their first year together. And as hard too, he discovered six months later, when she grew bored and left him. Her hands were long and slender, the skin unbelievably soft, but it was her hair she loved most. Chestnut brown, stretching down in lines of silk almost to the base of her spine. Katherine loved to feel the touch of it against her naked back; loved to feel it billowing beneath her, or fall, cascading, round her face, sticking to the dampness of her, while she made love. Yes, she was a beautiful woman....

"A product of my mind," she told herself, making small, circular movements with her shoulders; a relaxation and mobility exercise. Her breasts rose slightly with each upward movement of her shoulders, the nipples so dark they seemed almost black in the reflection.

"From the mind comes power." It was a tenet she believed in; upon which she had based her adult life, and for every thirty minutes she spent exercising her body, she spent twice as long training her mind. Sitting with her back resting against the mirror she was looking into now, her legs folded beneath her and her eyes closed. Searching for the Void, emptying her mind of the petty distractions that dominated the lives of others. Searching for power, because she knew that without it she could accomplish nothing.

Katherine rose from the bed, saw the muscles in her thigh split as she did so. She raised her arms straight above her head and stretched, one arm at a time reaching for the ceiling, as if grasping the rungs of an invisible ladder. Katherine felt her spine respond, slowly, sleepily, like a waking snake. She saw her breasts flatten slightly. Katherine continued her exercises for the next five minutes, until her skin was warm and reddened. Then she picked up the towel and rubbed it first over her back, shoulders and arms, then her breasts, belly and thighs. The clothes she had chosen were draped over the back of her dressing-table chair, and when she had finished with the towel Katherine turned her attention to them. She dressed slowly, enjoying the touch of the different fabrics against her skin. She had only just fastened her skirt, when Jon Chaney rang the front doorbell.

* * * * *

Jane Swift had been to self-defence classes, two hours every Wednesday for six weeks, but she was still pleased when she arrived safely at Anne's house. Walking alone at night was not something she enjoyed.

'Then why the hell do you do it?' David had asked, a hint of anger in his voice, when she first revealed her fear to him. 'Why don't you drive?'

'Because women should be able to walk out at night. You don't expect me to become a prisoner in my own house, do you?'

David sighed loudly; it was one of his favourite ways of expressing his anger. 'You can hardly call yourself a prisoner when you've got access to a car.'

'That's not the point.'

'Then what is the point?' David folded his newspaper and threw it on the table.

'The point is, that I, as a woman, have the right to go where I like, to walk where I choose, and I'm not prepared to give up that right simply because I might one day be the victim of an assault.'

'But you only run that risk because you insist on taking unnecessary chances!'

'I will not be put off.' Jane was adamant.

'You will continue walking?'

'Yes.'

'Even though it scares you to death?'

'Yes...'

Jane had been scared tonight, but was quick to assure Anne that her fear had been unjustified.

'It was the Johnson boy,' she said. 'I didn't recognise him in the dark. He followed me most of the way here, but then, of course, he would do.'

The Johnson's house was less than a hundred yards from the Chaneys'.

'It was knowing there was somebody behind me, but not knowing who it was, that was the problem.' Jane picked up the mug Anne had placed before her and added two spoonfuls of sugar to her coffee. 'At least I was able to remember what I was taught on my self-defence course. I had decided what I would do if he...well, if he had been a real attacker.' Jane tapped the spoon on the rim of her mug and laid it against the sugar bowl.

'Would you have tried to fight him off?' Anne inched the biscuit plate towards Jane. She shook her head.

'I certainly wouldn't give in.'

'But don't you think you would be more at risk if you tried to fight back? Don't you think it would be safer to just ....do as you are told?' Anne picked up a digestive, broke it in half.

'Survival isn't the issue.'

'Then what is?'

'Pride.'

'Oh.' Anne took a bite of her biscuit. "Sometimes," she thought, "Jane so reminds me of Kay."

'You ought to go on a self-defence course.' Jane picked up her drink. 'It would be really useful.'

'You mean, it would give me some pride?'

Jane blushed. 'No, no of course that's not what I meant. It's just that you spend so much time here alone, in the house. It must worry you sometimes.'

Anne smiled wistfully, dropped the remaining half of her biscuit onto her plate. 'It's funny, isn't it? Jon's away so much you would think I'd get used to it, but I never have. - Not that I'm scared of burglars, or anything like that. No, it's the loneliness. That's what I haven't been able to come to terms with. Spending so much of my life alone.'

'It doesn't have to be like that.'

'It doesn't have to be, but it is.' Anne blinked, once, twice, and Jane saw the moisture in her eyes, the tears threatening to spill out.

'I'm sure things will get better.' She returned the mug to the coffee table and leant across, squeezed Anne's hand, received a grateful smile.

'It's something I try not to think about. It doesn't pay to brood.' Anne stood up, breathed in noisily through her nose. 'Now,' she exhaled, 'you came here to see my latest picture - although I must warn you, it still isn't finished. So why don't we take our drinks through into the study and take a look?'

'Sounds like a good idea to me.' Jane came to her feet, her coffee in one hand. 'Lead on, Picasso.' She smiled at her friend. What she was about to do scared her more than the Johnson boy ever had.

* * * * *

Chaney heard her footsteps in the hallway, heard the latch turn, heard the chain slide out of place. Katherine opened the door. She was wearing a simple mauve blouse of pure silk, brought in at the waist by a black, soft leather belt, in a way that accentuated the tightness of her stomach, the slimness of her hips. The hem of the blouse was cut away at the sides like a man's dress shirt, revealing the contours of her thighs and hips beneath the tight-fitting black, woollen skirt. Against that, a final patch of mauve curled gently down, covering her groin; drawing Chaney's attention to it.

'Well?' Katherine moved slightly to one side, allowing him access. Her shoes were also black. Her legs were bare, the skin a golden brown. 'Are you going to stand there all night? Because if you are I'll close the door and find something else to occupy me. This isn't my idea of fun.'

Chaney blinked and stepped inside, realising how cold he was.

Katherine pushed the door with just enough force for it to shut. 'Now that's better. It's certainly a little more private.' Katherine slipped her arms round Chaney's neck and kissed him gently on his lips, teasing him, staring into his eyes. She felt Chaney's hands on her hips, his thumbs pushing against her pelvic bone. Keeping her at bay. Katherine ran the tips of her forefingers across Chaney's forehead, and then down, following the line of his cheekbones, the contours of his face, until they met and stopped, beneath his lower lip. 'You look tired.'

Chaney lowered his head slightly and kissed her fingers. Katherine smiled and pulled away. 'Why don't you hang your jacket up, while I pour us both a drink?'

'Yes.' The movement her bottom made as she walked into the lounge entranced him. Not the deliberately affected swaying motion so many women displayed, more the economical pumping action of the well-trained athlete.

-Chaney grabbed her hair, twisted it, felt her hands clutching his wrists. Marched across the room, leading because it hurt more. Forced her down onto the table. Face down. Heard the thud of her forearms and elbows against wood. Saw the fingers opening and closing. Grasping. Pressed down hard with his left hand between her shoulder blades. Felt the ridges of her spine. Grabbed the skirt. Pulled it up. Struggled with it. Got it there. Ripped the flimsy covering away. Kicked her ankles further apart. Pulled his left hand away. Used it on her. Held himself in his right. Saw the hands grasping. Gasping. 'Now...Oh God, now...please..now!' Thrust inside her.-

'Your drink's ready.'

'...Right. I'll be there.'

'What's taking you so long?'

Chaney slipped his jacket off and hung it on the walnut coat stand by the door. 'I was... er, looking at the new addition to your collection.'

'The mirror?'

'Yes.' Chaney walked into the lounge. 'What the hell is that all about?'

Katherine was sitting on the floor, her back resting against the settee, her legs splayed out in front of her. Chaney sat on the settee next to her and took the offered glass.

'It's just a...a Chinese pattern. One that I have always liked.'

'Seems bloody stupid to me.'

"Yes, it would to you," thought Katherine. "Because you don't understand the real nature of power. And for as long as you are mine, I'll make sure you never do." 'It's just something that pleases me,' she said resting her head against Chaney's knee.

Katherine had spent four years at a university in Ohio, studying for a degree in Eastern philosophy. Not that she ever intended to pursue a career as a lecturer. Her study had been a purely personal one, the result of a growing desire to understand the workings of the universe, the nature of man. 'True power comes from understanding,' she had read once. 'Consider the words of Sun Tzu: 'Know your enemy and know yourself; in a hundred battles you will never be in danger. When you are ignorant of your enemy but know yourself, your chances of winning or losing are equal. When you are ignorant both of your enemy and of yourself, you are always certain to be in danger.'

Katherine sipped at her drink. Her understanding, her power,was increasing daily and still she strove to develop it further: the tortuous workouts in the gym; the periods of meditation, of emptiness; the relationships with men like Chaney. So much to learn.

'Aren't you going to ask me?' His voice was like an explosion beside her.

'About what?' The ice in Katherine's glass clinked as she placed it on the the carpet beside her left thigh.

'Tonight's interview.' Chaney shifted on the settee.

"He's irritated," Katherine thought, "because I haven't asked him yet." 'I don't need to ask you."'She looked up at Chaney, kept her face expressionless.

'Did you watch it?' he asked.

'No.'

'Then what are you, a mind reader?'

Katherine smiled. " Appease him now," she thought. " I don't want him out of control tonight. Not like that anyway." 'I am when it comes to you, darling.'

'Sometimes I think you are...'

'I know that your mind is too sharp to let a man like Hyndman beat you.'

'Then you did watch it?'

Katherine smiled again. At his puppy dog excitement.

'I saw about two minutes. Then my mother phoned. By the time I got rid of her, you had already finished.'

Chaney nodded. 'It's a pity you missed it. It was one of my better performances.'

'I hope you've still got one left for me.'

Chaney stroked her hair. 'It's good to know there was one person who had faith in me.' He said it without meaning to.

'I have complete faith in you,' Katherine said. "Faith in you to be yourself. And I know exactly what that is..."

'Then you won't be surprised by what I have got to tell you.'

'What?' Katherine straightened, leaning against the settee with her right arm. "Is this enthusiastic enough for you?"

'I'm to have my own series.' Chaney finished his drink.

'That's terrific. Whose idea was that?'

'That's a bloody stupid question.' Chaney stood up. He daren't lie. Not to her. 'Do you want another drink?' Katherine shook her head...

'What's it going to be about?'

'Me.' Chaney unscrewed the bottle top. 'It's going to be a look back at the past...'

'A look back at anger.' Katherine grinned.

'...A catalogue of my favourite interviews.' Chaney had not heard her. 'Anything I choose. We're running ten programmes and the idea is, each one will deal with a different year. We play the extracts I select, and then I give an update on the characters involved.' He shrugged. 'Apart from that, it's up to me. Mine to do with as I like.'

Katherine saw the red glow of excitement on his cheeks. 'It sounds really good.'

'It will be.' Chaney almost emptied the glass with his first swallow.

"You over-indulge," Katherine thought. "With everything. It's the cause of your weakness."

'Think about it, I've got a captive audience,' Chaney enthused. 'They have watched me for years, they won't stop now. Especially when they realise that it's my own series.' He drained his glass, poured himself another whisky. 'The beauty of it is, I have so much material, there's no reason why it should be a one-off. I'm sure that when the powers-that-be see how well it goes, they will want at least a second series. Maybe a third.'

Katherine smirked. 'You are going to be a very popular man.'

'That doesn't concern me.'

'Oh? What does?'

'Being successful. There is a difference.'

'But you already are successful.'

'I know, but there is always room for more. That's what keeps you at the top.' Chaney sat down beside her. Katherine observed his lack of balance and co-ordination; felt his weight sink into the settee, and remembered Isaki...

'Eiyaah!' The small Japanese in the dazzingly white outfit exploded into motion with such speed and ferocity that Katherine Durham gasped and raised her hands instinctively in front of her.

The afternoon's lecture was the first in a series about Zen Buddhism, and to mark the occasion a Kendo master who occasionally taught at the university's club, had agreed to give a demonstration of swordmanship and then talk to the students about the relationship between Zen and the martial arts. His name was Isaki, and when Katherine recovered from her shock she found herself intrigued by the awesome power of his movements and the serenity of his countenance. She questioned him about it afterwards. 'Power,' he said, 'comes through facing the self without fear or expectation. Every day I take up my katana, my sword, and use it in a battle against my self. Every day I face a new challenge and, because of that, every day I grow a little stronger..' He picked up a plastic cup from the table beside him, took a jug of water in his other hand.

'People are like a cup,' he said. 'If they become too full,' he began to pour the water, 'of their own desires, of their own self importance, they are of no use.' The cup was almost full now. 'And in time they can cause harm. To themselves,' the water began to spill over onto the floor,' and to others. People should therefore learn how to empty themselves, how to let go. In that way they will always develop. They will become strong...'

Chaney burped. 'You are very quiet all of a sudden.'

'I was thinking, that's all.'

'What about?'

'Your series.' The realisation came to her as she spoke. 'It will mean you will be spending more time in the city.'

'Yes. I've been thinking about buying a flat, or something. Perhaps now I will.' Chaney parted her hair, ran two fingers down the nape of her neck. Katherine felt him try to force them inside the collar of her blouse.

'Careful...' She pulled away, pulled her feet underneath her. 'These things cost money, you know.'

'I can always buy you another one. Another dozen if I come to live in the city. If you move in with me..'

Katherine saw the movement behind the curtain, looked towards it. Chaney followed her gaze.

'What is it?'

The curtain bulged again. Chaney placed his glass on the seat beside him. Saw a flicker of a smile cross Katherine's face; saw Soul's tail waft lazily as he settled on the window sill. 'Bloody cat.'

Katherine stood up and crossed the room. As she pulled the curtain back Soul stretched up to meet her downcoming hand, purring loudly as he pressed his head against her palm.

'He's watching the night.' Katherine let the curtain fall back into place.

'He's got nothing else to do.'

'What the hell is that supposed to mean?' Katherine's smile was replaced with a frown of anger. Below the curtain the tail flicked from side to side. 'C'mon, tell me, what point are you trying to make?' She raised her voice as she advanced on him.

-Yes. Always the same. The only time I ever really touch you. A worthless cat. Its head crushed on a dark night.-

'You understand what I am saying, why pretend that you don't?'

-You surprised me. When I found out. I could never have guessed. Not from the first time.-

Katherine Durham walked into the restaurant and recognized him instantly; sitting alone at the bar, staring into his drink as if it contained pictures that only he could see. She had time for a drink, her table was not booked for another twenty minutes, and as Katherine walked towards him she realised that she would have changed the booking if necessary. He was a man she desperately wanted to meet; to be with. Indeed, Katherine had only begun using this restaurant because she had heard that it was one of his favourite places.

'May I?' Katherine gestured towards the stool next to him.

He looked up; his face impassive. 'Why not?'

Katherine sat down, ordered a Scotch on the rocks. Waited just the right amount of time. 'Do you often eat here alone?'

His eyebrows raised, he looked at her over his shoulder.

'Do you often begin conversations with strangers?'

'Never with strangers.

'You know me then?'

'I have watched you.' Katherine was aware of the power of him, like a rock, difficult to penetrate. She had been right in her estimation of him. He was everything she required. The perfect test.

'So now you would like to join me for dinner?'

Chaney's face expressed no invitation.

Katherine took a peanut from the silver bowl, popped it in her mouth. 'I would really like to join you for much more...'

'For Christ's sake, he's my cat!' Katherine was shouting now. Stood before him, her right foot dangerously close to the glass she had left on the floor. 'How I treat him is my affair. I certainly don't need advice from you!'

'I don't give a damn about the animal. I just don't understand why you're so scared.' Chaney smirked. 'And that intrigues me.'

'What do you mean?' Katherine calmed suddenly, took a pace back.

'The cat is replaceable - you can easily get another. You've got nothing to lose by letting him go outside.'

'That isn't the point, you know it isn't.' The tone in Katherine's voice changed as she sank down to the floor by Chaney's feet. 'I have to keep him in. To keep him safe.' Pleading to be understood; ashamed that Chaney had recognized her fear.

'He's a cat. He deserves a life outside.'

-You wouldn't last five minutes in front of the cameras.-

'That's not true. If I let him outside he'll die. At least my way he will live a full life.'

'A longer life.'

'No!' Katherine shook her head, forcing back the tears. 'I won't let him out. Ever!' Thinking: " I couldn't bear to lose him. To be alone. No-one should ever be completely alone."

Chaney watched her internal struggle, waited until she had almost regained control. 'Then he will remain a prisoner.'

Katherine's anger flared again. 'How dare you say that!'

'He has no right of choice. You deny him that.' Chaney laughed softly. 'He might as well be dead.'

'Why don't you leave?' Katherine saw the surprise on his face and realised her mistake. If she didn't stop him he would go; his pride would make him go. And she didn't want to lose him. Not yet. Not until she mastered him. 'I'm ... I'm sorry, Jon. I've just had a hard day, that's all.' She reached for his hand. He let her take it. 'Don't leave me, please. You know I don't want you to.' Katherine raised his hand, rubbed her cheek against it.

-Underneath you're just like all the rest.-

'Stay and make love to me..'

Chaney came to his feet. Katherine looked up at him, holding his hand between hers.

'And if I buy a flat in the city, you'll sell this and move in with me?'

Katherine ran her left hand along the inside of his thigh. She thought: "I'll give up nothing for you." 'Can't we talk about that later? There are more important things now...'

Chaney pulled her to her feet. Katherine placed her palms against his chest. 'Where?'

He considered. 'The bedroom.'

Katherine smiled. 'Why don't you let me get there first?'

Chaney watched her leave the room, watched the movement her body made beneath the skirt. The door closed behind her and Chaney turned his attention to the bookshelves, lined with works he had never heard of, written by authors with names he could not pronounce. All of them relating to aspects of Eastern religion or philosophy. Chaney considered Paul and his similar interest; how different he was from Katherine.

-But only on the surface. You must never forget that.

I never do.

You must always go deeper.

Of course.

Penetrate to the heart.

And then?

Do with it as you will.-

Chaney made his way into the bedroom.

* * * * *

Jane Swift sat down gingerly in the offered seat. 'It's alright. I know they look awful, but the paint's dry. It won't come off on your skirt.' Anne sat in the grubbier of the two chairs, the one nearest the easel. 'I'm such a messy worker that I need a separate room. Besides,' Anne looked around her, 'This is the one place in all the world that I think of as truly mine. Not to be shared with anyone else...' Anne's voice trailed off.

'That must be nice.' Jane shifted slightly in her seat, trying to find a more comfortable position.

'Having your own private place. A place where you can be so creative too. To be honest with you Anne, I envy you.' She laughed nervously, not wanting to be misunderstood. 'Not because I want somewhere to escape from David. It's nothing like that. It's just that you have a place you can identify with. A place that represents you and no-one else. A real haven.'

'Yes..' Anne's face paled, staring at the desk covered with tins of paint, jam jars filled with brushes. The memory was there again, unwanted, unbidden, as loud and colourful as it had been some years before when ...

'Anne? Anne, are you alright?' Jane leaned forward, her own nervousness heightened by the sudden change in her friend. 'Anne?'

... When she arrived home, her newly bought paints and canvas in her arms, her face flushed with excitement, eager to transform the sun lounge into her study and begin her first painting. Surprised to see her husband's car in the drive. Confused and frightened by the noises she heard coming from the room that was to be hers. Rushing into the dining-room. To see the french doors open; to see the curtains closed across the patio door; to see Jon and Kay. To hear him groan...

'Anne?' Jane grabbed her by the shoulders. 'What's the matter with you?'

'Oh!' Anne shook her head, refused to see anymore.'Nothing, I'm alright. Really.'

'Are you sure?' Jane frowned. 'It was almost as if you were having some form of fit. I couldn't get through to you. I didn't know what to do.'

'It's nothing to worry about. Honestly.' Anne wiped her brow with the back of her hand, remembered the party and shivered.

'You don't seem alright to me.' Jane stood up. 'I think perhaps I ought to phone the doctor. Make you an appointment for tomorrow.'

'No!' There was desperation in Anne's voice as she grabbed Jane's hand and held her. 'I really don't need to see a doctor. Please sit down.'

Jane hesitated.

'Please.' Anne calmed. 'Sit down and forget it.'

'Are you sure?'

'Yes, I'm fine.' Anne smiled. 'I had a bit of a headache this morning. It was probably something to do with that.'

'O.K. Jane picked up her coffee and lowered herseslf carefully onto the flimsy chair. 'But if anything like that ever happens again, I want you to promise that you will see a doctor.'

'I promise.'

'Cross your heart?'

'You sound like you are advertising bras.'

Jane laughed. 'Alright, let's change the subject.' She looked about her. 'Where's this new picture I've been hearing so much about?'

'It's here.' The board was on the floor, leaning against a desk leg. The picture was almost complete.

'I'm afraid it's not quite finished yet, so you will have to use a little imagination.' Anne placed the board on the easel, turned it to face Jane. 'Well, what do you think?'

'Er...I'm quite surprised.' Jane realised she was frowning.

'What do you mean?'

'Well, it's not very...' she struggled for the right word; gave up, 'pretty, is it?'

'No, but then it isn't meant to be.'

'I see.'

'I think he was a stray. I took a photo of him during one of my afternoon walks. I only had time for one, which was rather unfortunate, but I couldn't get him to stop. He just looked at me over his shoulder as he trotted past.' Anne smiled. 'I think if I'd kept Sly's camera, I wouldn't have managed even one photo, and that would have been a terrible loss.'

'Yes.'

Anne's smile broadened. 'You don't need to be polite about it. If you don't like the picture I will understand. Besides, I'm not drawing him to please anyone else.'

'Then, why?' Jane struggled to keep her voice calm. She wanted to shout, "Why? Why are you doing this, when we had so much faith in you. When we have taken such a chance?" The dog was ugly. The sort of creature you would expect to find scavenging from dustbins. The sort of creature you would drive away with a half-brick and feel no sympathy for. 'Why are you doing this, Anne?'

'It is a real challenge for me. Concentrating on something scruffy and uncared-for. Unlike all the others. I look at some of those and you know, I don't really like them anymore.

'Why not?' This was turning into a nightmare. Jane's hands encircled her mug, squeezing it hard, as if somehow that would wake her. "God damn Kay Chaney and her bright ideas!"

'They seem so pretty. So perfect.'

'What's wrong with that?'

'Oh I don't know.' Anne blushed as she tried to organize thoughts. 'It's as if, by painting or drawing the animals, I remove them from the real world. I seem to paint out any faults that I see. Playing God with my paints...I told myself that that was what an artist should do, strive for perfection, and if that meant changing the model slightly, well... I was lying of course.' Anne looked again at the desk. 'An artist's responsibility is to reveal the truth, warts and all..'

'But who would want to put that on their wall?'Jane nodded at the picture. 'I mean, with the best will in the world, it isn't very nice to look at.'

Anne removed the board from the easel and returned it to its original position on the floor.

'I'm not a professional, I don't have to worry about pleasing other people. That's something I'm only just beginning to realise.' Anne paused. 'Besides, this type of work is more of a character study than anything else. It doesn't need to be pleasing to the eye.'

'How do you mean?'

'It's the dog's personality that I'm concentrating on. Trying to convey his attitudes, his character, through his expression and posture. You see, with a work like this,' Anne warmed to her subject, 'they are the areas of primary concern. The fact that he isn't wearing a collar and his coat's dirty is of secondary importance.

'It's like when, oh, I don't know, when you're travelling on a bus and you look at somebody and you just know they've had an interesting life. You don't need to talk to them, you can see it in their face. They are the people who will have been to all sorts of different places, broken all kinds of rules. They are completely independent, self-sufficient, and the way they look tells you that.' Anne glanced down at the picture. 'It's the same with him, only he's an animal not a person.'

The mug in Jane's hands had grown cold as the liquid cooled, but she didn't notice.

'That's amazing.'

'What is?'

'The way you talk about the picture. I thought when I first saw it that you were making a big mistake - moving away from the things you do so well, but now I can see that I was wrong. This is the sort of challenge you need if you are going to develop your talent. Of course it is.' Jane's confidence returned. 'And although I don't like - no, that's not the right word, - although I don't appreciate this particular picture, I'm sure there are many people who would.'

'You make it sound as if it's going on public display.' Anne smiled, saw the flush of colour in her friend's cheeks. 'Now what have I said?'

Jane shivered, realised for the first time that the room was not heated, that the cold had penetrated the thick curtains. 'Do you mind if we go back into the lounge?'

'Oh, I'm sorry. I spend so much time in here that I'm used to the cold.' Anne stood up. 'I just didn't think..'

The lounge was warm and bright and Jane chose the armchair nearest the fire. Anne sat opposite her on the settee, placed her mug on the small, rosewood coffee table that was positioned between them; Jane kept hold of hers.

'Now what is it you were going to say?'

'When?'

Anne saw Jane's back stiffen, saw the tension in her shoulders. 'Before we came out of the study. There was something you wanted to say, I could tell. We've been friends too long for you to hide it from me.'

'Yes, I should have known. Should have got straight to the point.' The shoulders relaxed slightly.

'Go on then.'

'It's to do with your art work.' Jane began hesitantly. 'Kay and I both think you are wasting your talent by not showing at least some of the work you have done.' Jane paused, staring into the bay window. 'We think an exhibition would be a good idea.'

Anne laughed nervously. 'Oh no. I could never do anything like that. Really. That's not why I paint, you know that. My pictures are too...too personal, I couldn't possibly share them. Especially with strangers. No, no, I don't think so.'

'That's nonsense and we both know it is.' Jane forced herself to be stern, to look directly at Anne. 'We have known each other for too long, remember? The real reason you don't want an exhibition is because you're scared. Of what people might say about your work. That it isn't good enough. That you won't sell any. That it might not be a success. Well, Kay and I both think that your work is good enough. That it's time you stopped wasting yourself.'

'Even if that is true, I couldn't organise an exhibition. I wouldn't know where to begin.' Anne was rubbing her hands together as if washing them, her fingers occasionally interlocking. 'I've never done anything like that before in my life. I mean... I just couldn't do it.'

'You don't have to.'

'What do you mean?' Anne's hands were suddenly still, clasped in prayer.

'Kay and I have arranged an exhibition for you.'

'But ... but that's impossible. Nobody's mentioned it to me. You couldn't have done such a thing without me finding out.'

Jane smiled with relief; the worst part was over now.

'We could and we did. We knew that if we discussed it with you in the first place, you would find a reason for not going ahead. This way you don't have any choice.'

'Why not?' Anne blanched.

'Because the exhibition is next Sunday.'

'What?'

'It's only in the village hall. Nothing too grand, not to start with anyway. We have booked the hall for the day, but the exhibition is only for three hours in the afternoon. We'll need the morning to prepare everything, to hang all the pictures.'

'Who knows about it?'

'Only Kay, Paul and myself. Oh, and David too. We've only invited a few friends, and some of Kay's business colleagues from the city, so there is nothing to worry about.'

'Have you discussed it with Jon?'

'No, I think that's ...er...going to be Paul's responsibility. Unless of course you want to tell him yourself?'

Anne shook her head. 'I really don't know what I want to do. The whole thing has come as such a shock. I never expected anything like... Anne's eyes opened wide, childlike, as the realisation dawned on her. 'My God! Next Sunday! You said next Sunday! That means we've got little more than a week to prepare, and there's so much to do!'

Jane laughed.

'Not to worry. Everything is under control. Kay has it all planned, down to the last detail. All you have to do is select the pictures you want to show. You can leave the rest up to us.'

'There's something else I must do first.'

'What?'

'Finish the picture of the dog.' Anne came to her feet, her face flushed with excitement; Jane followed suit. 'I must have him there next Sunday, although he won't be for sale.' She laughed. 'He'll be my lucky mascot!'

They gripped each other's hands above the coffee table; their reflection was just a blur in the polished wood.

* * * * *

Scream you bitch, scream! ...I'll make you...I'll make you do it... do everything ... all night.. I won't stop...I'll kill you with ...kill...kill...Aaah!

Apart from the bed, the bedroom contained a row of built-in wardrobes with glass-panelled doors covering one wall, the long, gilt-edged mirror, a dressing-table - done out in white and pink to match the bed linen and carpet - and a bedside cabinet on which stood a telephone and a heavy marble ashtray. A naked woman lay on the bed,her hair flattened beneath her like a chestnut halo, her thighs raised, gripping the waist of the man above, the fat on his buttocks trembling as he thrust himself into her with such ferocity it seemed he desired to hurt rather than pleasure.

Katherine Durham opened her eyes. Chaney held his torso off her, his arms straight, locked into position. She studied his face, ignoring their more intimate connection, refusing to think about the lies - the words, the noises; the things she had done to please him. Chaney's eyes were closed, tightly shut, the skin lined around the sockets, as if in the glare of a powerful light. His jaw was clenched, the muscles in his cheeks pulsing, working to the rhythm he had established. His head rocked from side to side, the movement increasing in intensity as he neared his orgasm.

Katherine looked into the gilt-edged mirror; saw the things she could not see. Began to use her own power to draw him out. Pressed against the base of his spine with her heels - pushing. Saw him quicken; saw the perfect shape of her thigh, her hair on the pillow. Saw it all as if it were someone else's dream. Felt nothing.

SEVEN

Paul Chaney had not slept well that night. For the most part he had lain in bed staring up at the ceiling, his hands behind his head; his wife breathing deeply beside him.

It had been a mistake, he realised, to mention his new job when he had. Not that he had planned to. It had been a spur of the moment decision, provoked by Kay's insistence on watching his father on television. That was something she always did, partly, Paul suspected, because she knew how much it annoyed him. Still. After all those years... Annoyed him because of the way Kay insisted on flirting with his father; because of her strange fascination - no, say it - desire, for him; because ....well.

Kay shifted, turned on her side. Paul felt her shoulderblades touching his elbow: bone against bone. No, he should have said nothing about the job, not yet. Instead he had used it as a weapon, lashing out with it in the hope that he would hurt - who? Perhaps himself - or his father. Certainly not his wife. Not deliberately anyway. Paul sighed. For better or for worse...

When he viewed his marriage as a whole, Paul wasn't sure which. That was the trouble. Sometimes love just wasn't enough. Sometimes it wasn't in evidence. Paul shook his head, pressed his teeth against his lower lip. If only he had kept his mouth shut...Now he would have to undo the damage and that would not be easy. Kay would almost certainly continue to dismiss the idea out of hand, no matter how much it secretly excited her. She would not lightly forgive or forget the way he had used it against her.

"But she forgave the way - No, don't think about that again, don't bring that into it. Don't let anything influence you now. It's too important for that."

Kay's breath deepened into a snore and Paul nudged her with his elbow; made her grumble angrily to herself. The snoring stopped.

"So what do I do if I can't change her mind? If she gives me an ultimatum? I want this job. It's a chance to get away. To make a fresh start. For both of us. God knows that's something we could do with. But what happens if she is too proud to admit that? Or if she genuinely doesn't want to leave? I want this job and I love my wife. -So what the hell do I do then?"

Paul Chaney had not slept well that night.

Katherine Durham had. When Chaney rolled off her she waited five minutes, until she was sure he was asleep, and then got up, showered, and went into the lounge where she performed thirty minutes' meditation. It was not her preferred place, but she did not wish to share the practice; dare not risk Chaney waking up. When that was complete, Katherine returned to her bedroom, lay down beside Chaney and slept for six hours. She woke, without the aid of an alarm clock, at the exact time she intended to; dressed in a pink Nike sweatsuit and a pair of light blue training shoes and went out into her small, walled back garden to perform her morning Tai Chi exercise.

The movements were slow and deliberate, designed to promote health, flexibility, and to cultivate the Chi, the internal energy, which, the masters said, gave the body power far beyond its physical parameters. As she practised, Katherine became aware of the city slowly waking up around her, felt the chill in the morning air, heard the sounds her shoes made on the wet grass.

Sitting on the window sill, looking out through the glass, Soul watched her exercise, and was aware of none of those.

'Hello Daddy.'

'Hello son.' Smiling, his teeth even and white. Such beautiful teeth. 'Are you looking after Mummy for me while I'm away?'

'I promised I would.' Squirming up onto the end of the bed. Sitting by his feet, playing with them as they moved beneath the white tight bed covers. Grabbing his toes. Giggling.

'How long are you going to stay here for, Daddy?'

'Oh, not very long, I shouldn't think.'

'Really?' Eyes wide. Bouncing with excitement.

'Really.'

'Is that a promise?'

He isn't smiling anymore.

'I want you to leave your mother and me alone for a while. I want you to go downstairs and buy me an evening paper from that little bookshop near the door where you came in. I want you to do it now.'

He's got a coin in his hand. He wants me to take it.

'But I want to stay with you, Daddy.'

'Son! Do as you are told!'

He's angry. I can tell. His eyebrows meet when he is angry.

I don't care. 'I want to be with you!' His feet have moved half-way up the bed, he's leaning towards me. He is shaking with anger. I can see his right hand in the air. He is going to slap me. I close my eyes. Screw my face up tight.

Nothing happens.

'Please son, fetch me a paper.'

I open my eyes. My Daddy is crying.-

Chaney woke with a start; sat up in bed and looked around him. He was in Katherine's bedroom. One of the wardrobe doors was half-open. The bedroom door was closed. He was alone.

Chaney ran the palm of his right hand round the back of his neck, felt the sweat there. He looked into the gold-edged mirror; his hair was dishevelled; there were still dark rings under his eyes. He could feel his heart pounding, triggered by the dream. Chaney snorted, sank back into the bed and began to breathe deeply, counting the breaths, reducing them gradually until he was breathing only eight times a minute, until his heartbeat was strong and slow.

-It is only a dream.

But I cannot lose it.

You pay too much attention to it.

I don't search it out.

You should disregard it.

It wasn't always a dream.

It is now.-

Chaney exhaled loudly, pushed the covers away and swung his legs over the side of the bed. He had a slight headache which he hadn't noticed when he was lying down. Chaney dropped his head forwards, until his chin was resting on his upper chest. Then he pressed the first two fingers of each hand together and placed them on either side of his neck, at the place where the skull rises behind the ears. Applying pressure, he rotated his fingers in tight anti-clockwise circles, feeling the muscles and ligaments moving slightly beneath his fingertips, the hardness of the bone. It was the way he had always relieved his headaches. For as long as he could remember; the way he had always known. Without ever being told.

Chaney dismissed the thought, no longer prepared to consider the mystery of it. Within minutes the headache had disappeared.

He stood up. His clothes were strewn on the floor between the door and the bed - the place where Katherine had undressed him. Chaney gathered them together and dropped them on a corner of the bed. Then he sat beside them and dressed slowly, struggling with his underpants and trousers because he refused to stand, managing in the end only because he lay back to fasten the final two buttons on his trousers; giggling at his game.

When it was over Chaney stood up and stretched, feeling awake now. His stomach rumbled and he needed to piss. He glanced once again in the mirror - a distinct improvement - and then quickly round the room, making sure there was nothing he had missed. Chaney was opening the bedroom door when the phone rang. He crossed the room swiftly and picked up the receiver. Said nothing.

'H - Hello?' A man's voice, cautious, hesitant, vaguely familiar the way all telephone voices are. 'What number is that?'

Chaney waited, violently aware of the pumping of his heart. 'Guess.'

The line went dead. Chaney lowered the receiver slowly, watching it as if it might suddenly explode.

-Secrets...are a figment of other people's imaginations.-

Katherine Durham was standing in the doorway.

'Oh.. You are awake now.'

'Yes.'

'Did I hear the phone ring?'

'Where were you?' Chaney noticed that she did not move towards him. There was a faint sheen of persperation on her forehead.

'Outside. I was..er..exercising.' Katherine smiled with conviction, cocked her head as if in apology. 'What about the phone?'

'Oh, yes. It rang.' Chaney nodded slowly, the movement lending authority to his statement, to the seriousness of it. Questions hung in the air between them, touching them both, daring to be asked.

'Who..er..who was it?'

Chaney raised his eyebrows in a gesture of ignorance, breathed in deeply, filling his lungs. Exhaled.

'It was a ...wrong number.' He said finally.

'Oh I see. I thought perhaps with it being so early in the morning it would be someone from the office.'

Katherine spoke quickly. 'They often call me about this time. Last minute changes and all that.'

'I see.' Chaney walked towards her. 'It's funny they've never done that when I have been here before, isn't it?'

Katherine paused only briefly and then linked her arm through his and guided him out of the room, through the hall, the lounge, and into the kitchen.

'Don't be silly, you are not here that often, you know.' Katherine's manner was light, girlish. 'If you were, there wouldn't be much point me having a telephone next to the bed. - I'd never get a chance to use it.' She halted their progress by the small, pine table. 'Now why don't you sit there while I make us both some scrambled eggs?'

Chaney did as he was told.

'And while I'm doing that, you can tell me about your plans for the day.'

'I'm spending some time with Russell Tobin.'

'The publisher?'

'Uh-huh.'

'Something to do with the book?' Katherine turned away from him began to busy herself at the cooker.

'He thinks he is going to change the publication date.'

'That sounds serious.'

'I don't think so.' Chaney could see the line of Katherine's underwear through the sweatsuit pants.'So why don't you tell me about your day?'

Katherine shrugged. 'Work, as usual.'

'What time should you start?'

'Nine-thirty. Why?'

Chaney reached across, crooked his fingers inside the waistband of Katherine's pink trousers. 'You're going to be late.'

* * * * *

Paul Chaney was sitting in the lounge reading the notes he had made for his morning lecture, when Kay came downstairs. He was wearing a blue shirt, white tie, and a grey two-piece suit, the size of the lapel and the flare of the trousers indicating that it had been purchased in the previous decade. His socks were green and his shoes were brown: fashion was not one of Paul's greater considerations.

'Did you know your sports bag is at the bottom of the stairs?' Kay kicked at it angrily; in her sleepy state she had almost fallen over it.

'I'm playing squash with my father this afternoon.' Paul did not look up from his notes.

'I think you ought to give it up. It's a pointless exercise.'

'What makes you say that?' Paul frowned.

Kay entered the room. 'You always lose, and unless you know something I don't, you always will.'

Paul straightened, covered the sheets of paper with the palms of his hands and ignored her gaze, staring instead at the wall opposite.

"Because you only want to win...I need to.."

Paul heard the words echoing in his head; felt a tingling in his nose, down the length of his spine, shivered.

"I doubt the truth of it, father."

Paul had been surprised when his father asked to join him at squash, delighted that, for the first time, he had knowledge to impart that the other could not refute.

Chaney had insisted that he book the court for two hours for their first session: allowing one hour for competitive play. Paul had argued that one hour was sufficient - it was a strenuous game, men had died playing it. He had been overruled. In that second hour they played four games. The first one was close, the other three were not. Chaney won them all.

They continued to play, once, sometimes twice, a week and occasionally Chaney managed to win every game without losing a point. That had not surprised Paul, for even as a child his father had beaten him mercilessly at every game they played. As an adult, Paul came to realise that squash was the instrument of his revenge. Not that he ever began a game expecting to win. Indeed, he was quite prepared to accept the possibility that he would never beat his father, but he could make him run and sweat and occasionally stumble. That was Paul's victory. Although he did not experience a feeling of joy, or even success, when it happened, just a strange burning sensation in the pit of his stomach - a nothingness, because he knew of no way to describe it.

"There is a safety within it," he thought. "I will never win, but the points I score mean that I will never have to treat him as I should ...Punish him as I should..."

Paul had heard a car pulling up, looked outside and been surprised to see his mother getting out of a taxi. Even at that distance he could see the dishevelled hair, the tears. He raced outside. His mother ran towards him, almost collapsed in his arms. Paul held her tight; felt her soundless sobbing, her stomach heaving as if she were about to retch.

'Oh...oh...P...Paul!'

'It's alright...it's alright..'He stroked her hair; his mind racing.

'Oh God Paul!...I...didn't mean...to see it...I didn't want to...I...' Her voice came in great raking gasps.

'It's alright now.' Paul eased her away from his chest, keeping his palms on her elbows for support. 'You can tell me what it was. Tell me what you saw.'

His mother raised her head and looked directly at him for the first time. Paul felt himself tremble, resisted the temptation to look away. She seemed to have aged ten years overnight: her forehead was lined, her skin was pale, streaked with black mascara below her eyes. Her mouth hung open as if the jaw was unhinged; Paul felt a tremor of fear. Grabbed her more firmly by the shoulders.

'For God's sake, what is it?'

The mouth opened and closed soundlessly; the eyes staring vacantly at some spot behind him.

'Tell me what you saw!' Shaking her now, scared by her silence, not caring what words she used to fill it.

'I...' Anne took a deep breath. '..was going into my study to...to start a picture..'

'And?'

'Jon and Kay were there. They...'

'What do you mean mother? What were they doing?'

'By the desk. I heard their noises.' Anne's head shook rhythmically from side to side as if denying the vision that was still before her. 'He was just about to...going to...he was...' Anne's head stopped moving, her eyes blazed with a sudden fury. She grabbed Paul's upper arms, pulled him close, her fingers like talons.

'Your wife! Do you understand, she's your wife! You can't blame him! You should learn how to..'

Paul staggered back and Anne followed him, her fists beating against his arms and chest.

'I hate!..I hate!...I hate !...'

'You haven't heard a word I've said, have you?' Kay sighed deeply, for Paul's benefit.

'Oh...No, I'm sorry. Really. I was miles away.' Paul closed his eyes, ran the thumb and forefinger of his right hand along the bridge of his nose; erased the memory. "For a time. It will come back. I know it will. It always does."

Paul looked at his wife, standing arms akimbo. 'What were you saying?'

'It doesn't matter, but what I'm going to say now does.'

'Why?'

'Because I've come to a decision about your new job.'

'And?'

'I've given it as much thought as it deserves,' Kay said, enjoying her sudden hold over him., 'and I've decided that you will have to make a choice. Between me and the job...If you take it, I'll leave you.'

'But...but that's ridiculous.' Paul half stood, his notes fell on the floor. 'You've had no time at all to think about it, and... and we've hardly discussed it.'

'I thought we discussed it sufficiently last night.' Kay said.

Paul sank back into the chair. 'I'm sorry about last night,' he said. 'I know I introduced the subject in an awful way. I was just a bit uptight, that's all.'

'Oh, I see. A change of approach now, is it? You think that will be more successful, do you?'

'Of course not. I was apologising for a mistake I made.' Paul's voice hardened. He felt the first knots of tension in his stomach, blamed the lack of sleep. 'It's an important decision. We need to consider it calmly, together.'

'I am perfectly calm.' Kay's speech was cold and deliberate. 'And you didn't give the impression last night that you wanted us to reach a joint decision...'

'I've already apologised for last night!'

'..Rather that you simply wanted me to agree with you.'

Kay's voice took on a melodramatic tone. 'The man has made his decision!'

'That's not true! I only want what's best for us.'

'Well, I've told you my decision.'

'But for God's sake, we've got nowhere.' Paul hit the chair arm in frustration.

'That's not quite right, dear.' Kay backed towards the door, watching for his reaction. 'It's me who's going nowhere. You can go where you choose.'

'And suppose I do?' Paul rounded on her. 'Suppose I leave you? Suppose I take the job and clear off to the other side of the world? What the hell will you do then? What will you do when I sell the house?'

Kay's lip curled into a slight smile. 'It won't cause me a problem if you sell the house, darling.'

'Why?' Kay's assurance tempered his anger; forced the question.

'Because if you ever do, I'll move in with your parents. I'm sure your father won't mind.'

'You stupid cow. You...' Paul was on his feet, raging. His notes tore beneath his brown two-tone slip-ons.

'Careful, darling.' Kay laughed and opened the door.

'It wouldn't do your career prospects any good at all if I divorced you on the grounds of cruelty, now would it?' Kay disappeared into the hall. Paul stood, unmoving, letting his turmoil subside; wondered why his hands were shaking. He saw the sheets of paper scattered on the carpet around him and realised the damage he had caused. Kneeling, he began to gather them together. When that was done, Paul glanced at his watch. 'Shit!' His lecture was due to begin in forty-five minutes.

* * * * *

Russell Tobin's office was red. From the carpet, which was a pale red, studded with flecks of black, to the wallpaper, a blood red with lines of embossed gold, in threes, running from floor to ceiling. Even the two chairs facing his desk, placed equidistantly from the walls and sufficiently apart to prevent a private conversation between the occupants, were made of red leather.

Red had not always been Tobin's favourite colour. Indeed in many ways, the fact that he had made a choice went against his general principle. Tobin was the managing director and majority shareholder of one of the largest and most successful publishing houses in the country. His success stemmed from his ability to make calm, rational decisions: determining the worth of a manuscript in a cold, clinical manner. Russell Tobin was not possessed of an artistic temperament. He was a business man, who had made his fortune selling work that, occasionally, others described as works of art. He was emotionally unaffected by all the books he published. He had no favourites. At work or at home. Tobin was a bachelor, dedicated solely to his profession and to the art of making money. He had no need for favourites of any kind. And then he went to Spain. For a holiday. Soaked up the sun and the booze, enjoyed the architecture and the women. And went to a bullfight.

Tobin went because his host, a writer, Tobin always tried to mix at least a little business with his pleasure, invited him. As he took his seat, Tobin was determined not to enjoy himself. He had already decided that, when his host asked him afterwards, he would calmly describe the event as 'a spectacle'. It was, he felt, a suitably English description, sufficiently remote to indicate neither horror or fascination. As it was, he had been entranced. Following the swirling movement of the cape as determinedly as the bull. Sitting on the edge of his seat, aware that he was twisting and swerving, following the matador's movements, but unconcerned by it; by the smiling locals around him. Before, he had always wondered at the bull's stupidity, attacking a square of cloth that it couldn't hurt, that posed no threat to it. Now, he understood: the red flag, signalling danger, risk and possible glory; as demanding as the hypnotist's watch, as sincere as Judas. And when the matador rose high on his toes ...Tobin saw also why his host had described him as 'a Nureyev of death'... and plunged the blade downwards into the bull, as clean and easy as running a knife through lard, he saw the blood red spill over the heavy black shoulders of the beast and watched the bull drown amid the cheers of the crowd.

Tobin went to the bullfight twice more before his holiday came to an end, and he returned to England with his first - and only-favourite.

Chaney had only been to Tobin's office once before, on the occasion of their first meeting, when the publisher had suggested that Chaney write his autobiography. The idea excited them both and within six months the book was complete, apart from a few minor editorial changes that Tobin performed personally. Now there were only the formalities to determine.

"Let's get the fuckin' thing published." Chaney told himself for the third time that morning as he climbed the stairs to Tobin's outer office. "We don't have time to fuck about."

-Is that what you think?

No. It's ...it's what people say.

You're not like other people.

No...

You have success and power.

I'm in control.

Then you have as much time as you need.

As much time as I want.

Ha! You understand. There is a difference.-

The secretary was different to the one Chaney had seen before. This one was young, in her early twenties, with dyed blonde hair and a white nylon blouse that revealed her bra.

'Mr Tobin is expecting me.'

The cups of her bra were three-quarters lace, showing patches of pink and a hint of darkness in the centre. Chaney moved back a pace, away from the desk. Her legs were crossed, her left thigh clearly visible. She coughed. Chaney lifted his gaze, saw a slight colour in her cheeks - she had seen him look. No matter, she was a cheap, oversexed secretary. Chaney had seen women like her so many times. They could fuck and still make a hundred words a minute.

'Who shall I say is here?' She pushed her chewing gum to one side of her mouth as she spoke, a slightly aggressive tone in her voice.

'It's your job to know.' Chaney shrugged, dismissed her, and glanced round the room. Three grey filing cabinets, two chairs covered in a brown fabric, too low to be comfortable, beside an equally low, oval table with a teak finish, and one painting - a bullfight scene - on the wall behind the secretary's desk. Like a dentist's waiting-room, Chaney considered.

-Or a doctor's-

The secretary was watching him expectantly, still waiting for an answer.

'Chaney. Tell him Jon Chaney is here.'

She leant forward, no hint of recognition on her face, and spoke into the intercom. 'There's a gentleman here to see you, Mr Tobin. Says his name is Mr Jon Chaney.'

-It is.-

Her legs were still crossed, her left foot bobbing up and down to a beat only she could hear.

-'Do you want me?' She pushed against the desk with both hands, her chair rolled back. 'Of course you do.' She smiled, stood up. Her lipstick was of the purest red. 'You know how I like it.' She walked round to the front of the desk - in front of him. He could smell her now. 'I'll leave my shoes on.'- shiny, black, high-heeled - ' They will make it easier for you.' She turned her back to him, wiped the two trays and the letters from the desk with a sweep of her arm, using both hands to push the typewriter off. She pulled her skirt up round her waist, wearing nothing underneath, and bent forward onto the desk. 'I'm ready now...Now! Chaney moved towards her.-

'Jon! How are you?' Russell Tobin came out of his office looking cool and immaculate, wearing an expensive light grey suit and a red silk tie.

Chaney rocked on his feet, regained his composure. The secretary continued with her letter, pausing to correct an error and tut-tutting to herself as she did so.

'You're looking a little shaky, Jon.' Tobin grinned, extending his right hand in greeting. 'Late night, last night?'

Chaney felt the softness of Tobin's palm against his and squeezed harder than was necessary. 'I've never felt better.' He increased his grip. 'How about you?'

Tobin paled and laughed nervously. 'I'm in danger of losing my hand.'

Chaney raised his head slightly in agreement, felt the tightness in his groin diminish. 'We can't have that.' Chaney released his grip and saw Tobin surreptitiously wriggle his fingers. 'Not when we have so many other important things to discuss.'

'That's right.' Tobin backed away, his voice lacking the confidence it had displayed earlier. 'You had better come through into my office. We can't spend all day out here, and there are other people I've got to see.' Tobin gestured towards the open door and Chaney, accepting the invitation, led the way.

The secretary finished her letter and then slipped a hand under the desk, tugged nervously at the hem of her skirt. "Arrogant bastard," she thought. "Russell was right, he thinks he's God almighty..."

Tobin closed the door behind them; Chaney paused in the centre of the room. 'Take a seat, Jon.' Tobin patted one of the red leather chairs as he walked past them. 'I'll get us both a drink. ...Unless it is too early for you.'

'I'll have a Scotch.'

'Fine.' The drinks cabinet was in a corner behind his desk. Tobin opened it and poured two equal measures, adding a shot of soda water to one. 'I think we should drink to a future bestseller.' He turned; Chaney was standing by the window, looking down to the street below. 'Because I ...er...I'm sure that's what it is going to be.' His smile faltered. 'You are happy with it still? No change of heart?' Tobin crossed the room as he spoke.

Chaney waited until he was close. 'I'm happy with it.' He took the offered glass. 'And there isn't time to change it anyway.' Chaney looked out of the window. The road was lined with traffic. A boy fell off his bike, landing heavily on the pavement. Pedestrians hurried past.

'Well...er, that isn't strictly true. ' Tobin moved away again, taking his seat behind his desk. 'There is always a certain flexibility in these matters. To allow further revision, or...whatever.'

Chaney nodded. The boy mounted his bike and fell again: the chain was damaged. Chaney turned away abruptly, approached the desk. 'You want to change the publication date.'

Tobin's eyes widened in a protestation of innocence. 'I want to do what is best for the book, and for you as an author. That's my job.'

'Your job is making money. Let's not pretend otherwise.'

'Of course, we are a business, but we are only a successful business because we look after our writers, market their products properly.' Tobin leant forwards, surprised that his nervousness had disappeared, encouraged by it. 'Your work has enormous potential. You are a household name, so are the people you write about, but you're not the professional in this business, Jon. I am. If your book is going to maximise its potential, you will have to listen to my advice. To accept it. I mean, after all, I wouldn't dream of telling you how to conduct an interview.' Tobin smiled, tried to lighten the tone.

-There isn't anything you could tell me.

But you need this man.

I don't need anyone.

You need to use him.

Yes.-

'What is your advice?' Chaney sat down.

'I think we need to consider when is the very best time for publication,' Tobin began quickly. 'We can expect your book to sell well whenever it is brought out, but if it's timed properly it could be...well, enormous.' Tobin paused, drank thirstily. 'A mistake on my part now could, I believe, cost you a great deal of money, Jon.

Chaney sniffed. 'Suppose I don't agree with what you've got to say? Suppose I trust my own judgement more than yours?'

'I don't think that will happen, but if it does, well...'Tobin rubbed his hands together, '..I will be forced to overrule you. Unless of course your reasoning is so persuasive that it changes my mind.' Tobin smiled. 'Although realistically I don't see that as a possibility, do you?'

-He's rushing in.

Like a fool.

He can't see the danger.

How could he, he hasn't heard about it?

He should sense it. He lacks awareness.

Yes.

That's his weakness. Exploit it. Punish him for it. Let him exhaust himself first. There's no hurry.-

'When do you think would be the right time to publish?'

Tobin pursed his lips, clicked his tongue several times against the roof of his mouth before answering. 'We've decided not to publish until November.'

'That's almost ten months!' Chaney felt a surge of anger and dissolved it. There was no need for it.'Why should I be prepared to wait that long?

'It's when the market is at its best. Just before Christmas. People are always looking for something new, something different. They will buy your book in droves - I guarantee it.'

'Are you saying that if you publish it earlier in the year, people won't buy it at Christmas?'

'No I'm saying that if we publish in November we are sure of launching the book with a bang. It's better for everyone if we sell a vast amount of copies in a short space of time. I'm sure you can see the logic of that.'

'Yes, I can. It makes a lot of sense.' Chaney's voice was soft, congratulatory. Tobin beamed, stretched back into his chair and relaxed.

'I'm pleased you see it that way, Jon. I can't tell you ...'

'That's why I think you should publish in the summer.'

'You think what?' Tobin came forward with a start. His voice took on a high pitched note, his cheeks the colour of the wallpaper.

'You should publish in the summer. When the demand will be greatest.' Chaney contained a smile; regretted having to end the game.

Once he had driven a hundred miles just to be with a woman. An older woman he had never had before. A woman he wanted. It took him ninety minutes to reach her house and in that time he hardly noticed the roads or the traffic; his mind filled with thoughts of her. Her body. The things she would do for him. The ways he would have her. Chaney realised that day that pleasure is determined by anticipation, that an action is only made good by the thoughts that precede it: the looking forward; and when the moment arrives, and hopes become a reality, there is no climax. Only a draining away ...

'For Christ's sake, Jon!' Tobin's right hand thudded against the desk. 'I thought I'd explained all that. I thought you understood. Christmas is the time when demand will be greatest.'

'I heard what you said. And I know that you are wrong.' Chaney paused, making it last. 'You see, there's something you need to know about. Something that will change your mind.'

'What?'

Chaney licked his lips. 'Something of mine that begins in the summer. It's called 'Chaney's Choice'.'

When Paul Chaney arrived home that lunchtime, he found a note on the dining room table. It read: 'Jane phoned just after you left. Everything is going ahead as planned. Mummy wants you to tell Daddy ... so do it this afternoon. I will be home late. K.'

Paul read the note twice and then dropped it and watched it drift down onto the table. The last thing he needed now was a bloody stupid exhibition. He had more important things to worry about.

"No, that isn't fair." Paul corrected himself. "I can't blame Mum, not for my mistakes."

Paul walked into the kitchen and poured himself a Perrier. "I've got two weeks to save my marriage and get the job that I want, and in the middle of that I'll have to lose a couple of days helping my mother.'" Paul shrugged, took a swallow of his drink. "And of course I'm given the job they are all scared to do."

He opened the fridge, chose a cold chicken leg for lunch. "I'll tell him this afternoon. I don't really have any choice." Paul pushed the fridge door to with his knee. "But what the hell will he say?"

'An art exhibition!' The plimsoll dropped to the floor. 'You must be out of your minds!' Chaney's voice reverberated round the changing room. Paul groaned inwardly.

'I was afraid you would take it like this. But if you will just listen -'

'What for? You've told me everything I need to know!'

-That isn't true.-

'Jesus Christ!' Chaney came to his feet, kicked at his sports bag, sent it sliding across the tiled floor. 'A bloody art exhibition! What's the next bright idea you're gonna get?'

-Listen to him.-

'What a bloody absurdity. I mean -'

-Listen.-

Paul saw his father turn away abruptly, silencing himself, then walked across the room in the direction of his bag, his right fist tapping against his left palm. When he reached the bag he stopped, but made no attempt to pick it up. When the tapping stopped Chaney spoke again, a tremor in his voice.

'Who already knows about this?'

'All the family. And...and the Swifts.' Paul saw the head nod twice but otherwise his father was motionless, staring at the wall.

'You made sure I was the last.'

'It wasn't deliberate.' Paul lowered his gaze as he spoke, an instinctive reaction. 'It just worked out that way.'

'I'll bet it did.' Chaney bent suddenly, picked up his bag and returned to his place on the wooden bench. 'Tell me, whose idea was it?'

It was Paul's turn to look away. 'It doesn't matter.'

Chaney smirked. 'Kay's. I might have known. It's about all she's good for.'

'For Christ's sake! It doesn't matter!'

-That's better.

Yes, it's what you should have said in the first place.

You were lucky it was Paul.

I was...I was surprised. That's all.

You were shocked.

No, no, that's not true. It just took me by surprise. I didn't expect ...

It must not happen again. Surprise is a dangerous thing. It can destroy a man. Completely. It must never happen again.

No, never again.-

'I mean I keep telling myself that I should have got used to you after all these years of fighting and arguing,' Paul had not finished, 'but the stupid thing is, I haven't! I still keep expecting - hoping - that one day you'll stop being so fucking destructive!'

'Me!' Chaney slapped his own chest with the palm of his hand, his voice louder than Paul's. 'You tell me I'm destructive -'

-Prey on his fear.-

'- and yet when your bloody wife comes up with a stupid idea and pretends it's to benefit your mother, you go along with her because you haven't got the balls to stand up to her, or the sense to see what damage it'll cause! Jesus Christ!'

-I know you too well son..-

'My mother needs something!' Paul screamed, his face white with rage. 'She's got a husband who doesn't care and a talent she doesn't recognize. She needs someone who is prepared to try - and I am!'

-...For your own safety.-

'It amazes me how a sexless frump and a recognized bastard could ever produce such a saint.'

'Listen -' With two strides Paul was at his father, his hands reaching down to grab his shirt collar.

Chaney rose to meet the challenge. 'No, you listen ...' Paul hesitated; backed off. '...your mother's just like the rest of us.

She had a life. The chance to do with it what she wanted. And she did. She made her choice a long time ago. She chose to hide away!'

'How can you say that?'

'Because I watched her! Why the hell do you think she married me?

'Because she loved you.'

'Bullshit! She married me because I offered her somewhere to hide - someone to hide behind - and if you think anything else you're a bigger fool that I took you for'.

'That doesn't justify the way you treat her; the things you do.' Paul was sure he was right, but something his father had said touched him, rekindled the fear he had felt when Kay first told him.

'We need to do something positive for your mother,' she had said. 'To get her out of her rut, to give her a feeling of accomplishment.'

'What do you suggest?' Paul was reading the morning paper, only half listening.

'An art exhibition.'

The silence forced him to lower his Telegraph. 'Are you serious?'

'I've been thinking about it a great deal. It's precisely what your mother needs.'

Paul shrugged. 'Suggest it to her, see what she says.'

'No, that's not the way to do it.'

'Oh?'

'We will arrange it and then tell her. Give her no choice in the matter. That way it's sure to happen.'

'She might not want that.' Paul frowned. 'She might prefer to carry on the way she is.'

'Nonsense.' There was a determined edge to Kay's voice.

'People are always looking for ways to improve themselves.'

'I'm not sure -'

'Well I am, and I'm going ahead with it. So I'd suggest the best thing you can do is help me.'

'I don't think you can just bulldoze your way into other people's lives like that.'

'For God's sake Paul, she is your mother!' Kay pointed a finger accusingly. 'It's about time you did something to help her.'

'And what happens if the exhibition's a failure?' Chaney sensed Paul's uncertainty, pursued his advantage. 'What if she doesn't sell a painting? If people laugh at her?'

'That's a chance we will have to take. It's unavoidable.'

Chaney nodded. 'That's right. Only you're not the one taking the chance. She is. And if it is a disaster, you can be sure she will never recover from it - and it will be your fault.' Chaney bent forward, began to put on his plimsolls.

Paul watched him in silence. "He's right. I should have warned her, given her the chance to say no," he thought. "If it does go all wrong, I can't possibly turn round and tell her I am leaving the country. That would leave her with no-one. Hell!"

Chaney straightened and took his racket from his bag.

'It's too late to worry about it. There's no turning back for you now.'

'I wasn't. I was just wondering if you were going to be there. We'll need all the help we can get.'

'I'll be there.' Chaney stood up, tapping his racket strings against his fingertips. 'But I'm too busy to help you with the preparations. Something's come up at work. I haven't told anyone yet, but -'

'You'll be busy, I know. You always are. It's what I should have expected.' Paul glanced at his watch.

'We are due on court.'

'Right.' Chaney put his bag in his locker, fastened it, and followed Paul out of the changing rooms. The two men walked along the corridor in silence.

-He didn't listen.

He didn't want to know.

I'll tell him later. After the game.

That would be stupid thing to do. There is no need to hurry. You have all the time you want.

But I thought ...

Relax! It's only in a village hall. It will be forgotten in a couple of days. Then it will be your turn. Do you understand?

Yes.

Timing. Without it you are nothing.

But I wanted to tell them today...-

The court was empty and Paul closed the door behind them, throwing the ball to his father. 'Ten minutes warm up?'

Chaney took his position in the right-hand court, massaging the ball in his left hand. It was cold and soft. 'Make it five.' He threw the ball gently up in the air, waited a brief second until it was level with his face and struck it with his full force. Saw it thud against the far wall some two feet above the green line.

-Burn, you bastard.-

* * * * *

It was Kay Chaney's favourite coffee shop, with real wooden beams on the ceiling and maybe a dozen walnut tables - some round, some oblong - with matching chairs. Not a hint of plastic in the place.

Kay visited the shop three, sometimes four, times a week, according to her schedule, and she always sat alone at the table for two furthest from the entrance. She used her time there in various ways. Sometimes working quietly on documents brought from the office, on other occasions simply taking the opportunity to relax. Today she did neither of those. Today was different. Today she had to consider - force herself to consider - the possibility that her husband might accept a post abroad. No matter what she said.

Kay put a spoonful of brown sugar in her coffee, holding the delicate silver spoon at an angle above her cup, watching the granules fall slowly, silently, into the liquid. Paul's unexpected announcement - surprising her as it had - was evidence that he had changed; had been changing over the years. Changed gradually, imperceptibly like sugar granules falling from a spoon, and Kay could not be sure how much was hidden from view; that she could still control him. Today was the second most frightening day of her life.

'Do you mind if I join you?' He was already sitting down, a tall well-dressed man carrying a burgundy coloured briefcase.

'I ...suppose not.' Kay glanced around the room. There were several empty tables.

'It's nice to get a break.'

Kay returned his smile and moved fractionally in her seat, so that she was no longer facing him. The one day she wanted to be left alone..

'I actually use this place regularly. It's a real delight. A haven from the hassle of the real world.' He smiled again. Kay looked away, made a point of not replying. She had never seen him here before.

'I take it you work nearby?'

Kay sighed and considered telling him to piss off. 'Yes.'

'So do I. I thought I'd seen you around.'

Kay took a drink of her coffee, a larger swallow than normal. The man copied her.

'You have the look about you of a business woman. Who do you work for?' He leant forward as he spoke, resting his right forearm on the table. It creaked beneath the weight. Kay could smell his aftershave.

'Look, I've got a lot on my mind at the moment. If you want someone to talk to why don't you go somewhere else?' Kay moved again, turning her left shoulder towards him.

'I apologize. I didn't mean to cause offence. I'll move to another table if you prefer.' He straightened, reached down for his briefcase.

'No, it's alright.' Kay smiled, faced him. 'I've just had a bad day, that's all.' There was no point causing a scene, she would have to leave in a minute anyway. She could consider Paul later. At home. When she had a bath.

'Pressure of work?' His hands encircled his cup. They were powerful builder's hands.

'Something like that.' Kay glanced at her watch, felt his foot touch hers.

'Are you in a hurry? Perhaps I could drive you somewhere?' He was leaning forward again, his brow furrowed, his eyes hard, threatening. The memory leapt out at Kay, making her gasp.

'I think you ought to -'

His foot was on top of hers, pressing down, hurting her. 'I'll take you anywhere you want to go.' His hands began to move across the table towards her, 'If you understand what I'm saying'

Kay struggled to move away, but the memory grabbed her, dragging her further...

'Why don't we leave now?'

Kay lurched to her feet, caught the underside of the table with her knee and stumbled against it. Realised too late that it was falling. Heard a cup break as it hit the floor. Saw the man stagger backwards, his hands covering his groin. Ran out of the coffee shop, tears streaming down her face...

* * * * *

'There really is nothing to worry about, Mr. Chaney.'

The doctor smiled reassuringly. 'It is quite a routine investigation, and not at all uncomfortable - the local anaesthetic makes sure of that.' He was a young man, wearing the traditional white coat, and carrying a clipboard in the way some people wear a badge.

Chaney coughed. 'I'm not worried. Just bored waiting.'

He did look very young.

'Then you will be pleased to know that you will have to wait no more.' He glanced at his clipboard: a double check. 'You seem to be suitably prepared. You did hand any valuables over to the nurse earlier?' Chaney nodded.

'Splendid.' The doctor squinted quizzically. 'You are sure there are no problems at all?'

'None that a good meal won't solve.'

'Patience, Mr. Chaney. It's what you are and what you need at this present time.' The doctor laughed. 'Time to be going, I think.'

Paul expected his father to be on his feet within seconds, cursing, lashing out wildly with his racket. It took him considerably longer than that to realise something was wrong.

'Dad? Dad, are you alright?' Paul crossed the court in three strides, dropped to his knees beside his father. Chaney felt the support beneath his shoulders, his head hung down, his vision blurred.

'So if we just open wide..' Chaney saw the doctor beside him - recognized the coat - as he pulled gently on his chin. Chaney felt his mouth flop open.

'That's terrific. Now if we can just keep it like that. Nurse...' The doctor turned away. A girl in blue appeared by his right side.

Chaney wanted to speak to her. The doctor was there again, leaning over him. With something in his hand. A tube. An enormous black tube.

'Now you really won't feel a thing..'

Chaney was aware of the tube entering his mouth, sliding down his throat; wondered why he wasn't gagging.

The face blurred into focus. Paul was holding him by the shoulders, shaking him.

'I'm alright.' Chaney pushed him away with his right palm.

'We'll have to stop the game.' Paul watched his father climb shakily to his feet.

'Only if you've pissed yourself.' Chaney swallowed, ran his fingertips up and down his throat.

'But you can't carry on after that.'

'After what?' Chaney spoke aggressively, walked back, ready to receive service.

'I ... I don't know.' Paul shook his head. 'But it seemed more than just a faint, I couldn't get through to you at all, and you were mumbling something.'

'What?'

'Something about a doctor. I couldn't make out the rest.'

The first doctor - the older one, the specialist - had made no promises.

'I am going to send you for a series of tests. Internal examinations. Until I have seen the results of those, it will be impossible for me to reach a proper diagnosis.' He paused, wrote a hurried sentence and then with great deliberation laid the pen on the desk. When he looked at Chaney again his face was emotionless. 'I must stress, it is imperative that you undergo these tests, and I see the results, as quickly as possible. I don't want to seem an alarmist, but I feel it only fair to warn you. You could be seriously ill, Mr. Chaney...'

Chaney snorted. 'Just the brain playing tricks. You can't take any notice of what a person says when...' He licked his lips, noticed how dry they were. 'I must have hit my head when I fell, knocked myself out.'

'I didn't see you.' Paul had still not recovered from the shock. 'I don't think it's wise to take chances with such things.'

'Bollocks.' Chaney slapped his racket against his thigh. The pain made him hiss with anger; told him he was alive.

'What are you going to do?'

Chaney bent his knees slightly, took his weight on the balls of his feet, began to rock gently from side to side.

-Win.-

-But you didn't, did you?-

Steam filled the shower room; swirled around him, isolating him.

-Did you?-

The heat of the water made him sweat more and he rubbed both hands over his body, mingling the two. It was a timeless place.

-Did you?

No.

You cannot retrieve that.

It is only a game. Everyone loses sometime. It only happened because ...

Because of what? Go on. Give me your excuse.

I don't have to tell you anything.

You don't need to tell me anything.

It is only a game. It doesn't matter!

Winning doesn't matter?-

It was dark before they left the squash club, the sudden darkness of a winter teatime.

Paul was jubilant. He led the way out of the building, unconcerned by his father's silence, seeing the winning shot again in his mind: a ball he had played from deep in his own backhand court, struck with a force he had not known he possessed; leaving his father wrong-footed and beaten. Beaten. It was an omen, Paul decided. An indication that things were going to work out. No, that he would work them out. Paul smiled and decided not to tell Kay. He stepped outside, made no attempt to hold the door open for his father, and all thoughts of the future disappeared from his mind.

'God, it's cold.' Paul fastened his jacket, pulled the collar up round his ears.

'When are we playing again?'

'I assumed next week as usual. Why?' Paul hesitated, waited until they were side by side.

'I thought that you might want to stop. Now that you've won a round.' Chaney's breath turned into mist in the cold air.

Paul laughed, loud enough for his father to hear.

'You're way off the mark. I'll carry on playing you for...for as long as I'm around'.

'Good.'

They continued walking. For some reason Chaney had parked theJaguar in the far corner of the car park, as far away from the entrance to the club as possible. It stood alone, barely visible in the gloom. Paul noticed that his father's pace was slowing, that he was now a yard behind and to his right.

'What's the matter?'

Chaney raised his right hand, pointing with his forefinger in the direction of the Jaguar. 'By the car.' His voice was the merest whisper.

"Distanced," Paul thought, "like a final echo..."

He stopped and peered towards the car. Saw nothing. 'What can you see?'

Chaney felt his sports bag slip from his grasp, was barely conscious of it. Let himself be drawn, the sensation inside him growing as he neared the car. Taking him over until it flooded his being, ending the internal dialogue, filling him with rage.

'What the hell is going on?' Paul was ten yards behind, but he still sensed the change in him and he shivered.

There's nothing there!' His father did not stop - was almost at the Jaguar now - and Paul grabbed his bag and hurried after him.

The two figures seemed to come from nowhere , "They must have been kneeling by the other side of the car," Paul realised late and they converged on Chaney. He stopped dead, made no attempt to face either, and when Paul saw that his hands were in his jacket pockets, he screamed in fear.

'Look out!'

His shout made one of the figures hesitate, but the other continued his attack, his hands reaching for Chaney's face. At the last instant Paul saw his father's right hand free itself, moving between his attacker's outstretched arms, as he pivotted to meet the threat. The hand appeared to make a sudden 'Z'-shaped slashing movement when it came into contact with his assailant's face and Paul heard a gasp of pain. The hand moved again, as if scratching with the finger nails, and as the other man backed off, Chaney followed him, somehow managing to avoid the hands that were desperately trying to protect the flesh from further punishment. Suddenly the hands dropped in an act of submission, and Paul watched in horror as his father took advantage of the opening. His left hand snaked out - Paul had forgotten about that - grabbing the hair on the side of the head above the ear, pulling the head down until it was almost at waist height, twisting it so that the face pointed up at the sky. Then the right hand began again, scoring the face, and as the screams subsided, turning instead into a barely audible pleading, it seemed to Paul, watching in the darkness, that the hand never made

'For God's sake, leave him alone!'

The shout came from his left and Paul swung round, almost grateful for the distraction. The other man was still there, and as they stared at each other Paul saw the same fear and panic on his face as he felt welling inside himself. And something more besides..

'You stupid bastard!' Paul leapt towards his father, galvanized into action by the sudden realisation. 'Leave him alone!'

Paul reached him, reached instinctively for the right hand that was still covering the man's face. Grabbed the wrist with both hands, managed to move it, to force it away. Heard himself scream with terror, forced himself to hold on. The face, from the lips to the forehead, was lined with shallow, jagged cuts, both nostrils had been pierced, but, worse still, the left cheek was punctured and was spilling blood over skin and hair and clothing.

'For Christ's sake, you're killing him!' Paul struggled to control his father's arm, felt his strength wane as he saw the key, dull and bloodied, protruding from between his thumb and

'He's only a boy! He didn't mean any harm!' Paul was losing the battle. He saw the boy's mouth open, the tongue moving weakly around the lips as if parched. Felt his father's renewed effort. 'Oh my God, not that!' Paul glanced wildly over his shoulder, desperate for assistance. The other boy had fled. He tried one last time.

'You're killing a child! Look at him! Look at him!' Chaney blinked, inclined his head as if shying away from a powerful light or sound.

'Look in his eyes!'

It was a voice he knew, distant but irresistible. Chaney looked into the face. A tremor racked his body. He released his grip and stumbled back a pace. The boy fell to the ground, making no attempt to break his fall with his hands. Chaney reached out, felt the roof of the Jaguar and used it as a support. Paul was kneeling beside the body, peering at him, his hands hovering above his face.

'He was trying to steal the car.' Chaney's voice was dull, emotionless. 'You saw what he was trying to do.'

The boy groaned.

'I didn't see anything!' Paul shouted. 'How the hell could you?' The boy moved slightly, his forearm resting against Paul's shin; forced the thought from his mind.

'What are we going do?' Paul stood up. 'We can't leave him here like this.'

'What are you saying?' Chaney forced himself to breathe deeply, forced his shoulders down.

'You've seen what you've done. He needs hospital treatment!' Paul's voice was loud, insistent. 'Fuck you! He's disfigured!' Paul advanced on his father.

Chaney realised he was still holding the keys. 'No, he'll get better. Nothing permanent.'

The car roof was wet.

'There were two of them.' Chaney straightened. 'Where's the other one? What happened to him?' He grabbed the collar of Paul's jacket. 'What happened to him?'

'I...I don't know.' The key was only inches from Paul's face. 'He must've run away.'

'Shit!' Chaney released Paul and spun round to face the car. 'We've got to get out of here, he'll have gone to fetch help.'

'But what about him?'

Chaney had already opened the car door.

'We can't just leave him.'

And climbed inside.

'Watch me.'

Paul heard the roar of the engine. 'But the boy needs help.'

'Then stay here and give him it.' The door slammed to.

'No..'Paul grabbed the bags, ran round the other side of the car and jumped in. 'This is a terrible thing..'

'Tragic.'

The Jaguar shot forwards, missing the boy's head by inches.

EIGHT

"Doors are made for opening. It is the premise upon which I based my career."

From: 'Life and Death: Standing Somewhere in Between.' By Sir Henry Seymour-Jones. V.C.

Kay Chaney did not go back to work that afternoon. Instead she walked the city's streets, finding solace in the noise and bustle. She was spoken to on only two occasions, the first time by a drunk asking for money, whom she ignored. The second time, an hour later, by a tourist seeking directions, and Kay stopped and spent at least five minutes drawing maps in the air with her forefinger. After that Kay slowed her pace, began to spend time window shopping, and finally gave in to temptation and bought an evening dress she did not need. When she arrived home it had been dark for almost three hours. Kay tried to fit her key in the front door, found that she couldn't and rang the bell, stepped back a pace and wrapped her arms around her to fend off the cold.

'C'mon Paul, it's freezing,' she muttered, stamping her feet. Although the curtains were shut, Kay could see that the lounge light was on, but she could hear no movement, no sign of life. She rang the doorbell again, three short impatient bursts.

'What the hell are you doing in there?'

Her question received no answer, so Kay rattled her knuckles angrily against the bay window. She thought she heard a groan, muffled and low, come from the lounge and she paused for a second before tapping again, a note of urgency in her movement.

'Paul?' Despite her growing concern, Kay's voice was hushed, reserved.

The groan was there again, louder this time, followed by a movement, a shadow that flitted quickly past the space where the two curtains didn't meet.

'Paul?' Shouting now, all thoughts of the neighbours forgotten. 'Who is it in there?' Memories of her afternoon encounter came flooding back - and of the time before...

The latch turned suddenly, making Kay's heart leap, and as the door opened she was already moving backwards, towards the safety of the street.

'You're ... late.' Paul's right hand gripped the latch as he swayed uncontrollably in the doorway. 'Where...have you been?' He grinned aimlessly, like a ventriloquist's doll, as he struggled to be coherent.

'You're drunk.' Kay's voice deepened, hardened, as her fear dissolved.

'You noticed.' Paul grinned again, almost lost his balance. 'Pissed out of my brain actually.'

'Jesus Christ!' Kay brushed past him, making him stagger, then almost fell over his sports bag. 'What the hell is this doing here?'

'Resting.'

Paul leaned forward, nudging the door, to, with his forehead.

Kay took her coat off. 'I think you have got some explaining to do.'

Paul turned his back to the door. 'Who, me or the bag?' He giggled.

'What are you doing?' Kay screamed, throwing her coat to the floor. It crumpled against the wall. Paul fell backwards as if under attack, and hit his shoulder blade against the latch. It knocked the breath out of him. They were both suddenly very aware of the silence.

'You never drink too much,' Kay said, her voice a fearful whisper.

'No.'

For a reason she did not understand, tears welled up in Kay's eyes and she rushed forward, threw her arms round her husband. 'Hold me!'

Paul responded, squeezing Kay's upper back with his forearms, squeezed his eyes shut.

For almost a minute they did not move, just hugged in a way that should have hurt but didn't, and then they sank slowly to the floor. Still clinging to each other, their tears mingling.

Let their fears overwhelm them.

* * * * *

Chaney slept alone that night, unmoving. The next morning he could remember none of his dreams, and he showered, dressed, and left the house without having breakfast. There was a busy day ahead and as Chaney walked towards the car he dismissed the possibility that the boys had reported the assault to the police, that he was wanted for questioning.

-Forget them. They won't talk.

How can you be sure?

They were trying to steal the car. They can't admit to that.

Of course.-

Chaney reached the Jaguar; reached into his jacket pocket for the keys.

-That is what they were trying to do?

I saw them.

Paul didn't.

You have never had doubts before.

Today is a ... different day.

Trust me.

I am afraid.

Remember who you are...-

Chaney held the key between his thumb and forefinger and peered at it in the half-light. It was difficult to tell, so he opened the car door and sat down, his feet still resting on the gravel, his back to the gear box. The light situated above the windscreen confirmed it: the key was stained. On both sides. Small patches of brown that had to be removed. Just in case..

Chaney raised the key to his lips and aimed a slow stream of spittle at the dulled metal. He missed, felt a pain in his eyes as he tried to focus on the key just below his nose, and failed to move his legs quickly enough to prevent the fluid landing on his trousers.

'Shit!'

Chaney searched his pockets for a handkerchief, didn't have one, and so dried the dark grey woollen material with the the palm of his hand. That done, he considered returning to the house to wash the key under a tap, but decided against it. He had heard Anne moving around upstairs just before he left, and didn't want to be confronted by her; was not in the mood for a conversation. Chaney shrugged, swung his feet inside the car and pulled the door to. He would take care of it later. There was no hurry. It wouldn't go away. These things never do.

-You have a series to think about. Put things in perspective.

That's easy to say.

Deal with the things you know. That's the only truth.

A changing truth..

You're contradicting yourself.

I wish I knew.-

Chaney turned the ignition. The Jaguar started first time. He was at work within the hour.

* * * * *

Peter Randal looked up and dropped the pen on his desk as Sylvester Harris entered his office. Everything else would have to wait now.

'My God, you look half-dead.'

'Thanks,' Sly poured himself a coffee and sat down.

'And on the day when I needed you at your brilliant best.' Randal smiled, but Sly detected the note of concern behind it.

'There's nothing wrong with my brain. It's only my body that's suffering.' Sly sipped at his coffee and scowled; his throat felt as if it had been shredded.

'You shouldn't drink so much. You should take more care of your health.' Randal jogged every day, usually at lunchtime.

'You should worry more about your lungs than my liver. All the pollution you breathe in while you're running round the streets,' Sly hissed, shook his head, 'very nasty. A real killer, if you ask me.'

'And booze isn't?'

'You don't understand. You choose to run, and pretend that it's good for you. I need to drink and know that it isn't. Sly paused. 'Besides, it softens the blow when I see all that hard earned money disappear.'

'Then you shouldn't gamble.' Randal grinned. 'And you've never earnt any money the hard way in your life. You'd do this for nothing if you had to.'

'That's not true. If I hadn't been good enough to earn top money, I'd have found something else. Something that I did excel at.'

When the war had finished, Sly was returned to the city. He said goodbye to the countryside, the farm, and the people in it, and gratefully accepted their parting gift: the camera lent to him shortly after his arrival. Six months before his departure a letter had arrived, in a formal, brown envelope, which informed the old couple that their son would have no further use for it. There had been tears in the farmer's eyes when he gave Sly the camera, told him to keep it, and said goodbye.

It had been a most profitable gift. Back in his original home, Sly spent all his free time wandering round the city, taking photographs of the decimation; of the beginnings of reconstruction. From the dozens he took, Sly chose his favourite twelve photos and delivered them personally to the offices of a national newspaper, explaining that they were for sale and that he was going to be a professional photographer when he grew up. The boy caused quite a stir among the tough, uncompromising professionals, but his work staggered them; made them realise that he had a gift. The editor agreed to publish the photos, paid a minimal sum for them, and wondered if the boy had considered a title. He had. He said the series should be called 'Wildlife in the City.'

Sly finished his coffee, dropped the plastic cup in a bin near the door, and perched himself on the corner of the smaller table to the left of Randal's desk. 'What time are you expecting Jon?'

Randal glanced at his watch. 'Any time now. I phoned him last night and said that I wanted to see him.'

'Did you tell him why?'

'No, and the strange thing is, he didn't ask. It was almost as if he wasn't interested.'

Sly frowned. 'That doesn't sound like Jon.'

'No, it doesn't. To be honest, it came as such a surprise I didn't know what to say. I'd spent so much time preparing my little speech, and then I didn't have to use it.'

'You'll get your chance. There's no doubt about that.'

'Yeah, that's what I'm afraid of. The point is, I'd have preferred to have delivered it with him on the other end of a telephone line, not on the other side of a desk.' Sly smiled. 'Yes, it will be interesting to see how he reacts.'

'How can you be so calm about it, Sly? I've often wondered. I mean, doesn't he worry you at all?' Sly looked down at his shoes and pondered the question. It was one he had asked of himself many years before, when his relationship with Chaney was in its infancy, and he knew the answer - just wondered how much to give.

'I don't believe in it,' he said finally, mildly amused by Randal's puzzled look. 'I think if you are talking about killers, worry has to come at the top of the league. Besides, it's a pointless exercise, you never benefit from it. No, I don't worry about Jon. He could no more change himself then I could the future.' Sly shrugged. 'Might as well just sit back and wait. It'll come round anyway.'

'What will?'

Sly whistled, a single blast, that faded away like a falling bomb, the result, it semed to Randal, of a private thought he could not fathom. 'Whatever it is,' Sly said. 'Today, tomorrow, next week, it'll be there when the time is right for it.'

'How does that help me?' Randal asked, looking at his watch for the seconfd time. Chaney was late.

'I didn't realise that was the point of the exercise.'

'Thanks, you're a great help.' Randal picked the pencil up and began tapping it against the desk top.

'That's not what I'm paid to be.' Sly's voice was suddenly non-committal. 'Unless they have changed my contract without telling me.'

Before Randal could reply, there was a sudden cursory knock on the door and Jon Chaney entered the room.

'Peter, my man, I - ' Chaney froze, his voice stopping in mid-sentence, when h.e realised that Sly was also present. 'I see.' He looked from one to the other and then back again. 'Party time.' Chaney closed the door with a flick of his wrist, paid no attention to it.

'Morning, Jon.' Sly made no attempt to move, and smiled only slightly.

Chaney nodded in response. 'I didn't realise it was going to be a team meeting.' Chaney turned his attention to Randal. 'If I had I wouldn't have been so punctual.' Sly shook his head in wonderment. 'Like a sixth sense, and no matter how many times I witness it, it still amazes me.'

'What are you talking about?' Randal felt suddenly outnumbered.

'The man knows something is wrong,' Sly said. 'Don't ask me how, but he does. So there's no point beating about the bush, we might as well get straight down to business.'

'That's right.' Chaney crossed the room and sat down in the chair nearest Randal. 'You know what they say, Peter? A bird in the hand is worth two in the bush. -The question is, who's the bird?'

Randal glanced at Sly before he spoke. 'Its nothing that serious, Jon. I think you are both over-reacting a little.'

'Then why are you looking so worried?' Chaney leant forwaard, resting his arm on the desk top. 'If we are only here to discuss details for the new series?'

'Well, there is something else. Another possible alteration.'

'A change of plan?'

'Only a suggestion at the moment.'

'One that you have been aware of for some time?'

'That's not strictly true. You see - '

'In other words, someone lied when they gave me the information in the first instance.'

Sly stiffened as Chaney turned towards him. 'I told you the facts, Jon. You've never known me do otherwise. It's just that some people have got other ideas'

'About what?'

'About your future now that you are to have your own programme. Let's be realistic, if it goes well - and there's no reason why it shouldn't - you have got enough material to do a second, maybe a third, series. The argument is that that wouldn't leave you very much time for anything else.'

'People make time.'

'You have been around too long to know it's not that easy,' Sly said.

'What exactly are you telling me?' Chaney put the question to Randal.

'It has been suggested that you reconsider your role within the "Living Today" programme, and to be honest with you Jon, I think you should.'

-They want you out.-

'In what way should I reconsider my role?'

Randal paused briefly before replying. 'The suggestion is that you leave the programme altogether. Concentrate solely on the new series.'

-I told you.-

'Who's suggestion is this?'

Randal shivered involuntary at the meance in Chaney's voice.

'Not ours,' Sly said. 'I told you before, I believe you should do both programmes. Taking you out off "Living Today" could - just could - have a detrimental effect on the potential viewing figures of the series. Peter and I are arguing that for that reason alone there should be no change.'

Chaney looked again at Randal. 'But you just said that you thought I should leave the programme. Who's lying here?'

'No-one's lying, Jon, I don't want you to think that.' Randal spoke quickly, looking alternately down at his desk and at Chaney. 'I feel it's in your own best interest to serously consider whether you want to go ahead with both, or concentrate on one. There's a lot of work involved. A lot of pressure-'

-Are you blind?-

'-From the stations's point of view, I have to argue that you should do both. It's a question of viewing figures and my only concern in that context is how best to improve them.'

-I can handle pressure.-

Randal smiled, opened his hands in a conciliatory gesture.

'I hope you can see now why I decided to tell you. Although in the end it might not matter what the three of us think. Ultimatley it's not our decision.'

Chaney nodded. 'When shall we know?'

'It's impossible to say for sure, the argument is still raging.' Sly eased himself off the table, a pain in his left buttock. 'But it can't go on forever. Decisions need to be made well before "Chaney" begins, in case they have to prepare someone new for "Living Today".'

-Of course.-

'Who is it likely to be? Have any names been mentioned?'

'Yes, a number of people have been discussed.'

Chaney noticed a slight uneasiness in Sly's manner, the first time it had been there since the meeting began.

'It's never that vague.'

'No.' Sly realised there was no point in delaying the moment. 'It's most likely that if you leave the programme they will ask Michael to replace you.'

Randal flinched despite himself as Chaney thrust his chair away for the desk and came to his feet. Sly returned slowly to his position on the table edge.

-Michael.-

'Who's on the programme tomorrow, Jon?'

-The devious bastard!

You've been set up.

I am.

He conned you. Perhaps thay all have. They don't think you are good enough any more.

I am.

It's already decided. They've given you your own series to keep you quiet. They don't think you will fight.'-

'I am!' Chaney roared.

Randal was on his feet, his hands open in front of his chest. 'I'm ... I'm sorry Jon, I don't quite follow you...'

'It's my series!' Chaney's hands rigid and tense clawed at the air like a tormented lion. 'Mine!'

'Which -'

'And they still are.' Sly interrupted quickly before Randal did further damage. 'Nothing's changed, Jon.'

'Yet.' Chaney calmed only slightly.

'And we are doing our best to make sure that nothing does.' Sly continued as if Chaney had not spoken. 'But there is no personal vendetta involved. They wouldn't be stupid enough to try that against you, Jon.'

'Michael knows...'

'No,' Sly shook his head emphatically. 'No-one is supposed to know. Not yet. Not even you.'

Chaney nodded thoughtfully. When he spoke again there was no hint of anger in his voice. 'So it's still in the balance?'

'Everything always is.' Sly was a Libran, his astrological sign a pair of scales. It suited him, he believed in a balanced approach. 'While it's not possible to be certain, I think we can reasonably assume that, in the long term, the status quo will be maintained.'

'That's what I want.'

-You are a better man than Michael.

Yes. I believe that.-

'Well,' Randal sighed, sat down again, 'I'm pleased we have sorted that out.'

'It isn't finished yet.'

'No, no of course not. That wasn't the impression that I wanted to give.' Randal reacted quickly to the look of anger that flashed across Sly's face. 'What I meant was, at least we are now all aware of the situation.'

'All three of us.'

'Yes,' Randal faltered slightly and then hurried on.

'So let's get down to more serious business. I ..er.. I wondered what thoughts you might have had about your series, Jon. Any bright ideas?'

Chaney grinned. 'Peter, you disappoint me, I thought you would have realised by now,' his voice had an obviously sarcastic ring to it, 'I'm full of bright ideas...'

* * * * *

Katherine Durham was working in the kitchen, preparing lunch for her expected visitor. She had phoned the office earlier that morning, complained of a migraine and said that she hoped to recover within twenty-four hours. Her condition was accepted without question - as Katherine had known it would be, she was rarely ill - and now she looked forward to her first few hours alone with a very special man.

As she put the finishing touches to the salad, the radio D.J. announced the lunchtime news, and at the same moment the doorbell rang. Katherine smiled at his punctuality, wiped her hands on a towel and hurried out of the room to receive her guest. She opened the door to find Jon Chaney leaning against the wall outside.

'Jon.' Katherine felt her heart leap with fear, a sudden dryness invade her mouth, as she realised the awful danger she was in. 'What a surprise.'

'You see, you can't keep me away.' Chaney stepped inside.

'Although you don't look too happy about it.'

Katherine closed the door behind him. 'Don't be silly.' She forced a laugh. 'It's just come as a bit of a shock, that's all. I wasn't expecting you.'

'I've got an appointment in the city, and a couple of hours to kill, so I thought I'd take a chance on you being home.'

'Yes, I...I had a bit of a headache this morning. Thought I'd take the day off.' Katherine steered him into the lounge.

'Good job I didn't stay last night.' Chaney leered at her. 'Are you cooking something?'

'Quiche.'

'Smells good.'

'I'm afraid it won't be ready for some time.' Katherine smiled apologetically. 'Do you want a drink?'

'Why not?' Chaney stood by the fire while Katherine poured him a whisky. 'Why aren't you having one?' he asked as she handed him the glass.

'I'm not really in the mood' Katherine selected the armchair nearest the front window and sat down.

'What's the matter, are you afraid it'll unbalance your internal forces?' Chaney felt the heat of the fire against the back of his legs.

'What are you talking about?'

'Yin and Yang. The mirror in the hall. That's what it's all about, isn't it? The Chinese concept of the universe?'

'Y - Yes, something like that.' Katherine pressed the fingertips of her left hand against her forehead as if in pain from it. 'It's a Taoist belief - the two controlling forces in nature. Yin is - '

'Feminine, I know. The more subtle force.' Chaney grinned savagely. 'What a schoolboy would call "silent but deadly." '

'How...how do you know - about this?'

Chaney reached into his jacket pocket and produced a small paperback book, with the Yin and Yang symbol on its front cover. 'I borrowed this off your bookshelf. I thought it was about time I became... enlightened.' He used the word deliberately, like a cudgel, brought it crashing down around her, daring her to respond aggressively.

'Well, did you... enjoy reading it?' It was all she could think of to say.

'I didn't read it for enjoyment.'

'Then why did you?'

'Because I wanted to learn something.' Chaney paused deliberately, giving Katherine the opportunity to speak. She refused it.

'And I did.'

'What?' The question was wrenched from her.

Chaney sipped at his drink and glanced out of the front window. Katherine trembled with fear. 'I learnt that people who write books like this don't know what the fuck they're talking about.' He threw the book to her, and Katherine caught it in her lap. 'Yin and Yang didn't exist until someone invented them. It's just a theory made up by someone with nothing better to do.' Chaney snorted. 'People who live and work in the real world don't have time for theories. They're too busy.' He rocked back on his heels, felt the heat from the fire sting his calves.

Katherine watched Chaney walk slowly across the room to the settee. His revelation had shocked her and she silently cursed herself for having treated him with such little caution. She had determined that he was too introspective - and too interested in her - to pay much attention to his surroundings. Katherine knew now that had been a mistake.

'He's researching me,' she thought with horror. 'As if I'm a guest on his programme. He wants to destroy me.' Chaney sat down and tugged several times at his trousers below the knee.

'No, that's not true.' Katherine corrected herself. 'He only wants the capability to destroy me. He isn't thinking of doing it, not now, that's not why he's here.'

A car passed by outside.

'It must be very important,' Katherine said.

'What must?' Chaney frowned.

'Your appointment, if it's dragged you away from your work.' Katherine leant forward slightly, resting her forearms on her thighs, her hands clasped in a position of prayer.

'Oh yes, my appointment.'

-I'd forgotten about that.-

The telephone rang. Anne Chaney got to it first. 'Hello? Yes, he is. Who's calling please? Oh.' Anne lowered the receiver, a puzzled look on her face.

'Who is it?' Chaney was already standing in the doorway. He had been in the shower and he was naked but for a towel wrapped round his middle. Water dripped off him onto the carpet.

'A Doctor Matthewson,' Anne replied, 'He says - '

Chaney brushed past her as he strode across the room.

'Chaney here.' He was speaking even as he raised the receiver. 'What have you got to say?'

There was only the briefest pause, and when the doctor spoke his voice was calm and assured. 'I apologize for the lateness of the call Mr. Chaney, but I felt it necessary to contact you at the earliest opportunity.' Chaney felt a finger of fear run down his spine. 'I'm not worried about the time.'

'Very well.' The doctor coughed and went on. 'I received the results of your tests this afternoon. We need to discuss them.'

'We can do that now.' Chaney's heart thudded against his chest, threatening to drown out the sound of the other man's voice.

'I'm afraid that is inappropriate, Mr. Chaney. I need to see you in person.' There was a sudden sternness, a finality, in the way he spoke that made Chaney sit down.

'When?'

Anne moved towards him, her hands raised, steepled, her fingertips pressed against her lips. Chaney saw the movement out of the corner of his eye; it seemed as distant as a speck on the furthest horizon.

'There are only two occasions in the coming week when I am available. I'm afraid you will have to re-arrange your schedule around mine.'

'I will do that,' Chaney said, trying to work some moisture into his mouth. 'I will be there whenever you say...'

'Well?' Katherine smiled and secretly wondered at his silence.

'What?'

'You still haven't told me who your appointment is with.'

'Oh...it's connected with the new series, that's all,' Chaney said. 'Nothing very important really.'

'It's obviously enough to make you forget something important.' Katherine deliberately turned her gaze towards the vase filled with more than a dozen red roses.

'What are you talking about?' Chaney frowned when he saw the flowers.

'It's my birthday,' Katherine said.

'Shit!' Chaney slammed his fist into his open palm, felt a twinge of pain.

'Don't worry about it,' Katherine said, 'no-one else forgot. I've been able to celebrate.'

Chaney looked again at the roses. 'Who gave you those?' he asked.

'Why, do I detect a sign of worry, a hint of jealousy perhaps?' Katherine teased him.

'No, I just asked you a question.' Chaney's voice was hard, demanding.

Katherine forced a laugh and reached her decision. 'My parents sent them to me,' she lied, 'they arrived this morning. Don't you think they are beautiful?'

'Roses?' Chaney was not convinced.

Katherine shrugged. 'Why not? They are my favourite flower. I thought you would have known that by now.'

'I know more important things about you than that.'

'Oh? That's a very arrogant statement.' Katherine made sure he heard the playful tone in her voice.

'I'm a very arrogant man.' Chaney stood up and walked towards her, a half-smile on his face. 'It's why you came to me in the first place. It's why you will celebrate your birthday with me in a very special way.'

He was standing in front of her now, so close that his feet were touching the chair, his groin level with her face, only inches away.

Katherine looked up into Chaney's eyes and saw the anger that always took control at moments like this. Already his breathing was short, terse. Katherine did not move when he rubbed his left hand over her cheek and then forced it round - as she knew he would - to the back of her head. Neither did she show any pain when his hand moved crudely over her ear, pressing it against her skull. She was running out of time, that was her only concern.

'Do it for me.' Chaney's voice was a hoarse whisper. Katherine felt the pressure against the back of her head increase. 'The curtain's open,' she said.

'It's a quiet street.' Chaney was struggling to undo his trouser belt with his free hand.

'But what if someone walks past and sees?'

'They'll think you're a whore.' His breathing quickened. The belt was unfastened. It hung limply against the inside of his right thigh. His hand moved with even greater urgency.

'We will make love?' Katherine reached out, began to undress him herself.

'Later.'

'Good.' She paused deliberately. 'You are sure there will be time?'

'Why not?' The anger was in his voice now.

'Your appointment. You didn't say what time it was exactly.'

'For Christ's sake, stop questioning me about it!' Anne backed away, but only a pace. 'I'm concerned, that's all. You hadn't told me you were seeing a doctor.'

'Because it's not important!' Chaney roared. 'It's a routine matter!'

'Then why don't you want me to mention it to anyone?'

Anne's fear gave her courage.

'Because it's my body!'

Anne shook her head defiantly. 'No, we are married. We share things.'

'Is that what you think?' Chaney advanced on her.

'Is that what you bloody well think?' His left hand grabbed her right shoulder, his thumb digging painfully into the flesh. 'Tell me, you stupid bitch, is that what you think?'

Anne paled, the pain robbing her of her certainty. 'I... I think..I...I...don't...'

'I'll show you.' Chaney marched her across the room without releasing his grip. 'I'll show you how much you want to share. I'll show you what sort of wife you've been.'

'Please..Jon...I didn't -'

Chaney released her suddenly and Anne clutched instinctively at her throbbing shoulder. He grabbed the note book that was kept by the phone and began frantically scouring the pages. 'I'll show you...what you want... what you - here!' Chaney jabbed repeatedly with his right forefinger against a number on an otherwise empty page. 'Here it is! This is what you want. A chance to share something. Here!' He thrust the book at her, towards her face, and Anne tried to palm it away as if it were a stinging insect. 'Take it! This is what you want to know! The doctor's phone number, ring him up and ask him for yourself! Go on! Do it!' Chaney was no longer trying to force the book into Anne's hands, but striking her palms with it, the blows increasing in intensity as his voice grew louder. 'Show me how much you want to share! What you want to know! C'mon, I'm giving you the chance. Do it. Show me. Face it!!'

Anne dropped to her knees under the onslaught. She was sobbing uncontrollably, tears streaming down her face.

'Please...stop...no more... please... I can't take...I...'

'Then say it!' Chaney hurled the book against the wall, above the fire.

The words seemed to come from deep inside Anne's stomach. 'I don't want to know!' She fell forwards, her belly heaving, her forehead coming to rest against the back of her hands. 'No more please.'

The book was lying face down and open in the hearth. It looked as if some pages were torn.

Chaney staggered back, his hands fumbling with his trousers. 'I've got to go.'

'But I thought you wanted...to celebrate?' Katherine rose quickly, despite the disappointment in her voice.

'There isn't time.' The trousers were fastened, the belt hung loose, forgotten. 'I've got an appointment.' 'Well, if you are sure you can't stay...' Katherine moved towards the lounge door, Chaney following her in a daze.

'No. I'm sure,' he said.

Katherine led him into the hall and waited, her left hand resting impatiently on the door latch, as he searched his pockets for his car keys. Her heart pounded, in another minute he would be gone- she was so close now - and with every passing second her fear increased.

Chaney produced the keys and held them in front of him as if they were a trophy. 'I killed a man with these.'

'What?' Katherine blanched, and moved away from the door despite herself. 'What are you saying?' She thought she could see a stain, a light brown, on the largest key. Chaney smirked, his eyes, no longer dull, sparkled with life, as if reliving a treasured memory. 'It's not true,' he said. 'You can ignore it.'

'I'm pleased.' Katherine's laugh was a mixture of anxiety and relief. She resisted the temptation to ask about the colouring on the key. She did not want to know. 'When will I see you next?' Katherine asked, her hand returning to the door.

'I don't know,' Chaney murmured, his attention focused on the key he was holding.

'Oh. Well, phone me sometime - but don't leave it too long.' Katherine tried to distract him, to encourage his departure.

'I need to use your bathroom,' Chaney said, turning on his heels.

'I - I thought you were in a hurry?' Katherine raised her voice as he moved away from her, back into the house.

'There's something I need to do...'

He was gone almost three minutes and when he returned the key was still in his hand. Katherine had opened the door.

'Alright now?'

'Mmm.'

'Good. You promise you will phone me?'

Chaney nodded and Katherine smiled and glanced down at the key. It was shining like new and Katherine wondered if her imagination had been playing tricks on her. She kissed his cheek. 'Have a good meeting.'

Chaney hesitated in the doorway, looking not at Katherine, but out into the street. 'Count on it,' he said, and then strode away without a backward glance.

Katherine closed the door and hurried into the kitchen.

Her guest was late - but she now had the opportunity to ponder his absence. It was not what she had expected, and she wondered if she had misjudged the man, as she had Chaney. Chaney. Katherine was suddenly still - preparation momentarily forgotten - a knife in her right hand, as she considered the wisdom of the decision she had made earlier. Yes, she nodded gently, he would have to be disposed of, replaced. Perhaps by her latest acquisition. Katherine rubbed her thumb across the cutting edge of the blade, only dimly aware of the steel pricking at her skin.

Chaney was becoming too dangerous, too much of a risk. There was nothing to be gained by prolonging the relationship - and a great deal to lose. Katherine smiled softly. She would enjoy ridding herself of Chaney. Indeed, the ending of a relationship required more planning, more finesse - satisfied her more - than its creation, and she knew exactly how to deal with Chaney. She would reach to the heart of his weakness and expose it, and when he saw what she had done, realised the awful truth of it, he would be unable to face her. Ever again. Katherine laid the knife on a work surface next to the sink. So simple really.

The doorbell rang and Katherine ran to answer it, deciding how to react to his excuse for lateness. A delivery boy was standing on the step, an enormous bouquet in his arms.

'Yes?' Katherine frowned, this was becoming a day for surprises.

'Would you sign please?' The boy awkwardly thrust a receipt book and pen towards Katherine and she scribbled her signature. 'Thanks very much.'

Katherine took the bouquet from him, cradling it in her arms, without thanking him and pushed the front door to with her foot. She returned to the kitchen and laid the gift on the pine table. It was a wonderful mixture of long stemmed pink rosebuds, white peace lilies and mauve singapore orchids, with a cluster of freesias at the base. The greetings card was in its own small envelope and the message it contained answered Katherine's questions and made her smile. 'I cannot make it at lunchtime - something's come up at work. Please, please accept my apologies and these flowers and meet me for dinner at six...'

Katherine dropped the card onto the cellophane wrapping. Yes, she told herself again, the perfect replacement. Jon Chaney's days were numbered.

* * * * *

The door was black - shining black - wooden and solid. The centre of it was divided into four rectangular panels, creating the shape of a cross in the spaces between. On the wall to the right of the door was a gleaming brass plate giving the name and qualifications of the occupant in two lines of black, orderly writing. The door handle was also of brass and as Chaney wrapped his hand around it the coldness of the metal made him shiver. He paused on the white-washed step.

'Shall we say two thirty on the afternoon of the thirteenth? Splendid. I will see you then'

-Not looking forward to it.-

Chaney looked at his watch - the third time in ten minutes. Two twenty-five. He was early but he couldn't wait any longer. He looked briefly at the street and took two deep breaths, filling his lungs with air, trying to overcome the feeling of nausea in his stomach. Chaney opened the door. Stepped inside.

Anne Chaney was filled with a mixture of excitement and fear. She had tried to decide which pictures she wanted to show, but had so far been unable to make a permanent decision. The work she selected that impressed her in the morning, looked awful when she reviewed it in the afternoon; the pictures she thought were her worst, were precisely the ones the others thought she should include. The situation became more confusing the more she considered it, so Anne ordered herself to ignore it for a day, to spend the time instead putting the finishing touches to the charcoal sketch of the stray. It was, she believed, her most significant work to date.

'Here we are then.' Jane Swift entered the study. She was carrying two steaming mugs of coffee.

'Thanks.' Anne pushed her chair away from the easel.

'Why don't you put them on the desk? We can drink them there. It's time I had a break anyway.'

'I agree.' Jane sat down. 'You don't want to push yourself too hard. You've got to make sure that you are fighting fit for Sunday.'

Anne stood up slowly, an ache in her lower back, a cramp in her right hand. 'I don't think I have slept more than two hours in total since you first told me,' she said, flexing her fingers. 'But the funny thing is, I'm not at all tired. Usually if I don't get eight hours' sleep I'm exhausted the next day.'

'As long as you are alright,' Jane said. 'That's the main thing.' She nodded in the direction of the easal.

'Can I see it?'

'Of course you can.' Anne picked the sketch up and laid it on the table between the two mugs. 'There he is. Almost finished and ready to take pride of place in the exhibition. What do you think?'

'I still don't like it,' Jane said. 'I mean, it's incredibly life-like, the damn thing looks like it could jump off the paper and bite you, but...well...it's just not my sort of picture.'

'Don't sound so apologetic.' Anne encircled her mug, its warmth soothing her hand. 'I'm going to have to get used to people being critical of my work, so don't worry about it. I like this sketch and that's all that matters. In fact, the more I look at it, the more pleased I am with it. I only wish I could say the same for some of the others.'

Jane shook her head in disbelief. 'You know, I can't get over the change in you in the last couple of days. I don't think I have ever seen you so confident.'

'Don't you believe it.' Anne smiled. 'I looked at the rest of my work yesterday afternoon and felt like chopping it all up. I assure you, I am just as scared as I used to be. You wait till Sunday, then you'll see.'

'On Sunday, we'll all witness a great success.'

'That depends,' Anne said.

'On what?'

'On whether or not I choose the right pictures to show.' The problem had not gone away.

* * * * *

Chaney tapped on the door - a formality-, and then entered the room. The doctor rose behind his large oak desk.

'Come in, Mr. Chaney. Please, take a seat.'

The leather on the chair creaked as Chaney lowered himself onto it. To his right the wall clock ticked loudly. Two twenty-nine.

The doctor was a tall, lean, silver-haired man, with long, delicate hands and shining fingernails. He smiled. It seemed to Chaney as if it was an apology for what he was about to say.

'I appreciate you being here at such short notice, Mr. Chaney. I trust that you have guessed at the urgency of the situation?'

Chaney nodded.

'There would therefore seem to be little point in wasting our time with...preliminaries.' The doctor paused, inhaled deeply, glanced at the clock and continued.

Two thirty-one.

'First of all, I would like to remind you of the tests we performed several weeks ago and explain again exactly how they worked. That way it should be easier for you to understand how we came to a diagnosis.' The doctor opened a blue envelope folder on his desk and removed a type-written sheet from it. He referred to it several times as he spoke.

'You came to me originally complaining of various problems. Erm, a cough that became particularly violent when you exercised, occasional pains in the chest, and you also reported noticing traces of blood in your sputum. The X-ray that we took indicated that there was a strong possibility of damage to your left lung, and it was vital therefore that we examined it in more detail.'

Chaney clasped his hands together; both palms were dry. He could still hear the clock, steady and sure.

'The bronchoscope revealed that there was a growth in the lung, and we were then obliged to remove part of it for further examination. This, as you know, we did, and the results we have now are conclusive.'

The sound of the clock was even louder than the beating of Chaney's heart, and it threatened to crush him. To crush both of them.

'I am afraid I have to tell you that there is a large carcinomatous growth in the bronchus of the left lung, just below the trachea. You have got lung cancer, Mr.Chaney. I'm sorry.'

The silence gave no warning. It simply settled on the room, surprising only Chaney. The doctor watched him struggle with it and said nothing. There was no point in hurrying now. He could not set the pace.

'There is no doubt?' Chaney said, finally.

'None.'

The next question came quickly, as it always did.

'What about an operation?'

The doctor sighed, steepled his fingers. 'You are strong enough to withstand an operation at the present time... but there really would be little point. The ...illness is at an advanced stage. The truth is, if we had been able to catch it earlier you would have had a good chance of making a full recovery. As it is... well.'

He collapsed his fingers, a sign of despair.

'How long?'

The doctor leant back in his chair, staring at a spot somewhere above Chaney's head, as if he had not considered this question before. He frowned, raised his eyebrows once and nodded curtly. 'With treatment you should be able to carry on as you are for a minimum of three and a maximum of twelve months,' he said.'I'm afraid it is difficult to be more precise...As time passes you will require more constant treatment to slow down the effects of the illness. And to ease the pain.' He paused and looked directly at Chaney for the first time since he had entered the room. 'Eventually you will become bedridden.'

'I see.' Chaney stood up and walked over to the window. In the street below people hurried past as if nothing had happened. 'I don't want anyone to know. Not yet.'

'Of course.'

'I'm going to leave now. I will...contact you later. Another day.'

'Please, don't leave it too long.'

Chaney opened the door and then turned back.

'Where did you say it is - inside?'

'In the bronchus. Just beneath the bifurcation of the trachea. Why?'

Chaney shrugged. 'It just seems strange, that's all. I'd never thought of myself like that before.' He closed the door behind him and felt a slight relief, as if the action had somehow trapped his illness, his death, inside that room. Chaney ran his fingers along the wood in a grateful caress and then turned and walked slowly along the dimly lit corridor towards the heavy, black door. The time was two forty-six.

* * * * *

Anne Chaney was talking excitedly about the exhibition. She had not yet drunk any of her coffee. Neither had Jane.

'I was wondering last night just how I would feel if someone buys one of my pictures,' Anne said.

'When someone buys one of your pictures,' Jane corrected her. 'And what did you decide, how will you feel?'

'I'm not sure. I thought, at first, that I would be wildly excited, because, well, it would be a sign that my work was of a certain standard. You know, that it was good enough to sell.'

'But?'

'But now I think I would be embarrassed.'

'Whatever makes you say that?'

'I can see every little mistake in every picture.' Anne explained. 'In fact, in some of the pictures the mistakes aren't so little. If someone actually offers me money for one of my pieces, I think I would be obliged to point out the errors, to give them a chance to change their mind.'

'That's ridiculous,' Jane said. 'People don't buy things if they don't want them, and don't think about under-charging, Kay and will check the price on every piece on Sunday morning. This isn't meant to be a charitable function you know.'

Anne raised her hands in defeat. 'Alright, alright, I give in. But I'm still not convinced that anyone will want to buy anything. I mean, no-one's ever offered to buy one of my pictures before.'

'That's because most people haven't had a chance to see them.' Jane hoped that she sounded more confident than she felt. She had made exactly the same point herself to Kay, during a telephone conversation the night before.

'A number of pictures will be sold,' Kay had said.

'There's no need to worry about it.'

'But how can you be so sure?'

'For God's sake, you are beginning to sound like Anne. Why don't you just believe me? Sales will be made.'

'But she has never sold any before. People might not like her work.'

'What ever else happens, some people will buy some pictures. I guarantee it.'

Something in Kay's tone warned Jane that the subject was no longer open for discussion, and also raised a question in her mind. How could Kay possibly guarantee how a number of people would react? Jane chewed on her lower lip as she searched for possibilities, and then clarity dawned and Jane shook her head as if to erase the problem. The answer was obvious: she could not. It was an impossibility.

'What time will David be there, on Sunday?' Anne wanted to know.

'Oh...er...he'll be there all day, helping out. If that's alright?'

'Yes, the more the merrier I should think,' Anne said, and Jane remembered what she had not asked.

'What has Jon's reaction been?'

'Oh...' Anne looked down at the sketch, 'we haven't really discussed it much. Paul said that he was quite calm about it when he told him, but I think he's too busy at work to be able to spend much time helping. I know he is going to be there in the afternoon.'

'Does it bother you?'

'What?'

'That he's not more involved.'

Jane was right, the dog did look as if he could leap up and bite you.

'I don't know,' Anne said.

Jane felt herself blush and she reached out for her coffee. The piece of paper it was standing on stuck to the bottom of the mug land Jane tugged at it with her free hand. The paper was freed, but Jane's sudden movement caused the liquid to splash over the rim of the mug. She instinctively jerked her hand away, expecting to be burnt, and in doing so worsened the situation. Almost half her drink spilled out, landing on the sketch, and Jane watched in horror as the paper soaked up the coffee and a dirty brown stain spread across the dog's features.

'Quickly!' Anne grabbed the sketch, but she was already too late, and as she raised it, angled, from the desk, Jane saw the stain spreading even more quickly.

'No! You're making it worse!' Jane lunged forwards, wanting to help, but Anne pushed her away using her shoulder and upper arm, as she clung to the picture.

'Leave it alone!'

Jane staggered back and Anne turned away from her, her head bowed as she studied the sketch.

'Please...let me...' Jane took a pace forwards reaching out with her left hand into the space between them. Anne's shoulders heaved as she sobbed silently and Jane hesitated. 'Let me see,' she tried again. 'See if there's anything we can do.'

'You can do nothing!' Anne spun round, her face contorted with rage. 'It's my picture! Mine! Do you hear? I didn't ask you to make it so important. I didn't ask you to get involved. What right had you got? Tell me!' Anne hurled the sketch at the desk and the wooden board that held it scattered paints, jam jars filled with brushes, and knocked her drink to the floor. The mug shattered and they both, inexplicably, focused their attention on the puddle of coffee that was formed on the rust coloured tiles.

'My picture,' Anne's voice was barely audible, 'It's ruined.'

Jane's tears ran swiftly over her cheeks, and down, leaving a salt taste on her lips. 'I'm so sorry,' she said. 'I didn't mean it. Please, believe me, I didn't mean it...'

* * * * *

The street was loud and busy and took Chaney's breath away. He paused on the white-washed step and rocked back on his heels until his shoulders were resting against the door. The street was not as he remembered it.

-When was that? Tell me... speak to me!-

Chaney gasped as if in pain. Pressed his shaking fingertips against his forehead, temple, the base of his skull; was aware only of the clammy feel of his skin. -What shall I do?-

People moving past stared straight ahead, paid no attention to him. Avoiding each other. Waiting to cross the road. No words, no couples, no conversation, but so much noise. So much...

Chaney staggered. A woman carrying a Harrods' bag caught his knee with it. A man glared at him as they almost collided. He was on the street.

'Watch where you're goin', mate.'

Chaney recognized the voice. The figure was already past him, wearing a black three-quarter length raincoat, the collar raised high around his ears.

'Wait!' The figure did not respond, continued moving away at an incredible pace, and Chaney was drawn after him, his mind filling with images of the man.

'Facing me tonight is Samuel Colbert, M.B.E. Originally a church minister, he resigned from the clergy some twelve years ago and went on to achieve fame as a best selling author, and as the country's most popular and successful charity worker. Tonight Mr. Colbert has agreed to openly discuss...'

-A man he had met only once.-

'...You recently organised a series of events to raise money for the Red Cross Famine Appeal.'

'I did. And I am delighted to report that we raised over half a million pounds. Another marvellous effort...'

'Mr. Colbert, how many people know that three years ago you opened a Swiss bank account?'

'What?'

'And that only two weeks ago a sum amounting to several tens of thousands of pounds was placed into that account?'

'You...you can't know that...'

-A man he had exposed as a thief.-

'Mr. Colbert, isn't it true to say that in recent years you have actually stolen vast amounts of money from the various charities you represent?'

'This is...slanderous nonsense...I..'

'No, Mr. Colbert. It's the truth. The painful truth.'

Chaney reached the figure, put a hand on his shoulder.

'Look at me.'

-A man who had died in a car crash while awaiting trial.-

'What do you want?'

Chaney recoiled. 'Nothing...I...I..'

The man scowled, tugged at his collar and walked away, glancing over his shoulder occasionally as he did so. Chaney squeezed his eyes shut and staggered into the road. The voice in his head the only sound he could hear.

-'Tell me, Mr. Williams, why did you lie to the Commons over this issue?...

'I want to know why you have been secretly funding an organisation known to be sympathetic to the I.R.A.?....

'Why didn't you inform your members of these facts before the dispute began. Why did you betray them?....

'Tell me...I want to know...why...Why...WHY?'-

'Jon!'

The voice reached him, even over the blare of the car horn, and Chaney opened his eyes, realised the deadly danger he was in. He saw the face through the windscreen, twisted in fear, as the driver slammed the brake pedal to the floor and the car did not stop. An indescribable clarity overcame Chaney - it seemed the most natural thing in the world and he knew that in a fraction of a second he would die.

'Look out!'

The voice was there again and a figure in a pin striped suit lunged off the pavement, pushing Chaney to one side, to safety. As he fell back Chaney saw the man trying desperately to regain his balance, to pivot on his left foot away from the car. There was no time but still the man moved, turning sideways, twisting, needing to make only a few more inches - the car struck his left leg a glancing blow, knocking him three, four, feet into the air and across onto the other side of the road. His head hit the tarmac first and then his shoulder blades. He lay, unmoving, his arms outstretched, in the path of an oncoming motorcycle. The rider could not possibly stop and abandoned his machine, throwing himself to his left, towards the pavement. He screamed when he felt the weight of the bike on his left leg, but then it left him and went skidding towards the prone figure, lying like a man crucified, on the greyness of the road. It missed his body, but his hand, his right hand, caught in the spokes of the front wheel and for the second they were together the body jerked, as if receiving an electric shock. Chaney thought he saw flashes of pink in the air above the wheel and then the bike spun away, on a different angle, until the same wheel struck the pavement and the bike somersaulted, leaping at pedestrians who scattered before it; crashing into a pram that had been abandoned by a young mother as she leapt for safety. The bike thudded into the heavy, wooden door of a bank and came to rest there. The pram was on its side; a baby cried.

The crowd surged forward, moving to surround the body on the road. Chaney forced his way to the front of it. The man was dead, his neck was broken. His eyes, sightless, stared up at the sky, his mouth was twisted in a last snarl of defiance.

-'Jesus.'-

Chaney recognized the face despite the mask; recognized it as he should have done the voice. It was the face of Russell Tobin.

A woman standing near to Chaney was pushed forwards by a surge from the people behind her. She felt something give beneath her shoe and she moved her foot to reveal one of the fingers that had been severed by the whirling spokes. She began to scream hysterically. A man put his arm round her shoulders and tried to force a path through the crowd.

Chaney ignored them, his eyes fixed on the body, not wanting to believe what he could see. Tobin's wrist had been severely lacerated and the last three fingers of his right hand had been torn away. Blood pumped from the wounds, forming a spreading red carpet below the hand.

'No...'

Chaney shook his head and backed away. Tried to force his way out of the crowd, but could not. Had to look again. Could not escape it, it was meant for him. The forefinger of Tobin's right hand - his one remaining finger was crooked, pointing upwards. At Chaney.

'No...not me..'

In a prophetic warning of doom.

NINE

The video had been playing for ten minutes: the interview was half-way through.

Chaney sat in an armchair, a note book on his lap, a biro in his hand. He had not touched his whisky since the interview began, even though he knew all the old soldier's answers before he gave them.

He smiled at the fire in the younger man's eyes, at his desire to destroy. He would not have made a very good soldier. No, he corrected himself, he would not have made a very old soldier...

'You must remember, Mr. Chaney,' he said, 'that it is always easy to condemn with hindsight. Had all the facts always been available, I might, on occasion, have acted differently. However...' he shrugged, the movement accentuating the thinness of his shoulders beneath the navy blue material. '...the fact of the matter is, a soldier, like any other person, can only do what he thinks is right at the time.'

Chaney, watching, made a note on the pad, his eyes barely leaving the screen. Two days had passed since his visit to the doctor and, so far, he had told no-one about his illness, about his...

The death of Tobin had been widely publicized. 'A tragic accident: a noble death' one paper had written, and Chaney had been obliged to give a brief interview for the evening news programme, in which he was forced to admit that, yes, he owed his life to the brave actions of his dear friend. A man who, only this week, had met Chaney to confirm the summer publication of his autobiography 'All The Answers'. It was, indeed, a tragic accident, Chaney said. He would mourn the loss of a man who had taught him so much, and he would pay his last respects in the way he felt to be the most fitting: by dedicating his book to him.

At home, Chaney refused to discuss the incident - and he had returned to the city only once. To collect a number of video tapes of past interviews - those he felt that were worthy of possible inclusion in the series. He also brought home a copy of the Seymour-Jones interview, but that was for a different, more important reason.

'In your recently published memoirs,' - the book lay on the table between them - 'you talk at great length about your attitude to retirement and growing old. Tell me Sir Henry,' Chaney crossed his legs as he spoke, 'Do you miss the excitement of your youth?'

'Not at all. I actually enjoy the peace and comparative tranquillity of old age. It gives one the chance to reflect upon the past, and to wonder about the awesome nature of the future.' The old man imitated Chaney's movement.

'You are talking about death?'

'Yes.'

Chaney nodded. 'Presumably as a soldier, death was a possibility you were forced to consider?'

'It is a struggle every military man has to undergo within himself.' For the first time there was no sign of humour on Seymour-Jones' face. 'You have to come to terms with the fact - particularly when in combat - that you are not immortal; that every day really might be your last. Of course, it is a two-sided coin. Not only do you have to face the possibility of your own death, you are also aware that, to stay alive you might have to kill someone else - someone who, almost certainly, feels exactly the same way as you. That is, after all, the nature of the job.'

'How has that background helped you in old age to face what is now, for you, the certainty of death?'

It was a cruel question. -Are you ready to die? It is your death we are talking about. Yours. How do you cope with that? Surely you are afraid?- But Chaney could see no other way to touch this man; to break him.

'I have no choice but to accept the inevitability of death,' Seymour-Jones said, 'but I will do everything in my power to resist it for as long as possible.'

The smile returned. 'Surrender' is not a term an old soldier likes to use, you know.'

'Are you telling me that death holds no fears for you?' Chaney let his scepticism show.

'Not at all.' Seymour-Jones rubbed his hands together enthusiastically, as if this was a topic he had longed to discuss. 'All good soldiers are afraid of dying, Mr. Chaney. That's what keeps them alive, what allows them to become old soldiers.'

'Like you?'

Seymour-Jones inclined his head graciously, suggesting that he had just received praise rather than an insult.

'There is, I believe, a time and a place for all things,' he said. 'Death obviously cannot be beaten in the way that an army or another chap can be. We all have to face it sooner or later, and if I can just prevent it from taking me by surprise, I shall be more than happy.'

'I am sure many people will be touched by such a quaint idea.'

'I hope so. I am, after all, a quaint old soul.'

Their eyes met and locked, and Chaney curled his lip and let a sneer spread slowly across his face. It had no effect, the old man's mien hardly changed, yet Chaney struggled to withstand the power of his gaze: became increasingly aware of the authority of the man, which neither age nor physical frailty could erode; the authority of a man who had killed others; of a man who could not be harmed by words. Chaney glanced down at his notes and continued quickly.

'As we near the end of the interview Sir Henry, perhaps you could tell me of your hopes for the future?'

Seymour-Jones laughed quietly at a joke no-one else understood and then replied. 'Throughout my adult life I have tried to face up to my duty,no matter how messy or unpleasant that may have been, without complaining or asking for special favours of any kind. I can only hope, in the twilight of my life, that when the time comes, I will have the strength to die as I have lived.'

'Sir Henry Seymour-Jones, thank you.'

-Thank you thank you thank you. So many fuckin' times.

Watch it again.

No. Not now. There are other things to do.

Dying is what there is to do.

No, I don't believe that. They make mistakes. They can make mistakes. After all, where ...

Ha! Go on, say it! Where there's life there's hope. That's it, isn't it?...That's a rather quaint idea. I don't have time for this.

You don't have time for anything....

If only they had found out sooner. If only I had known sooner.

Don't lie to yourself now, that's most important.

What are you saying?

You are doing it again...You knew. A long time ago. Felt it deep inside. Instinct. Intuition. You knew. You just daren't face it.

That's not true! I wouldn't turn away. I wouldn't kill myself!

Of course not...-

Chaney stood up, the note pad dropped to the carpet as he straightened. He walked over to the video machine, sank to his knees before it and re-wound the tape, returning it then to the plain black case with a white label on the spine. All the tapes of his interviews were colour coded, a different colour for each year he had been with the 'Living Today' programme, and on each label the initials of the interviewee and the month number. They were the only reminders Chaney needed; his work was never far from his mind.

'More than just work. So much more...'

Chaney tucked the video tape in between the recorder and the wall of the specially designed cabinet. He would watch it again later. Perhaps tonight when Anne had gone to bed, when there were only the sounds of the house to distract him.

"It's a living thing," he thought. "'Only you don't notice it when there are people around. You don't hear it then."

Chaney sat back on his heels and listened. He was alone; Anne had gone to the shops and then on to see Jane.

"People breathe life into a house. Every house. You can feel it in the daytime, in the silence. You hear it at night. Funny, no noises in the daytime." He smiled "So many people believing in ghosts and haunted houses and don't know how right they are. People haunt them every day."

Chaney heard a click. He recognized it as the kitchen door opening; a shuffling noise that stopped and then another click as the door closed again. Chaney rose slowly, effortlessly, to his feet. Apart from himself and Anne, only Paul had a key, and he was at work today, it could not be him. He moved towards the lounge door. Silently. The house did not betray him. As the door opened, Chaney raised his right hand in front of his chest, kept the other low, to protect his groin. He felt no emotion. Only the beating of his heart.

* * * * *

Kay Chaney had visited her psychiatrist that morning. A six monthly visit; she had been assured that a more regular consultation was no longer necessary. That was perhaps the case - Kay was prepared to accept the professional opinion- but for her part, it made the experience far more awkward, more embarrassing; no longer a regular commitment, simply a reminder. Of an event she would have preferred to forget.

'Good morning, Kay. You are looking very well this morning.' The doctor had smiled and taken her hand in his, squeezed it gently and then released it. 'Please, come and sit down.'

It was always the same. The same greeting, the same procedure, the same agreement to meet again.

'I think it is important that we continue, that we meet again. After all, you have said yourself that the memory still haunts you, and the dreams, although less frequent, are still recurring more regularly than I would like.'

'I need them to go away.'

'I understand that.'

'You cannot.'

'Why do you say that?'

'That's a stupid question.'

The doctor smiled, removed his glasses and began to clean them. 'You continue to display aggression towards me, do you to all men?'

'No.'

'Do you still flirt with them?'

'I ...I don't think so. Not all of them.'

'Do you still flirt with your father-in-law?'

Kay looked down, trying to hide the fact that she was blushing. 'Yes,' she said.

When Kay left the doctor's she was already late; she had told Anne to expect her by mid-morning. She drove her black Ford XR31 with less caution than normal, once having to swerve round an old man who unexpectedly stepped out into the road in front of her, but she did not stop - there was no time for that. Kay hurried towards her destination, spurred on by the need to be with someone who made her feel secure, someone she felt superior to. The art exhibition was going to be great success. Serve the bastard right.

When Kay turned the Escort into the drive, she immediately saw the Jaguar parked outside the garage and she wondered at its presence. Anne had said that she would be alone, that Chaney was, for some reason, spending more and more time in the city. Kay parked her car alongside the Jaguar. She switched off the ignition, undid her seat belt, and opened the door. There was a chill in the morning air that she had not noticed when she left the doctor's. It made her shiver. Kay swung her legs out of the car, her high heels crunched against the gravel. She paused, aware that her skirt was covering only the uppermost portion of her thigh. Kay glanced at the house, thought she saw a movement behind the curtain in the bay window, climbed out of the car. She did not realise, until she came to place the key Paul had lent her in the back door of the house, that her hands were trembling.

Chaney was waiting behind the door. The intruder opened it and hesitated. Chaney breathed slowly, lightly, not wanting to be heard. For a second he thought that the intruder was not going to enter the room, but then a floorboard creaked slightly as whoever it was stepped inside and the door began to close.

Chaney sprang forward. Kay's back was to him and the recognition that pierced his mind changed his intention. He was hard almost as soon as he touched her. Kay felt the sudden eruption of force behind her, but before she could turn to face it a hand clamped over her mouth, the thumb and the edge of the forefinger pressing against her nose, cutting off her air supply. Instinctively, Kay grabbed at his forearm with both hands, but it was too powerful for her and she could not move it. Chaney took advantage of her mistake and reached underneath her arms, his free hand squeezing into the flesh of her left breast. A scream died in Kay's throat when she felt his touch, but she had to ignore it, the desire to breathe, the need for air, was overwhelming. She scratched at the back of his hand with her nails, felt the skin tear, but still he would not let go. Chaney increased the pressure on her breast, sometimes pressing against it with the flat of his palm, sometimes squeezing crudely between his fingers. He felt her body moving urgently against his as she struggled to remove his hand from her mouth. Chaney pressed his groin against her buttocks and knew that, if he didn't release her, she would pass out soon. The burning in Kay's lungs was becoming unbearable; the pounding in her ears, drowning the sounds of her struggle. Something inside Kay told her that if she just closed her eyes the pain would go. The temptation was enormous. She could not resist him any longer. She had tried her best. There could be no suffering once the conscious mind had ceased to function. There was nothing to fear..

Chaney suddenly released his grip and stepped back, watching Kay stagger and then fall to her knees; listening to her greedily sucking in air to relieve the pain in her lungs, sobbing with fright.

'You scared me to death.' Chaney put a hand on her shoulder as he spoke. Kay trembled at his touch, a half-scream escaping from her lips.

'I thought you were a burglar. I didn't know you had a key.'

'P..Paul's...Paul gave it to me.' Kay's voice shook with emotion. She forced herself to stand up, to face him.

'You should have said something when you came in. Identified yourself.' Chaney said. 'I could have hurt you. Damaged you. It could have been a terrible incident.' Kay realised that he was staring at her chest, that two buttons on her blouse were undone. She turned away as she fastened them. Her breast was sore.

Chaney watched her, painfully aware of his erection. 'It's fortunate that I didn't hit you.'

'I..I don't believe you.' Kay walked towards the bay window as she spoke. 'You must have seen that it was me.'

'That's not true. I swear it.' Chaney waited until she was looking at him again before he continued. 'I...recognised you another way.' He smiled. 'Your blouse isn't damaged, is it?'

'No.' Kay blushed. 'Where's Anne?'

'Was she expecting you?'

Kay nodded. 'We were going to plan a schedule for Sunday.'

'Oh, that's very unfortunate then.'

'Why?' The fear had never left her; now it began to grow again.

'I'm afraid Anne isn't here.' Chaney took a pace towards Kay. 'She must have forgotten you were coming. It's hardly surprising really, she does have a lot on her mind.'

'Where is she?'

Chaney took another step. 'She will be at Jane's now.' He glanced at his watch. 'Having lunch I should think. Very civilized.'

'I..er...I had better go and join them.' He had almost reached her now. 'There are...there are things we need to talk about.'

Chaney stepped in front of Kay, halting her exit. They were almost touching.

-Come with me into the study. The desk is still there. I wouldn't be without it. A memento. A reminder. Anne doesn't like it, but then she's an artist, she must suffer for her cause. Come with me into the study. Show me what you know.-

Kay stepped back. 'Please..I have to go.'

-It would be very quick the first time. Very rough. I know how to please you.-

'Please..'

-We could leave the curtains open. It would be alright. No-one can see in.-

-I'm not scared of you.-

-I don't believe you. I didn't believe you then and I was right. I called your bluff and you pleased me. Fear adds to it.-

-I'm not scared of you.-

-In the study. A winter's morning. Greyness and cold. I will choke you.-

-I have no need to be scared of you.-

-You will have no space for words. I will fill you.-

-You have cancer.-

Chaney paled. 'What?'

'It's true. Honestly. I wouldn't lie. There's..'

'You cannot know. ' Chaney's eyes widened. He backed away, as from an apparition. 'You cannot see it. It's not possible. It's too deep.'

The sudden change in him shocked Kay almost as much as his assault had done earlier, but it offered an escape route for her; he was no longer blocking her path.

'I'm going.'

Chaney reached out a hand towards her as Kay moved past him, but it was a feeble gesture and she brushed it to one side.

'You can't do that. Stay here. With me.'

-You can't keep me.-

'You have to tell me how you know.' Kay's back was to him, she was opening the lounge door. 'You see, I didn't know. Until...'

-Of course you did. You've always known.-

'No, no, that doesn't make sense.'

-You had to have a weakness.-

'No, I'm different. I left nothing to chance.'

-That's the rule of life.-

'How can you know? How can you be so sure?'

The kitchen door slammed shut; Kay ran to her car.

-You told me.-

Chaney collapsed into the armchair he had been sitting in earlier and for several minutes he did not move, just stared at the luminous digital clock on the front of the video machine. The flashing dots between the numbers had an almost hypnotic effect, and it was only due to a great effort of will that Chaney was able to look away. The note book was still on the floor. Chaney picked it up and flicked it open. He had written only one word while watching the video and he stared at it now transfixed, the words of Seymour-Jones hammering inside his head.

'We all have to face death sooner or later, and if I can just prevent it from taking me by surprise, I shall be more than happy. More than happy. More than...'

-You bastard.-

Chaney ripped the page out of the book, screwed it up in his hand, and hurled it against the television screen.

'Bastard!'

The word he had written was 'hindsight'.

* * * * *

Paul Chaney sat on the table at the front of the small lecture theatre and read from the book with the calm, unhurried ease of the professional educator. The round, gold-rimmed glasses that he wore only for work, were perched precariously on the end of his nose, and he occasionally looked up from the page he was reading and peered over the top of them at the students seated before him.

' "Virtue is not bought by bartering pleasure for pleasure, and pain for pain, and fear for fear, and the greater for the less, like coins",' he read.' "There is only one sterling coin for which all these things ought to be exchanged, and that is wisdom. All that is bought and sold for this, whether courage or self-control or justice, is real. In a word, true virtue cannot be without wisdom, and it matters nothing whether pleasure, and fear, and all other such things are present or absent." ' Paul stopped and deliberately frowned in consideration of what he had read, hoping that the students would follow his example in thought, if not in deed.

'Plato is arguing that, of the four cardinal virtues, wisdom is the greatest,' Paul said finally, as a means of silencing the chatter that had begun on the back row. 'Bearing in mind the fact that Plato lived four hundred years before Christ, I would like you, in the coming week, to consider the ...appropriateness of his statement for people living in our contemporary society. Particularly, I would like you to pose the question: "If wisdom is the single most important virtue, how should it manifest itself in the life of twentieth-century man?" '

The clock at the back of the hall said two minutes before the hour. Paul waited until the students had finished jotting down his requirements.

'Make sure that you come armed with your answers for next week's session,' Paul said. 'In the meantime, if you have any difficulties you know when and where you can contact me.' He eased himself off the table. 'Thank you very much, ladies and gentlemen, that's it for today.'

As the class dispersed, mainly in twos and threes, a blonde-haired girl, wearing faded denims and a Greenpeace sweatshirt, detached herself from her colleagues and approached Paul.

'That was a really good lecture, Paul.' She smiled, her teeth were white and even, her eyes a sparkling blue.

'Thanks. I'm pleased you found it useful.'

'To be honest, I find nearly all the lectures useful, the problem is that most tutors don't make them as interesting as you do.'

'I appreciate the compliment.' Paul continued replacing his notes in his briefcase - a new one, in black leather, with his initials emblazoned in gold on one corner - a Christmas present from his mother.

'Great. I think it's important that we give you the same feedback with your work, that you do with ours. That's what makes the learning process so...' her eyes widened expressively, '..complete. Don't you agree?' She moved close to Paul.

'Absolutely.' Paul moved to the other side of the table to close the briefcase.

Sally was becoming a nuisance. Accosting him at every available opportunity. Asking for tutorials when there was really no need to bother him. Apart from her obvious desire to ..well.

Paul flicked angrily at the double catch on his brief-case. It fastened with a satisfying click.

'There, ' he said. 'Time to go and mark some essays.'

'I might see you in the week,' Sally responded. 'If I have any problems with the notes you've asked us to prepare.'

'I shouldn't think you will have.' Paul clutched the briefcase, holding it in front of his groin as he moved out of the room. Sally was an attractive girl, there could be no denying that. Her body was slim but shapely, and she was available. She had made that abundantly clear.

"She must be immature," Paul had decided sometime before, on the occasion when he had finally convinced himself of her intentions. "It's more like a schoolgirl crush than anything else."

"Then why don't you take advantage of it?" an unexpected voice in his head had asked. "Why don't you give her what she wants? You would be perfectly safe. No-one need find out about it."

Paul had rejected the idea instantly, shocked that he could even consider it. "I couldn't possibly take advantage of her in that way."

"Why not?"

"Because she's my student, I'm...I'm her teacher. And besides, I love my wife. I couldn't betray her like that."

"Is that all?"

"What else could there be?"

"Fear..."

'So if I run into any difficulties, you won't object if I come to you for help?' Sally was at his shoulder.

'If that really is the case, then no.' Paul sighed. 'But I believe that you are capable of dealing with the task on your own. I expect you to...' Paul turned abruptly into the nearest staffroom and shut the door behind him without saying goodbye. There were enough problems in his life without adding a further complication. He was not the sort of man who would deal in untruths.

"I couldn't lie to Kay," he told himself. "Even by omission. I wouldn't want to."

After their emotional greeting two days before, Paul and Kay had sat together in the lounge and discussed their future. It had been surprisingly easy, and Paul, who had been prepared for a major disagreement, was shocked to discover how similar their goals were.

'I would like things to be as they were when we first married,' Kay said. 'Things between us, I mean.'

'So would I.'

'I'm not sure how we can achieve that,' Kay went on. 'I'm not really sure how we got ourselves into this mess - we just seemed to inch our way into it - so changing won't be easy.'

'Change never is,' said Paul.

'I'm not one of your students.'

'Sorry.'

A silence ensued, during which Paul tried to summon up the courage to mention again his new job possibility.

'I've been thinking about what you said about moving abroad, making a fresh start.' It was Kay who spoke first. 'I think it might be just what we need. -If you've not changed your mind, that is.'

Paul had not changed his mind.

'We shouldn't tell your parents, anyone, until all the details are finalised,' Kay decided. 'Besides, your mother has got enough on her mind at the moment, worrying about that blessed art exhibition.'

'You sound as if you regret the idea.'

'Perhaps..'

Paul sat down on one of the slightly tattered armchairs and placed his briefcase on the stained wooden coffee table before him.

That blessed art exhibition...If it was a disaster, he would find it extremely difficult to tell his mother that he and Kay were leaving the country; that she was on her own. He could only hope that it was a success. He would pray for it.

Paul was suddenly very tired. He slowly opened the briefcase and took out the pile of essays he needed to mark. The first one was written in black ink. The writing was very small and Paul squinted at the sheet. "Ethical egoism: a theory or a way of life?" He read and sighed deeply. He really was very tired. Paul looked up at the ceiling, ran his left hand through his hair and admitted defeat. The essays would have to wait until Monday. He needed to conserve his energy. It was going to be a hectic weekend.

* * * * *

The next morning was the coldest morning of the new year. "Too cold to snow", Chaney thought as he left the house. Although it was a Saturday and he was at work by nine-thirty, Chaney was not at all surprised to discover that Sly had already been there for an hour. 'That was a bad business,' were Sly's opening words. 'You seemed very distressed by it.'

'What are you talking about?'

'Tobin,' Sly explained. 'Quite horrific, by all accounts. I'm glad I wasn't there.'

Chaney smirked. 'It would have made a good photo.'

'You are a callous bastard,' Sly said.

'Just honest. I'm pleased it was him and not me.'

Before the police and ambulance arrived, Chaney had covered the top half of the body with his jacket. That helped him. It was easier to control the crazy ideas in his mind with Tobin's face out of sight; with that finger no longer pointing at him.

'I saw the television interview you gave, ' Sly went on. 'You looked as if you were ready to burst into tears at any moment. One would have thought you had lost a soul-mate.'

-In one way.-

'I'm a professional, put me in front of the cameras and I'll give you a performance.' Chaney's smile was not convincing.

'I have only ever seen one person die,' Sly said. 'That was my mother. At home. In her own bed. She was sixty-eight and too tired to carry on. For the last hour she didn't even speak. Just lay there with her eyes closed and her mouth slightly open. Twice I thought she had gone and she hadn't. There was no mistaking it in the end though. I recognised the change in her instantly. I can remember thinking then how easy it all seemed. Just a letting go...'

-'Come on now, son. You can't stay there any longer. If you do the nurses will come and carry you off.'

'No! I want to stay here with you.' Clinging. Arms tight round my Daddy's neck.

'You can't do that. You must go home with your Mum. You promised me you would look after her, remember?'

He is lifting me away from him, off the bed. His arms are shaking. Mummy holds my hand. We walk away. I keep looking back, but she tells me off. The people in the other beds are watching us. One man has a strange sort of smile on his face.

'Why are all these people in the same room, Mummy?'

'Because they all have an illness, like your father.'

'Is it the same illness?'

'It can be, or something very like it.'

'Some of the people in here are very old, Mummy.'

'Yes, some of them are, dear...'

Mummy's shoes make a very loud noise as she walks.

'Why is Daddy so thin?'

'Don't be such a silly thing, Daddy hasn't lost any weight, that's only in your imagination.'

That isn't true. I can remember what my Daddy looked like before he came into hospital. I've seen photos of him.

'When are we coming back, to see Daddy again?'

'Soon. As soon as possible.'

'And when will Daddy leave the hospital?'

We are outside now. Mummy stops walking. She holds both my hands.

'I don't think he will have to wait very long..'-

If Sylvester Harris had not known better, he would have sworn that he saw tears forming in Jon Chaney's eyes.

'Are we in front of the cameras now?'

'What makes you say that?' Chaney asked aggressively.

'Oh...just my imagination.'

-Daddy hasn't lost any weight...-

We don't speak for a time. We just continue walking very quickly into town. Away from the hospital.

'Does it hurt Daddy when he coughs?'

'I think so..'

'Why?'

'Because of his illness.'

'Why did he get the illness?' I pull at Mummy's hand until she answers me. She keeps staring straight ahead.

'The doctors don't know for sure. They think it might be because of his cigarettes...'-

Chaney lit a cigarette.

'Good God.' Sly's voice was a mixture of admiration and surprise. 'I never thought you would start that again.'

Chaney sniffed. 'Times change.'

'If it was anyone else I would wonder if the pressure was getting to them.'

A silence developed. Chaney looked down at his shoes and sucked on the cigarette; imagined the smoke whirling round in his lungs.

'I'm pleased I saw you today,' Sly said at last. 'I wanted to be the first to tell you.'

'What about?'

'The 'Living Today' series. A decision has been made. -In record time too, I think.'

Smoke trickled lazily out of Chaney's nose. " I wonder if you can get cancer of the nostril?" he thought."I've never heard of it."

'What's so funny?' questioned Sly. 'Aren't you interested in the programme any more?'

'Of course I am .'

-How would you smell if you had cancer of the nose?-

'I'm pleased. I was afraid for a minute that all our hard work on your behalf had been for nothing.'

-Bloody awful.-

'It isn't a fucking joke!'

'Who said that it was?'

Sly moved back instinctively and ordered himself to hold his ground. 'We have treated the issue with the utmost seriousness and never said or done anything to suggest otherwise.'

-I need to tell somebody.

You poor little man.

That doesn't work anymore. It's only words. They're not real. If I don't tell somebody, I'm going to explode.

I doubt that...but still, you go ahead. Share it with him.

...I have to tell some-one!

Don't we all?-

'Are you going to stand there all day?' Chaney asked. 'Or are you going to tell me their decision?'

'I presume you are ready now?' Sly's forehead creased in irritation. 'You would like me to continue?'

'For Christ's sake! ' Chaney growled. 'If you've got something to say bloody well say it. Otherwise piss off!'

-To be sure. To be sure.-

The X-ray indicated...the bronchoscopy revealed...the results are conclusive..

I keep telling you.-

'Michael isn't going to be offered a place on the 'Living Today' programme,' Sly said. 'Why aren't you interested?'

'Would you like me to cry with excitement?'

'No, there's no need to break the habit of a lifetime.' Sly tried a different tack. 'But you could offer to buy me a drink. As a small token of thanks for standing by you during your brief moment of crisis.'

'Monday night,' Chaney said finally.

'We'll go out and get drunk together.'

* * * * *

Katherine Durham had been so surprised when Jon Chaney phoned her, she had been unable to refuse him.

'What time do you want to come round, Jon?' she asked, her mind racing.

'Now.'

'Oh, I see. I hadn't realised you meant so soon. I...'

'Is that a problem?'

"No. No, of course not. It's just that -'

Click. The line went dead. Chaney arrived an hour later.

'There is something we need to talk about,' he said, having refused her offer of a drink.

'Tell me more.' Katherine sat on the floor in front of the fire. Her cat was sprawled out beside her, and her right forefinger gently caressed his ear and cheek. Chaney seemed subdued, there was no sign of his usual arrogance, and Katherine wondered what could have happened to have affected him in such a way. Not that it really mattered, not in the long term. She had not wanted to see him today, but now that he was here she would use the opportunity to find out what she needed to know before she could put her plan into operation. The plan designed to end their relationship.

'Are you afraid of death?' Chaney said.

'What?'

'Dying. Doesn't it tell you how to deal with it, in one of your fancy books?'

Katherine frowned as she struggled to gain control of her thoughts. 'Many of them deal with it, in their own way. Why, what makes you ask?'

Chaney did not meet her gaze, his face clouded and it seemed to Katherine that he was involved in a powerful internal struggle.

'Tell me.' She asked a second time, leaning towards him as she spoke, the cat forgotten.

'My appointment,' Chaney said. 'The one I was going to,' Katherine nodded, 'was with a doctor, a specialist.' Chaney paused. 'He wanted to give me the results of some tests that I had a short while ago. He wanted to tell me whether I was going to live or die.'

'And?' Katherine's heart pounded. With a little luck she would not have to rid herself of Chaney after all. Chaney stood up and walked to the other end of the room; looked out through the window as he spoke.

'There is a growth in one of my lungs just below the trachea; the tests were to find out whether or not it was malignant.'

Katherine held her breath.

'The doctor told me that there is no longer any doubt. The lump is harmless. I don't have cancer.'

'Thank God.'

Chaney beamed, his eyes shone feverishly. 'I faced it and beat it. D'you hear? I don't have cancer. I'm well, as healthy as...as anyone.'

'Oh, Jon.' Katherine thrust herself to her feet and moved towards him, her arms outstretched. 'Why did you do that? Why did you scare me in that way?'

Katherine put her arms round Chaney's neck and hugged him, keeping her face next to his, cheek to cheek.

'For a minute there, you had me so worried.'

-I don't have cancer. I don't. Listen to what I am saying. I don't have cancer.

Words contain a great truth.

Yes. Yes, I believe that. I do. My work proves it. Words cannot lie. If you can say it, you can make it so.

Yes! Yes yes yes. Words transform. Change, create, destroy. Words are real. I believe in words.

I know you do.-

Katherine felt Chaney's arms tighten round her waist.

'Don't hold me so tight. You will break me in two.'

She playfully nibbled his earlobe. The pressure increased.

'Jon! Careful. You're hurting me.' Katherine introduced a pleading tone into her voice; yielding before him. It was the most certain way she knew of calming his anger, of pacifying him. Only this time there was no anger, and Katherine winced at the pain in her lower ribs as he squeezed tighter still.

Kay's breast flattened beneath his palm until he could feel the breastbone itself. The body in his arms squirmed with life. He preferred to squeeze it, to feel its roundness; tugging at it, trying to isolate the nipple between thumb and forefinger. The body squirmed again. It excited him physically: her pelvis pressing against him, the way her breast could not resist his touch; straining for air, dying for it. Katherine. Kay. Katherine. Kay Kay Kay -

-Then you will help me?

How can I not?

I have a series to prepare. It needs to be so very good.

It needs to be the best. It will be the best.

Yes!

The most powerful words you have ever used. You must put them on display. Show them. Remind them.

Yes!

Prove to them that you cannot be denied.

Yes!

You have cancer.-

'No-ooo.'

Katherine Durham jammed her right palm against his face and pushed. Chaney released his grip. Katherine staggered away from him. The pain in her ribs seemed to increase when he released her, but she resisted the temptation to massage them.

'What the hell were you trying to do?' Chaney stared vacantly at the wall and his lack of involvement scared her, resulting in a tone of anger in her voice. 'For God's sake, Jon, you could have hurt me.'

'I don't have cancer.'

'You told me that.'

'I must make you believe it.'

'I'm not a bloody rag doll!' Katherine screamed. When Chaney looked at her, she saw the light of recognition in his eyes. 'You are the only one I've told,' he said.

'Why?' Katherine was breathing normally now, painlessly; her self-control returned. 'Why didn't you tell your family?'

'About what?'

'The tests! They must have worried you.'

'Oh.' Chaney shrugged. 'They were unimportant ...They mean nothing on their own.'

'Shall I pour you a drink?'

'Yes.' Chaney looked round the room as if for the first time. The shelves were lined with books. There was no sign of the cat.

'Here.'

Katherine offered him the whisky. Chaney nodded his thanks as he took it from her. 'The first of the day.'

'Well, it isn't that late.' Katherine wondered why he was lying; she could smell the alcohol on his breath.

'Most people don't start till the evening.' Katherine frowned and turned away from him. She remembered the keys. 'I killed a man with these.' Said almost without emotion, designed to create fear within the listener. And then today. 'He wanted to tell me whether I was going to live or die.' Intending the same effect, not knowing that she wanted to get rid of him - as permanently as possible.

"There is no time to lose," Katherine told herself. "I cannot afford to wait. I dare not. He is becoming too...unpredictable."

'Strange, isn't it,' she said. 'At the same time that you received the good news about your series - the most significant coup of your career - you were secretly worrying about your life.'

'What point are you trying to make?'

'I'm not sure, really.' Katherine smiled, her little girl smile. 'Perhaps something to do with Yin and Yang. Ups and downs. The way of the world.'

'I don't have time for that bullshit. I told you -'

'You're a busy man.' Katherine nodded in acknowledgement.

'So just how much time are you spending at work at the moment?'

'More and more, ' Chaney replied. 'And it's still not enough. Even if I spend half my time at home watching interviews, making choices.'

-It gives one the chance to reflect upon the past...-

'Still, I'm not complaining. I'm used to hard work. I'll do whatever I have to to make it a success.'

-..and to wonder about..-

'How have they reacted to the news?'

'What?'

'Your family. Your wife. What have they said about the series?'

'I haven't told them.'

-You shouldn't have said that.-

'Why ever not?' This time Katherine's interest was sincere, his purported reticence was totally out of character. Another sign of..something.

'Why are you so surprised?'

'Well, because I ..I thought you would want to share your success,' Katherine spluttered. 'I would have done if I had been you.' She paused. 'So why didn't you tell them?'

-An art exhibition.-

'I don't discuss my work with my family,' Chaney said. 'I never have.'

'But you do with me.'

'Sometimes,' Chaney corrected her. 'I discuss it with you sometimes.'

'Then tell me when your next day at the studios is going to be.' It was the question Katherine needed to ask; the answer would provide her with the one piece of information she didn't have.

'Tomorrow, why?'

Katherine sensed Chaney's suspicion. 'Oh, I just wondered how long I would have to wait before I could see you again,' she said.

'It won't be tomorrow,' Chaney said tersely. 'I have too much to do. Too many people to see.'

"Then it won't be at all," Katherine thought, forcing herself to control the feeling of elation that swept through her body. "You can have your pathetic little series, but you won't have me. Ever again. Ever."

Katherine put her arms round Chaney's neck and kissed him gently on the lips. She did not even flinch when she felt his arms circle her waist.

'Shall I tell you something, Mr Chaney?' she said, pressing herself against him. 'You have absolutely no idea how good you make me feel.' Katherine kissed him again. 'You really don't.'

* * * * *

'Are you sure?'

Anne Chaney asked the question, and Jane Swift nodded in reply without hesitation.

'Yes, I think it should definitely hang in the best place,' she said, laying the painting of the shire horse beside her on the settee. 'Possibly on its own somehow, away from all the others. That way I am sure you will sell it. In fact, I might even buy it myself.'

'Oh no, I couldn't possibly allow you to do that.' Anne's face filled with concern. 'Not after all the help you have given me. No, if you like the painting that much, you must take it, please. It's what I would like you to do.'

'Don't be silly.' Jane smiled. 'The point of the exhibition is to sell your work to people who don't know you personally, not to give it away to those who do.'

'Yes, but one painting won't make much difference, will it? Not when there are all these to go up.' Anne gestured vaguely at the paintings and sketches spread out on the Swift's lounge floor. 'I mean, you said yourself, if at the end of the day, we have only sold one or two pieces, it won't have been much of a success.'

'Yes, well, to be honest, when I said that I was merely quoting Kay. She seems to feel that we should be aiming to sell a substantial number of pictures. Myself, I'm a little more cautious. - Not that I think there is anything wrong with your work, it's not that at all. It's just that I think if you - we - expect too much, we might be disappointed at the end of the day. It is your first exhibition, after all. It's only a beginning, I think we should bear that in mind. Beginnings tend to be only small affairs.' Jane came to a sudden halt. It was unlike her to deliver such a lengthy speech and she was pleased with her performance.

This meeting was the first she had had with Anne since the afternoon when she had ruined the picture of the stray. They had both tried very hard to avoid mentioning it.

'I suppose you are right,' Anne said after consideration.

'I don't know why, but I keep going through phases when, for no reason, I feel really optimistic. They don't last very long, but they seem to be increasing in frequency as the exhibition draws near.'

'I'm pleased to hear it. That's how it should be.' Jane was quick to offer encouragement.

'Yes, I suppose so,' Anne said hesitantly. 'The only trouble is, I submit to an incredible feeling of fear whenever the optimism fades, and it seems the more confident I feel when I am enjoying one of my positive moods, the more scared I become afterwards. The two emotions seem to compliment each other - that's the strangest thing of all.'

'All that will change after Sunday,' Jane said. 'Success will dampen your fear, you wait and see.'

'There isn't that long to wait.'

'No.' Jane's smile faded, it was a sobering thought. 'There isn't, and I suspect the next few days will pass the most quickly of all. There will be less and less time to talk about it and more and more work to do.' Jane forced a grin. 'I think we can safely say that the final countdown has begun. Talking of which, have you heard from Kay lately? I tried phoning her twice yesterday, but there was no reply, so I presumed she was out with Paul.'

'Oh no! What have I done?' Anne's right hand fluttered nervously in front of her mouth.

'What's the matter?'

'Kay said she was coming to the house this morning. I completely forgot about it.'

'There's nothing to worry about,' Jane said. 'Everybody forgets something from time to time. I'm sure Kay will understand.'

'That's not the point!' Anne's voice was raised, revealing the growing panic inside her. 'Jon was at home this morning. He would be there when she arrived. They would be alone together.'

'What are you saying?'

-"She's your wife !...Do you understand?...You can't blame him..."-

'Oh my God!' Anne's eyes widened in fright.

'What's the matter, Anne? What are you scared of?' Jane understood the implication of what she had heard, but she wanted Anne to say more; she wanted her to refute it.

'Speak to me, Anne?'

'I have to make a phone call.' Anne stood up and Jane speedily followed suit.

At that moment the doorbell rang. Anne froze in her tracks.

'I'll get it.' Jane hurried past her and into the hall. She recognised Kay Chaney through the patterned glass panel in the door, even before she opened it.

'Hello.'

Jane's greeting was less than friendly, and as she stood in the doorway permitting no entry, Jane remembered what David had said about Kay when they walked home after the party.

'It seems a totally wrong match to me. He's quiet and studious - shy, almost, and she's...she's nothing but a flirt.'

'David! That's an awful thing to say.' Jane had secretly thought the same thing many times before, but to hear her husband voice the opinion, in his deep, authoritative tone, made the condemnation seem far more harsh, more damning.

'You must be aware of it yourself,' David said. 'I always thought that woman's power of observation was far greater than man's. To be honest, I only noticed because, well, I am incredibly astute,' a smile flickered at the corners of his mouth; it was lost in the darkness, 'and because I had first-hand experience.'

'What do you mean?' Jane clutched at his nearest arm with both hands, forcing him to stand still. 'Are you telling me that she flirted with you tonight?'

'Either that or she has no idea when she is invading someone else's space, and I find that a little hard to believe. Women don't usually press their breasts against a man's arm by mistake, do they?'

'It is possible, yes. I don't think it's fair to categorise in that way, David.' Jane chewed thoughtfully at her lower lip. 'I suppose, in the end, it depends how often it happens.'

'Three times in five minutes?' David's grin widened. 'I realise she has fairly large boobs, but they're not exactly huge. She must be able to control where she puts them.'

'Sometimes you sound like a real chauvinistic pig,' Jane said, starting to walk.

'Sometimes you take me too seriously.' David crooked his arm through hers. For a time they walked in silence, and Jane pondered what had been said.

'Did she really flirt with you?' she asked, finally.

'I believe so.'

'How did you react? I mean, were you flattered?'

'Not at all. If you really want to know, I gave her the elbow.'

Jane smiled despite herself. 'Why? Most men would have been delighted. She is a good-looking woman.'

'That's as maybe, but there's an old-fashioned streak inside me, that tells me I don't like pushy women. They insult my intelligence.'

When they arrived home, the Swifts made love, and Jane fell asleep with her head resting on David's shoulder, his arm curled protectively round her back. That night Jane dreamt of Kay Chaney revealing her breasts to her husband, of Anne's face thudding down into the body of the cat, and of an art exhibition, attended by many, ending in failure, without a single picture having been sold.

'Is Anne here?'

The question brought the other woman sharply into focus,.

'Yes, she is.' Jane couldn't help glancing at Kay's chest. 'She's in the lounge.'

'Can I come in?'

'I suppose you will have to.' Jane stepped back. Was it her imagination, or was there a wild look in Kay's eyes, was her hair slightly dishevelled?

Kay stepped inside. Anne Chaney appeared at the other end of the hall.

'I forgot,' she said simply.

'I realised that.'

'I'm terribly sorry.'

'Why should you be?' Kay asked. Her voice was hard, lacking intonation, and Jane was unsure if she was angry or not.

"Not that she has any right to be," she thought. "She's a scheming bitch."

'Jon said that he was going to be at home all morning,' Anne said. 'I ..I thought that -'

'You needn't have thought anything.'

Jane was sure now: a definite hint of anger.

'Oh, why?' Anne looked as fearful as she had when first told of the exhibition.

'Because he wasn't there. He obviously got bored sitting at home - and I can't say that I blame him. It's not the most exciting way to spend your time, is it?'

Anne didn't reply.

'Is it?' Kay pursued the matter. 'I mean, you should know, you're the expert. You must have spent half your life alone in the house, pretending you were doing something worthwhile. Still, I suppose you should always look on the bright side, if you hadn't been in that sort of mess in the first place, we most probably wouldn't have taken pity on you and organised the exhibition.' Kay shrugged and said without the least sign of interest, 'Funny how things work out, isn't it? I often wonder about that.'

'He...he wasn't there?' Anne stammered.

'No, he wasn't there.'

'He'd...gone out?'

'That's what I said.'

'Is that the truth?'

'On my mother's grave.' Kay walked brusquely into the lounge and put her foot through an oil painting of an Indian tiger. She promptly burst into tears and Jane, following, watched in amazement as Anne comforted her.

* * * * *

Katherine Durham also rose early that morning and while Sly wondered at the change that had come over Jon Chaney, she drove hesitantly along the main street of the village, searching for the road leading to the Chaney house. It was not an area that Katherine knew. She lived, worked and played in the city. It was the place where the risks were greatest. Where there was the most to win. Katherine had been surprised to learn that Chaney needed to escape to the country. It had been her first indication of his weakness, and it had helped her enormously, psychologically, in the first weeks of their relationship. Katherine had no need for escape. Indeed, she could have told him, for people searching for power, there is no possibility of escape; the true nature of the self cannot be avoided. It was a well-known principle.

Katherine decided to ask the way - she had no map - and stopped the car outside the small, village post office. As she approached the door, a poster in the window caught her eye. Katherine halted and looked at it again. It was not immediately clear why it should seem of interest to her, but there was something, something she had recognised. Katherine quelled her impatience and began to read the poster from top to bottom. When she found the word that had first attracted her attention, Katherine gasped with excitement. Not just a word, a name - Chaney - and another exciting possibility appeared before her. A way of improving her plan, a way of making it seem far more natural - and therefore successful - than she could ever have hoped. Katherine hurriedly obtained the information she sought from the postmaster and within minutes she had arrived at the Chaney house.

Katherine parked the car on the road and walked up the drive. It was a modern house - the redness of the brick in stark contrast to the greyness of the morning - with large Georgian style bay windows and a double garage off to the left. It was not the sort of house Katherine expected Chaney to live in. It was too new. As she neared the front door, Katherine realised her mistake.

'I don't live in the past,' Chaney had told her during their first dinner date together. 'That's one of the reasons why I've been at the top for so long...'

"Of course!" Katherine chastised herself. "I should have realised. I must learn to listen more closely."

Anne Chaney saw the stranger approaching the house, but made no move to open the front door until the bell had chimed for a second time.

'Mrs Chaney? Mrs Anne Chaney?'

'Yes.'

The woman was, in many ways, strikingly beautiful. The skin of her face and neck was smooth and unwrinkled and a golden brown in colour. Her hands were slender, the nails manicured and painted, but it was her hair that was her most impressive feature. Reaching down almost to her bottom, it moved in gentle waves as if possessing a life of its own.

'I'm Anne Chaney; can I help you?'

Anne flinched. The woman's eyes seemed to look right through her. They were tough, glittering with fire and life like diamonds. Anne made no attempt to return the look, allowing herself instead to be consumed with jealousy. This woman was everything she had always longed to be. Beautiful, elegant, but with no sign of weakness. "An individual in her own right," Anne told herself. "I bet she's not married." She glanced again at the other's hands and reviewed her opinion. "Her hair is not her most striking feature," she thought. "Her eyes are. I dare not even look into them."

'I sincerely hope so,' the woman said, and when she smiled her eyes changed their character so completely that Anne wondered how she could possibly have found them threatening. 'I believe you are an artist?'

'Well...' Anne's smile was one of embarrassment.

'There is going to be an exhibition of your work tomorrow?'

'Yes, that is true,' Anne confessed, 'but it is really only a minor affair. I doubt very much whether it would be of interest to someone...well, someone who doesn't live locally.' There was no doubt in Anne's mind that this woman came from the city, that she spent most of her time there.

'Unfortunately I cannot attend the exhibition tomorrow because of a business commitment,' the woman explained, 'but that is not really why I called to see you. No, I had something more personal in mind.' She glanced over Anne's shoulder, peering down the hallway.

'Oh well, in that case perhaps you had better come in.' Anne moved back, allowing her access. 'I don't have much time to spare today, but -'

'Of course, I understand, I don't want to hold you up. It will only take a minute.' The woman was already moving down the hall. 'By the way, my name is Katherine, Katherine Durham,' she said, over her shoulder.

* * * * *

Sly received the news as if he had been expecting it. Not a flicker of emotion crossed his face. Not a muscle moved.

'Is it just below the trachea?' he asked.

'How could you know?' Chaney felt himself blanch. He was suddenly very cold.

Sly shrugged. 'Just a lucky guess. You know how these things are.'

'Do I look ill?'

'Only on the inside,' Sly said and then went on with a sudden rush of enthusiasm, 'It could be the most important thing that has ever happened to you, professionally speaking.'

Chaney rocked on his heels, his strength draining out of him. 'What are you saying? I'm telling you that I'm dying.'

'I'm pleased to hear you admit it at last,' Sly responded. 'Now that you have we can think about your future. Your career.' Sly stopped suddenly and began to pace up and down, the tip of his right forefinger seemingly glued to his lips. 'I think you should have your own series,' he said at last.

'I have my own series.'

'No, no, nothing trivial like that,' Sly waved his comment aside. 'I'm talking about something major, something of stature. I'm talking about a documentary, about the last weeks, months, of your life. We could call it "Jon Chaney with so little time left - still dying to meet you"'

Chaney opened his mouth to speak, to shout, to scream, but no sound came out. Sly didn't notice. 'No, no, that's no good - too long. Still, details don't matter too much at the moment. What does matter is the concept of the thing. We need an angle. What scares you the most?'

A shiver went down Chaney's spine. The car keys were still in his hand.

'You're not going to tell me, eh? I suppose we can't expect too much in one day, and you have admitted the truth at least. At last. ' He smiled. 'I'll tell you then; one of us has got to.' He paused dramatically, his eyes mocking. 'It's not death. Well, that doesn't scare you anymore than it does the rest of us... No, it's losing that you can't handle. Being totally out of fucking control. That's your hang-up. And you are, of course. Out of control, I mean. It's got you beat. Under the hammer. Frightening thought, isn't it? Enough to make you sickle.'

He smiled again. 'We'll all say Bye Bye Chaney when it wants us to, not when you do. You've just got to wait your time. Serve your time. Bide your time. Have the time of your life. There's nothing else you can do.'

'You're lying.'

'Of course. There's always something you can do. There is a way round every problem, as my old dad used to say. He died of cancer in the end, you know. In a hospital. Very clean place.'

'What can I do?' Chaney shrieked. The reflection in the car mirror bared its teeth at him and changed its shape. Shedding its skin like a snake, until the face was once again recognisable. His own.

'Beat it,' it said. 'You have the power, you always have. Lose now and you destroy the memory. They won't remember anything else. They won't want to.'

'No' Chaney gasped. 'I can't allow that. I have to win... I have to...'

'And you will. You never lose. Think back, all the years of success..not one defeat... think of it.'

The old soldier nodded encouragingly. "Surrender is not a word an old soldier likes to use," he said.

'Fuck him,' the reflection snarled. 'That's meaningless. He only had men to fight.'

'Fuck you,' Chaney said. The old soldier disappeared. Only one thing matters. It always has... I can do whatever it takes.'

'To do what?'

'Win...'

A bead of sweat trickled down Chaney's nose. He shook his head to release it. The other face vanished. Chaney was sitting alone in the Jaguar in the underground car park beneath the television studios. Sly was upstairs somewhere, working, unaware of his illness. The car windows were steamed up. Chaney was sweating profusely. He put the keys in the ignition, but did not switch it on. He wound down a window. A figure loomed outside.

'Mornin', Mr Chaney. I thought I saw somebody sittin' 'ere.' The security man seemed somewhat embarrassed. He did not look directly at Chaney as he spoke. 'I-er-I wasn't sure who it was, you see. Thought I'd best come and 'ave a look. You can't be too careful. Not in a place like this.'

'How much do you earn?'

'I'm sorry, Mr Chaney?' The man's eyebrows disappeared into his hairline. Chaney repeated the question. 'Oh. Well, me and the missus, we 'ave enough to get by. Things bein' what they are.' He paused and gained confidence from the brief silence. 'To tell you the truth, Mr Chaney, I often wonder about the point of it all. You fight in a war, risk yer life to defend yer country, and how does it reward yer?' He looked around him. 'By stickin' yer down 'ere. Telling yer that yer not good enough for anythin' else. Good enough to go in the front line, tho', wasn't I?'

'You were a soldier?' Chaney croaked, his original line of questioning forgotten.

'All me life.' The security man grinned.

Chaney glanced into the mirror. 'Did you ever kill anyone?'

'Well, that's not somethin' that comes easy to talk about, Mr Chaney. Not to anyone. In those days, in those situations, I was a different man, you understand. Had to be to survive.'

'So?' The back of Chaney's shirt-collar was damp. The sweat was drying.

'I think I must 'ave done. One at least. I put two bullets in 'im fer sure, and not many men could 'andle that. Didn't seem to matter where the bullets 'it 'em. Just broke their will t' live, if yer know what I mean.'

'How do you feel about it?'

The security man whistled softly and patted a hand against the grey concrete pillar to the right of the Jaguar.

'Haunts me,' he said, walking off into the gloom.

-If I can just prevent it from taking me by surprise...

They are not your words.

It took me by surprise.

No...you must be strong.

Then why couldn't I face it? ....Why did I wait so long?

The past means nothing...Don't be so harsh. It's never too late.

Never...I can beat the cancer.

Say it.-

'I can beat the cancer.'

-Again.-

'I can beat the cancer.'

-Again.-

'I can beat the cancer'.

-How?-

'I'll find a way.'

Chaney did not race home.

* * * * *

Anne Chaney was talking on the phone, a note of irritation creeping into her voice.

'Do you really think that's necessary? I mean, I could walk round there now. It wouldn't take long and the fresh air would do me good. If I did that I would be able to see things for myself.'

Kay was patronisingly calm. 'That is not how we organised things, is it? We agreed that Jane and Paul and myself would arrange the display and that you shouldn't see it until we had finished. What has happened to make you change your mind? - Has that husband of yours been putting ideas in your head?'

Chaney was sitting in an armchair, staring at the blank television screen. He had not moved, or spoken to Anne since his arrival. If it had been any other day, Anne would have been concerned about his behaviour.

'How dare you say such a thing?' Anne retorted. 'We are talking about my exhibition. Not yours or....or anyone else's, and if I want to rearrange things, I have a perfect right to do so.'

'I couldn't agree more,' Kay said. 'I never meant to imply that you couldn't. But it does seem rather pointless discussing alterations before we have even finished putting it together in the first place.'

'I didn't say that I was definitely going to make alterations, I simply said that I wanted to see for myself.'

'And you have a perfect right to do so,' Kay replied, aping Anne's phrase. 'No-one is denying that. It just seems to me that you don't understand our reasons for asking you to wait just a little longer.' Kay chose her words carefully. Jane had spoken to her about the change in Anne's attitude and at their last meeting Kay had witnessed it for herself. She did not wish to be the cause of a major argument now. Not now, with the work almost finished and her usefulness at an end. Kay wanted to be around to see the fruits of her labour. To see the look on Anne Chaney's face, and -

'You have organized this whole thing simply to get back at my father,' Paul had accused her. 'There was not a good intention in your heart.'

'I had to find some way,' Kay shouted. 'Can't you understand that?'

'You didn't have to involve somebody else,' Paul replied.

'If you really felt that you had to do something, you should have... have found another way. A way that didn't risk any more upset.'

'That's so bloody typical of you, isn't it? It's alright if I'm the one who's upset, but if there's a chance that it could be anyone else in your dear family, you immediately start to worry.'

'That isn't true!' Paul was angry now 'And if you think it is, I pity you ...'

The memory of the argument was still embedded in Kay's mind, but she could smile at it now. Things had been so much better in the last few days.

'Exactly what are your reasons for asking me to wait?' Anne wanted to know.

'We don't want you to worry unduly,' Kay said. 'You will be the star of the show tomorrow, you will have enough to do then. We thought it best to give you a chance to rest today.'

'But I still don't see why -'

'Because we all love you,' Kay interrupted her, ' and because we want everything to go as well as it possibly can. We wouldn't have suggested the idea in the first place if we didn't care,' she added, knowing that it was a winning argument.

'I know that,' Anne said after a moment's consideration, 'and I appreciate it, I really do.'

'Then stay there till Paul collects you. It won't be long now.'

'Very well. If you think it's best. After all, you haven't been wrong yet.' Anne experienced a momentary feeling of guilt, and continued, 'I'm sorry for having been so awkward, I'm sure you must be really busy at the moment, it's just that I'm well... I suppose I'm a little tense.'

'That's quite understandable, and there's no need to apologise. We are family after all, remember?' Kay hung up before Anne could reply.

'What's happening?' Chaney's question was directed at the television set. It caught Anne by surprise.

'Oh... er... nothing really. Well, what I mean is, everything's going fine. Paul is coming to pick me up when they've finished at the hall.'

Chaney nodded, digesting the information as if he were a computer. 'That's the best way.' He gave his verdict. 'I suppose it's Kay's idea and she is right. You are better off here for the time being.'

'Yes, I can see the sense in that,' Anne was still not sure that she could, 'but one part of me says that I should have been there from the start. After all, it is my work.'

'That's precisely why you should stay away. You are too involved with it. Let the others arrange your work, that's their way of trying to share your glory - and don't believe any other reason they give you, no matter how convincing it sounds. They are not doing all this just for your benefit.' Chaney shifted in his seat and looked at his wife. 'You save yourself for tomorrow. No-one'll be able to help you then. If it all goes well you'll be permanently surrounded by the organizers. If it's a disaster, you won't see them. They you will find out what it's like to be on your own.'

'Yes.' Chaney's words scared Anne, but she was delighted that he was showing such interest. 'It really has been the strangest week for me,' she confessed. 'Such a... a mixture.'

A half smile played on Chaney's face.

'One minute I'm incredibly confident - more than I have ever been about anything, the next I'm sure that it's all one big mistake.'

'You'll get used to it.' There was a hint of encouragement in Chaney's voice. It thrilled Anne.

'Was it the same for you, when you first started working on television?' she asked. 'A mixture of fear and excitement so jumbled up that you don't really know how you feel?'

'How do you feel?' Sly asked, closing the dressing room door behind him.

Chaney raised one eyebrow contemptuously. 'I feel nothing,' he said.

'I find that hard to believe.'

Chaney's smile matched the coldness in his eyes.

'Tonight is your big chance,' Sly went on. 'Do what you promised tonight, and you will get a permanent spot in the series. Andrew is delighted with the idea of your joining the team - if you can prove your worth tonight.'

'I told you,' Chaney stood up, 'everyone has a weakness. If you ever doubt that, come in front of the cameras with me...'

'Yes,' Chaney said, 'I felt all of those things - particularly at the beginning, but most of all there was a sense of longing. I didn't just want to succeed, I needed to. That's the most important thing. You have to need it. When that goes, it's time to stop.'

-Stop. You are going to far. You don't need to tell anyone these things.

She's my wife.

In name only.

I have to do something.

To redress the balance? It's too late for that.

It's never too late.

It's never too soon.-

Chaney looked at Anne and smiled. 'You know, I can never decide which I enjoy most. The tension before, or the feeling of success afterwards. It's crazy really.'

'What about the bit in the middle?' Anne spoke hurriedly, desperate for his answers; not wanting the conversation to end. 'When you are actually there and everyone's looking at you. I would have thought that was the best time - if things are going well.'

'You only think that because you have no experience.' It was not a condemnation, there was no harshness in Chaney's voice. 'By that time you are too damned busy to be able to stand back and enjoy it. And if it is going well, the time passes so quickly.' Chaney paused and glanced again at the televison. Anne thought his eyes misted over.

'That's the ultimate problem,' he said, 'time.'

'What do you mean?' Anne's voice was soft.

Chaney gathered himself. ''Take a couple of pills tonight. Make sure that you sleep well. It'll be a tiring day tomorrow.'

'From what I hear, it's not only me who needs to rest.' Anne had not meant to be so forthright.

'Who else?'

But she was committed now. 'You. Paul says you ought to see a doctor.' She leant forward. 'Is there something wrong?'

-I told you. You went too far.-

Chaney thrust himself to his feet.

-You can't trust anyone these days.-

'Yeah. We had one kid too many.' Chaney stormed out of the room.

-Even yourself.-

Paul Chaney rushed into his parents' house and had entered the lounge before he realised how quiet it was. His father was sitting in an armchair, his eyes half closed. There was no sign of his mother.

'Oh. How long have you been here?' Paul asked abruptly. It had been a long day and he was tired.

'For a time.' Chaney's voice was mild, as if he had just finished a period of meditation. He turned his head slowly as he spoke.

"Like a lizard sunning himself," Paul thought. 'Then why didn't you come along to the hall and give us a hand?' he asked. 'You must have known how busy we were.'

'I had other things to do.'

'You don't seem to be doing so much right now.'

'Neither do you.' Chaney's eyes widened. 'Why are you here?'

'I've come to collect Mum. We are ready for her now.'

'Of course.' Chaney remembered. 'You've taken a long time.'

'Kay decided on a few last minute changes,' Paul said quickly. 'It means we are a little bit behind schedule.'

'Too far behind schedule,' Chaney corrected him.

'What makes you say that?' Paul frowned.

'Your mother left the house some time ago. I presume she got bored waiting.'

'Damn! She was going straight to the hall?'

'How should I know?' If you didn't see her on the way, perhaps not.'

'For Christ's sake, can't you do any better than that?' Paul asked angrily. 'She is your wife.'

-She is.-

'Why don't you sit down and have a drink? Relax for a while.' Chaney suggested.

'I don't have the time.'

'I suppose you're right,' Chaney conceded. 'You could still have a lot to do.'

'Why?' Paul was instantly suspicious.

'If your mother decides she doesn't like the display. You might have to start again.'

'I know, I've been thinking about that.' Paul was subdued. 'I can only hope that it doesn't happen.' He grinned wearily. 'To tell you the truth, I'm desperate for a bath. Parts of that hall were filthy when we started working there this morning. I've spent half of the day just cleaning up.'

'Somebody had to.' Chaney placed a hand on his son's shoulder. 'And none of the others would have been too keen.'

'Perhaps not.' Paul turned to go. 'Hey! Did Mum tell you about what happened yesterday?' Paul changed direction and approached his father.

'No.' This time it was Chaney who was cautious.

'A woman called. Here. A woman from the city. She had somehow heard about the exhibition - presumably she knows Kay indirectly, I don't know. Anyway the point is, she asked Mum if she would do a portrait of her pet. She left a photo. Even gave her an advance. Said that she had heard marvellous things about Mum's work. In fact, I'll bet the photo's here somewhere.' Paul had reached the mantlepiece almost before he had finished speaking. 'Yes, here it is.' He produced the photograph with a flourish from behind a gold carriage clock.

'What is it?'

The tone in Chaney's voice made Paul hesitate slightly.

'It's er... er... a cat. Why?'

The photograph was snatched from his hand.

'Soul.' Chaney's voice was no more than a whisper.

'What?'

-She's been to your house. Seen ... everything.

You understand what that means. You can't ignore it.-

'What did you say, Dad?'

'I wanted to keep her.'

-You cannot. She's laughing at you.-

'Keep who?'

-Laughing at you.-

'Why would she do that?'

'Are you talking about Mum?'

-Does it matter? Facts are facts.-

'No. Yes. Facts are facts. There is no turning back. She is laughing at me.'

'For God's sake, what are you talking about?' Paul wanted to reach out and touch his father, but he dare not.

'I have to finish with her.'

-Yes.-

'Show her that I understand. Punish her.'

-Yes.-

'There can be no second chance.'

-I thought you already knew that...-

'Dad! Dad, is there anything I can do?'

Paul's voice seemed unusually loud. Chaney lowered the photo.

'Find your mother.'

'But... but what about you? Are you sure you are alright?'

'I don't need you to look after me.' Chaney glared. 'So why don't you just run along.'

'If you're sure-'

'Now.'

Chaney waited until he heard the kitchen door close behind Paul before he looked at the photo again. He thought of Soul stretched out in front of the fire.

-'For Christ's sake! He's my cat! He might as well be dead... might as well be... dead.'-

Chaney slipped the photo into his inside jacket pocket. Above his heart. A cruel smile twisted his face.

Monday.

* * * * *

The next day, Sunday the day of the art exhibition, the weatherman forecast snow. He was wrong. Anne Chaney and her helpers arrived at the village hall at one o'clock, an hour before the exhibition was scheduled to start. Anne said very little but walked about the building, looking at, and occasionally touching, her work. By ten minutes before two, a small crowd had begun to gather outside the main doors. At three minutes past two, Anne overruled Kay and opened the doors to her audience. She felt not the slightest regret when someone she had never seen before bought a painting of the shire horse, and she realised it was no longer hers. For the first part of the afternoon Anne spent much of her time listening nervously to whispered conversations about her work, but as the afternoon wore on, and people realised who she was, she found herself becoming more and more the centre of attention. Anne was surprised how intently those around her listened to her observations about her work. She did not even notice her husband's arrival mid-way through the afternoon. By the time the last person left, Anne had been on her feet for over four hours, but she felt as light as a feather. She had sold fifteen pieces of her work.

The time had passed very quickly.

TEN

Sylvester Harris put the drinks on the table and sat down opposite Chaney with an ill-concealed look of delight on his face.

'So, by all accounts, it was a great success?' He was talking about the art exhibition.

Chaney grunted. 'You know bloody well it was. How many times do you need to be told?'

Sly's grin widened. Because he had been unable to attend the exhibition, he had phoned Anne on Sunday evening, to enquire after its success. What he had heard had secretly surprised him. 'I just wanted to hear the proud husband's reaction, that's all.' Sly said good humouredly.

'I take it you did go?'

'For a time.' Chaney remembered the other occasion he had used the same phrase, and his face clouded. The photograph was still in his jacket pocket; he had checked twice before leaving the house earlier in the evening.

'Am I to assume from that, you were not impressed?' Sly misinterpreted the look on Chaney's face.

'You can assume what you like.'

A group sitting at a table near them broke into laughter. Chaney shook off his melancholy.

'Actually, I know very little about art,' he confessed. 'I wouldn't know if she's got any talent or not.' He shrugged. 'From what I saw and heard most of the people there were impressed.'

'Another star is born...' Sly sipped at his gin and lime.

'Yeah. She's talking of having another exhibition in the summer. Bigger venue this time. If she can persuade the others to help her, of course.'

'She hasn't asked them yet?'

'No. I expect she will do that tonight.'

'Oh yes, the celebration party. I was invited too, you know.' Sly smiled. 'I must confess I felt somewhat guilty saying that I had already arranged a business meeting with you.'

'I'm sure you did,' Chaney said drily. 'I know how easy it would be for you to turn your back on an evening's gambling.'

The group at the next table laughed again.

Anne Chaney was almost drunk and she didn't care. 'This has been the most wonderful weekend of my life,' she said to no-one in particular. 'You can't possibly imagine how it feels.'

'I think we can,' Kay's voice lacked enthusiasm. 'We have all experienced success in our own fields. It isn't new to us.'

'But you are talking about success in business terms.' Anne took a hurried drink of her sherry. 'I'm talking about artistic success. The two are very different. There is, in fact,' she smiled condescendingly, 'no comparison.'

'I think, perhaps you have had enough to drink for one night.' Kay turned to Paul for support.

'I don't think that's any of your damned business,' Anne replied before Paul could speak. 'I think I have had enough of people making decisions for me. From now on I;m going to do what I feel is right, and if others want to join in and help, they can.' Anne blinked. The figures around her were becoming ever so slightly blurred. She took another drink of her sherry.

'I don't think anyone would object to that philosophy.' Paul said, ignoring the glare his wife directed at him. 'Or to your feeling of success, you've earned it, but you can't just ignore the assistance you received from those around you. It was a team effort, after all.'

'Yes, yes, you're right, of course it was.' Anne nodded her head vigorously. 'Wiothout my lovely family and friends there would never have been an exhibition. Without the lovely Kay,' Anne reached out and stroked Kay's cheek with her free hand, 'I would have spent the rest of my life painting pictures for no-one but myself. How can I ever thank you?'

Kay removed Anne's hand from her face and forced herself to smile. She had not wanted to waste her evening at a celebration party anyway. The other guests were the Swifts and Kay no longer had any desire to associate with them. Besides, from her point of view, the exhibition had been somewhat less than successful: Jon Chaney had been visibly unconcerned by the enthusiastic reaction to Anne's work. He had shown neither pleasure nor anger and he had talked to no-one throughout the proceedings. Kay's efforts had failed to touch him.

'Listen everyone,' Anne raised her voice as if addressing a large gathering. 'I have an announcement to make. One that affects you all.'

Jane and David Swift were at the other end of the room, where they had been talking quietly for most of the evening. They approached Anne, holding hands. Paul glanced at Kay and saw a look of irritation on her face. He struggled to contain a smile. Confirmation of his new post had come through today; they would be moving to Australia in the summer. Nothing else mattered.

'First of all I want to thank you for your work and support in the last few weeks.' Anne began. 'I must confess - although it's no secret - how scared I was when Jane first put the idea to me.' Anne paused and wondered briefly if she had said exactly what she had meant to. She finished her drink. 'Because of that, and because of the success yesterday, I have decided that for me now, there can be no going back. That was only my first exhibition. I intend to have many more, each one bigger and better than the last, and I would like you - all of you - to help me organize them.' Anne smiled at each one of her guests in turn, looking finally at Kay. 'And I would like Kay, particularly, to help me with my next exhibition. I intend to show my work in the city, sometime in the summer.'

'That's a wonderful idea!' Jane Swift clapped her hands in delight.

Paul Chaney turned to his wife and felt a sinking feeling in the pit of his stomach. They were going to Australia in the summer.

* * * * *

'You really ought to come with me, you know,' Sly said. 'It's a marvellous club, and if you don't want to gamble you can always continue drinking and look at the beautiful women.'

'And lend you money when you've none left,' Chaney said with a wry smile. The drink had relaxed him; he had married a woman with talent.

'Not tonight,' Sly replied. 'Tonight I'm going to win more money than I ever have before. In fact I'm going to buy two of Anne's paintings for a ridiculously high sum, out of the winnings.'

'What the hell for?'

'It's part of the agreement I've made. If I win a massive amount of money tonight, I have to buy some of Anne's work.'

'What are you talking about? Who did you make that agreement with?' Chaney was puzzled; he spoke with an aggresive tone in his voice.

Sly winked and drained his glass. 'Fate,' he said.

'Bollocks.' Chaney looked across to the other side of the bar. There was a beautiful woman there, sitting alone at a table.

-You will need a replacement. You are too old to change.- A sudden tension filled Chaney's stomach. He slipped his hand into his inside jacket pocket. The photo was still there.

'So you are absolutely sure that I can't change your mind?' Sly tried for a last time.

'I've told you. I have something else to do.'

'O.K. O.K, I suppose I should have known,' Sly conceded. 'You are too old to change.'

'What did you say?'

'I said ...' Sly stiffened; saw the anger in Chaney's eyes, realised the danger he was in. 'Nothing. It doesn't matter. Just a passing comment, it meant nothing.'

-Relax. Take it easy. Why are you taking everything so seriously? That's a sure sign of fear. Remember, you are only as old as you feel. And you are never too old...- Chaney nodded and rubbed his hands over his face as if washing it, 'bar-room talk.'

-... to die.-

Chaney stood up. 'I have to go. My business won't wait.'

'Well, if you are sure,' Sly pushed his chair away from the table. 'I had assumed we were going to have a couple more drinks.'

'There's no time ...'

The snow had started while they were in the pub. When Chaney walked into the car park it was already half-an-inch thick on the ground. Sly followed behind him.

'Shit,' Sly said, 'This wasn't forecast. What a bloody mess.'

Chaney said nothing. The flakes were large, drifting silently, in slow motion, towards the earth. The Jaguar's windscreen was covered beneath a white blanket. Chaney cleared it with his bare hand. The snow was cold and damp.

'I'll give you a ring tomorrow,' he said to Sly. 'There might be something I want to talk to you about.'

'Right.' Sly disappeared into his own car and quickly drove away. Chaney let the Jaguar's engine warm for several minutes, until the snow on the bonnet was beginning to melt, before he slipped the car into first gear and released the handbrake. The jaguar moved slowly out of the car park. There was no rush. He had a photo to deliver.

'For God's sake, why didn't you tell her?' Kay Chaney roared at her husband, slamming the wardrobe door shut as she did so. 'Why didn't you have the guts to tell her?'

Paul closed his eyes and tried to count to ten. Until this moment Kay had not spoken to him since his mother's unexpected announcement at the party. Her anger stemmed from the fact that Paul had remained silent; had not taken the opportunity to talk about their new plans; to explain why they would no longer be able to assist Anne with her career as an artist

'It was your idea in the first place,' Kay continued, 'a chance to make a new start. To break away from ... from all this. So why the hell didn't you tell her?'

'Because tonight was... well, tonight was her special night. You couldn't really expect me to ruin that, could you?' Paul gestured lamely. 'I'll go round there again tomorrow, when the excitement has died down, and talk to her then. It will be alright.'

'How do I know that?' Kay snarled.

'What?'

'Any of it!' Kay thumped angrily at the pillow on her side of the bed. 'How can I know that anything you say is true?'

'When have I ever lied to you?' Paul questioned hoarsely, his mind reeling from the shock of Kay's accusation.

'I'm not talking about your honesty!' Kay screamed.

'Then what-'

'I'm talking about your courage!' Kay was abruptly silent, as if her final shout had drained her of any strength she possessed. A fire suddenly doused. Paul looked down at the bed. 'I love my mother,' he said finally, 'but when I chose to marry you, I was making a public statement. A declaration. You come first now. You always will.'

'Paul, I'm sorry. I didn't mean...' Kay sobbed, her shoulders heaving. '...I didn't want to-'

'I will go to my mother's tomorrow,' Paul continued softly. 'I will tell her the truth, no matter how much it upsets her. We are going to live in Australia.'

Kay collapsed on the bed, burying her face in her arms as she cried. Paul sat down beside her; made no attempt to comfort her. The time had come to face himself.

"And perhaps - just perhaps - the week before we fly to Australia, I will go to bed with Sally. Just so that there can be no doubt."

* * * * *

The snow was falling more heavily now and Chaney drove slowly because of it.

-You are so full of fear... you can't even hide it any more.-

Chaney switched the car radio on; heard a pop song he did not like. His left hand automatically turned the appropriate button; turned the volume up. -If you do not want to do this, how can you hope to do more?-

'I feel alone.'

-You have always been.-

'The cancer is growing. I can feel it.'

-No! That is only the fear. It is unreal. Dissolve it.-

'Then what do you feel?'

-Nothing...-

'I have a series to prepare ...

-You must rid yourself of this woman.-

'...I have no choice...'

The speed of the Jaguar increased, the power of the machine soothing Chaney's fear. Not long now.

Sylvester Harris stacked the twenty black chips in front of him and smacked his lips with delight. He was winning tonight and the game was blackjack.

Two other players were also involved and Sly watched intently as the tall blonde haired woman in the black, low-cut dress, shuffled the cards and then placed the pack in front of the man with the red, thinning hair.

'It's time I got lucky,' the man said with a self conscious grin - so far he had lost more than either of the other players - and split the pack.

The blonde dealt from the bottom pile, delivering the cards with crisp economical movements. Sly received the jack of spades and could not prevent his mouth from curling into a slight grin when he saw the card. It was a simple game, the object being to get a score as near to twenty one as possible, without going above it, and higher than the hand held by the dealer. A picture card was an almost perfect beginning, needing only an ace to make the strongest possible hand.

When his turn came, Sly offered three of the chips, worth twenty pounds each, and received his second card. It was the eight of diamonds, giving him a total of eighteen. He had no choice but to wait.

The first player, a florid faced man in a black suit, bought twice more before he was satisfied, and Sly guessed that, with four cards in his hand, he would be difficult to beat. The red haired man tried the same, but his fourth card was too high, and with a look of disgust, he threw his cards onto the table and admitted defeat.

The dealer turned her cards over. She had a seven and a five, and Sly felt a knot of tension in his stomach. Only a ten could put her out of the game. The dealer's face showed no emotion as she took her next card from the pack. It was the five of clubs, and Sly knew without a moment's hesitation that she would not gamble further. He was going to win again and tonight he was going to continue winning. His horoscope had said so.

Chaney was forced to stop the car at a pedestrian crossing, as a group of late night revellers staggered in front of him, singing and shouting. To his left a crowd streamed out of a cinema, pulling up collars and putting on hats in defence against the snow. Chaney watched them with the dispassionate interest of a scientist studying life through a microscope. The car radio was playing at full volume.

'Got a black magic woman

I've got a black magic woman.

I've got a black magic woman.

Got me so blind I can't see...'

Chaney released the handbrake, his right foot moved from the brake to the accelerator. The Jaguar's speed increased, thirty, forty, fifty...

'I've got a black magic woman

Trying to make a devil out of me...'

The street lights cast an orange hue; buildings merged one with the other, shapeless, characterless, the snow that did not touch the car was light and harmless. Chaney saw the city flash past him, as unreal as a picture on a screen.

'Don't turn your back on me baby,

Stop messin' 'bout with your tricks.

Don't turn your back on me baby,

Just might...'

Chaney was travelling at fifty five miles an hour when the front nearside tyre burst. The Jaguar automatically turned inwards, towards the barely visible pavement, and as Chaney struggled to correct the skid, he became aware of the awful weight of the car for the first time. A building, black as night, loomed in front of him, and the image of a motor cycle spinning wildly into a screaming throng, filled his mind, threatening to blind him to the reality of his danger. Chaney shook his head, cleared his vision; saw his hands moving with a life of their own, spinning the steering wheel away, away from the pavement, urging the machine to obey their comand.

The snow helped him, gave the tyres something to cling to. The car straightened and slowed, and only then did Chaney apply the brake, caressing it with the sole of his foot, the movement in sudden contrast to the urgency of his hands. When the car stopped, Chaney switched off the ignition and got out. It was as he expected. The tyre was ruined. Chaney felt the adrenalin pump and he smiled a slow, satisfied smile, oblivious to the snow that was landing on him. He would walk to Katherine's, it could not be more than a mile. The fresh air would do him good. He was alive.

Katherine Durham lay back on the bed and groaned with delight. The man was trying to please her, and that mattered, it mattered so much. Katherine groaned again - for his benefit - and whispered his name, offering encouragement. She would tell him afterwards that he was the most wonderful lover, she would let him see the gratitude in her eyes. He was young and filled with the arrogance of youth, he would believe her. He would come to see her as another of his successes - as a symbol of his success - and slowly he would come to need her. When that happened, it would be time to find someone new. Katherine closed her eyes and decided that the time was right to end his ministration. Her voice increased its urgency; she felt him respond and Katherine altered her performance accordingly, no longer using words, but sounds. Just a few seconds more...

The sound of the doorbell shocked her. It was ringing continuously; not a polite request, but a demand. The man beside her stirred in his sleep and then woke.

'What's happening?' he mumbled, propping himself up on his elbow, his blond hair tousled.

'Some one's at the door,' Katherine's voice was stern.

'Leave it, they'll go away,' he lay down on his side, turning his back to the noise.

'No...' Katherine got out of bed, picked up the blue silk dressing gown from the back of a chair and put it on, tying the belt loosely round her waist. The embroidered picture of Mount Fuji that dominated the back of it was hidden beneath her hair.

Katherine left the bedroom door open and walked silently downstairs, her bare right thigh appearing and disappearing behind the silk. In the hallway the sound of the bell was even louder and when she opened the door, Kathering left the security chain in place.

The noise stopped instantly, as though controlled by the movement of the door, and when Katherine peered cautiously outside she saw nothing but the snow swirling silently in the light of a street lamp.

'H- Hallo?' There was no response, and Katherine, angered by her own timidity, released the chain, opened the door fully and took a pace forward. A snow flake, pushed gently by the wind, landed on the skin above her breasts, turning almost immediately into a single drop of water. Katherine, gasping at its touch, realized how exposed she was.

'I don't think it's very funny,' she told the night, stepping back to close the door. Tomorrow she would phone the police and ask them to keep a look out for children playing stupid games, disturbing other people's rest. This had always been a quiet area.

The piece of paper on the doorstep was almost covered with snow, and it was only by chance that Katherine glanced down and saw it.

'Who's been here...?' She picked it up, dusting the snow off it, realising instantly that it was not simply paper, but a photograph. A stab of fear penetrated Katherine's heart, paralyzing her, as she stared into Soul's green unblinking eyes. For a second Katherine was held motionless by her discovery and then the need to lock her door again spurred her into action.

The dealer turned her cards over; the jack of diamonds and the nine of clubs. It was a strong hand, and of the five players now gathered round the table, only Sly could beat it.

'How about that!' his exclamation was louder than was necessary; an empty champagne bottle was in an ice bucket beside him. 'Two beautiful big kings.' Sly pushed the cards arrogantly across the table and at the same time signalled for another bottle of champagne.

'I'm sorry to have to say this ladies and gentlemen, but I win again.' Sly leered at the dealer and added the chips she gave him to the neatly ordered columns he had built before him. They stood on the table like a wall between them. 'Deal me another card, beautiful lady.' The blonde obliged and Sly peered cautiously at it, aware of the small crowd that had gathered behind him. The card was the ace of hearts and Sly felt his heartbeat quicken. An ace ... the card he had been waiting for. Any picture card would go with it to give him a virtually unbeatable hand. Sly drummed his fingertips impatiently against the table top as he waited for his turn.

The man next to Sly scratched his nose, frowned with indecision, and then pushed three black chips towards the dealer. His second card appeared magically before him, and he raised it slowly, as if afraid of what he might see. Sly thought he detected a glimmer of triumph in the man's eyes and he wondered briefly what the card might be.

'Sir?' The dealer's eyebrows rose slightly as she spoke and Sly knew that by now she must have begun to hate him.

He glanced to his left and was surprised to see that his champagne bottle had been replaced. Sly paused in consideration and licked his lips; heard the rustle of movement behind him.

'Sir?' The dealer's voice had not changed, still cold and remote.

Sly looked again at the ace, then picked up three red chips, each worth five hundred pounds, and dropped them on the table midway between himself and the dealer.

No man's land.

The dealer did not hesitate, and as Sly's right hand reached out to cover his second card, there was an audible murmur of excitement from the crowd.

'Any picture,' he told himself. 'Any picture will do ... any smiling little picture ... just give me one picture ... that's all I ask ... just one ...'

Sly peered at the card and was forced to clench his right fist tightly to prevent himself from screaming with joy. The queen of spades. His smiling little picture. Barring a miracle, he couldn't lose.

'And that won't happen,' he reassured himself. 'It's my lucky night, not theirs.' Sly sipped hurriedly at his champagne, spilt some but didn't notice. 'And after this hand I'll stop. Get out while the going's good.. Walk away with a profit. A killing.'

The dealer had a score of fifteen; she dealt herself a ten. Sly pounded the table with delight.

'That's it! I must stop now. Give up my seat. It would be stupid to continue... stupid'.

The dealer shuffled the pack.

Katherine Durham dropped the photo of her cat and grabbed at the door with both hands. Her movement was fast, incredibly fast, fuelled by a fear that overwhelmed her, drove all rational thought from her body. Jon Chaney appeared from nowhere. Stopped the door from closing with his left arm and gently pushed it open as Katherine staggered back into the hall. Chaney stood in the doorway, his shoulders and hair speckled with snow, his eyes glittering as if on fire.

'Thought I'd come calling.'

There was a quality in his voice that Katherine could not recognize, but before she could concern herself with that, she heard footsteps on the stairs and realised with sickening clarity that what she felt before had not been fear. Only a pale imitation.

'Oh Jesus ...' Katherine backed away, away from the door, her arms hanging limp at her sides.

'What the hell is happening? What's going on down there?' The man had put on his trousers, but his upper body was bare; trim and muscular. He stepped into the hall and froze, his mouth open, his eyes wide and staring, only vaguely aware of Katherine moving erratically towards him.

Chaney heard the movement on the stairs just before Katherine did.

A man ... too heavy for a woman ...too clumsy ...a man ..she had another man ...she has...

'Michael.' Chaney said the word, but didn't hear it, was already moving. Forwards.

Michael isn't going to replace you on the 'Living Today' programme .. he's too busy ... fucking ...Who's on the programme tonight? ...smiling ...pretty ...who's on the programme, tell me.

-I am. I am. I am.-

'For God's sake, do something!' Katherine screamed, turning towards Michael. He stood rooted to the spot. 'For God's sake!' Chaney moved past her, ignoring her. Katherine felt the power of him, felt it emanating from him, surrounding him. Wondered how she could have ever been so terribly wrong. Chaney's hand dipped into his jacket pocket, came out with the car keys.

'I killed a man with these.'

'Look out!' Katherine screamed in horror as she saw the metal between his fingers. 'In his hand -'

Michael burst into action, lunging across to his right, away from the danger in Chaney's hand, bringing his left arm up to parry any attack to his face. Chaney's right arm was scything through the air, the keys stabbing down into the place where Michael's face had been only a split second earlier. Michael felt an intense moment of satisfaction and his confidence increased. Not such a wild man after all... Michael shifted his weight, began moving towards his adversary, ready to begin a counter-attack of his own. It occurred to him that Chaney had not yet realised that his opening strike had missed, he had made no effort to turn, to follow Michael, his first blow seemed to have thrown him off balance. Michael clenched his fists and drove a punch for Chaney's jaw.

Katherine screamed only a few words of warning and then her voice failed her, silenced by the purity of Chaney's movement. No longer the man who collapsed, ungainly, into an armchair, out of balance, out of control. A different man; a man possessed. Isaki flashed before her, his sword raised. Katherine's eyes widened in amazement as she saw the ease with which Michael evaded the first blow, and then, before it happened, she realised the awful truth. A feint... never intending to hit, but to distract... and her shout had helped. Katherine watched helpless, as Michael hurled himself on Chaney. She saw his lack of defence, she saw the openings he left, she saw Chaney pivot to meet him with the ease and grace of a great dancer.

Michael was committed now, there could be no turning back. His fist streaked past the other's hands, only inches from his jaw ... could not be stopped.

'Yaah!'

The shout broke like thunder in the hall and Michael doubled over in agony, pain raging inside him like a forest fire, all thought of attack forgotten.

Katherine saw the subtle change as Chaney eased his body weight onto his right leg. His left foot swung upwards in a seemingly slow, lazy fashion. It connected before Michaels fist, driving deep into his groin, destroying his forward momentum with a finality that made Katherine gasp.

Michael saw Chaney's hands reaching for him, almost casual in their manner. He tried to straighten to fend them off, but could not. Felt instead the fingers grabbing his hair, pulling him forward.

Chaney's left knee thrust upwards like a piston, slamming into Michael's downcoming face, breaking his nose, spreading blood and gristle across both cheeks. Katherine's voice returned.

'Let him go-ooo!'

The knee lowered and raised again, but not a random strike, this time smashing lips and teeth. Michael's last conscious thought was that he was going to choke on his own vomit.

'Please... leave him alone!'

The knee struck again and again and each time Katherine screamed for Chaney to stop. When he finally did, he hauled the body upright, holding it effortlessly in one hand, and pointed the face at her.

'Kiss your lover ...'

Katherine passed out.

-Lock the door ... You must lock the door fully.-

'Yes.'

-Put him out for the night.-

'Is that a good idea?'

-All good little boys should go out for the night.-

'Someone might find him.'

-He's garbage.-

'Yes ... He's getting heavy.'

-Let me help ...see how easy it is now?-

'Yes ... Throw me Daddy, throw me away into the water ...Whee! there he goes ...big boy... She's still asleep.'

-You can wake her up... but then what will you do?-

'I know Daddy. I can show you what Mummy did when you were poorly in the hospital... When I was hiding... Don't you know what that was? You'll make me cry Daddy. I thought you knew everything... I can show you...'

Katherine Durham opened her eyes. Chaney was standing beside her. There was a dark stain on the knee of his left trouser. Katherine began to cry.

'Stand up!'

'Please ... Jon ...I-'

Chaney pulled her to her feet. His face only inches away. Katherine saw in it only the vaguest resemblance of something human; of the man she had toyed with. Michael's body had disappeared.

'Come with me.' His voice came from somewhere deep inside.

'Jon. Jon. Listen to me.'

'Into the study. We'll use the desk there as we always do. It isn't quite the same Daddy ...'

'Jon ...please! ... What are you saying... What are you...'

Chaney pushed Katherine in front of him and bustled her upstairs, into her bedroom. The bed was crumpled; the cover thrown back. Chaney shut the door and stood with his back to it.

'Clean it.' He pointed to her dressing table. 'Wipe it all away!'

Katherine staggered back and fell onto the bed. 'I don't know what you mean... please!'

Chaney dragged her from the bed and marched her across the room. 'Clean it!' He ordered again, forcing Katherine's face down towards the dressing- table top.

'Wipe all the rubbish away. This is no artist's room. I know what you want. You needn't ask any more. Push it off with your arms!'

Katherine thrust her hands down onto the dressing table, locking her arms straight, trying to prevent him from forcing her lower. It was a futile gesture. Chaney knocked her arms aside with a nonchalant sweep of his hand, and twisted her head. Katherine's right cheek slammed down onto the table top, her cheekbone thudding painfully against a bottle of nail varnish remover. Chaney leant forward, pressing his weight over the top of her, and scattered the other bottles and canisters with his free hand.. Katherine felt his feet between hers forcing them apart.

'That's it ... that's it... mustn't make any noise ... it attracts little boys ... no noise, that's it ... we don't want little boys peering round doors ... seeing things they shouldn't see ...that's it.'Katherine gasped for air. Chaney kept his weight on her, pressing down with his left elbow on the pace between her shoulder blades. Katherine felt his right hand reaching her dressing gown, pulling it up, exposing the back of her thighs, her...

'Don't struggle Kay ... don't struggle ... no-one can see ... no-one's looking ... it's alright ... I've shut the door ... locked the door .. doors are made for ...'

The weight was suddenly gone and Katherine straightened, clutching at the dressing table for support, aware of a stabbing pain in her lower back. Chaney was by the door, opening and closing it, opening and closing.

'There is no lock!' he screamed. 'You want people to see!' Chaney hurled the door open - it struck the wall and ricocheted back - and approached Katherine with a murderous rage in his eyes.

Katherine lunged across the room, grabbed the heavy marble ashtray from the beside the bed, and prepared to use it as a weapon against him. Like a tigress trapped in her lair, she sprang to meet him, snarling now with rage rather than fear. Chaney saw her attack, saw her shrink in size as she neared him; felt the power and weight of his fist, as heavy as a boulder. He could not contain it and at the last instant, it smashed into her, knocking her across the room. Katherine did not see Chaney move, would not have stopped if she had. At the precise moment she thought she had reached him, Katherine felt the force of enormous power rushing towards her as inexorable as a tidal wave. It picked her up and hurled her across the room.

'I'm flying,' Katherine thought and then her head struck the gilt-edged mirror and her neck snapped.

Chaney let the picture grow around him, and as it did so, his rage diminished. Tiny bottles of different shapes and colours were scattered on the carpet; the marble ashtray was by his feet.

Katherine was lying, motionless, her head hanging at an obscene angle, against the bottom of the mirror. Chaney crossed the room and squatted hesitantly beside her; saw his own reflection in her eyes.

'Oh my God...' Chaney backed away, the terror he felt silencing him'.

"There is I believe a time and a place for all things..." The words filled the room and Chaney spun round, searching.

'Leave me alone!'

The old soldier smiled sadly, his skin as creased and delicate as old paper. 'I can only hope that ... when the time comes, I will have the strength to die as I have lived ...'

'You are dead!' Chaney roared, his voice echoing round the room. 'Dead, you bastard! You cannot-'

'Listen to him son..'

Chaney staggered, almost fell. 'What ...?'

'Think about your future, son ...'

'I killed her.'

'You have a cancer.'

'Yes...' Chaney stared at Katherine's body. Buried in the past. Unchangeable ... The past means nothing ... Just a shell. Meaningless ... without the future. 'I have to win!'

'You have a cancer.'

'I can beat the cancer!'

'How?'

A smile of triumph spread slowly across Chaney's face.

'I know.'

Kay Chaney screamed in fear as he kissed her neck, but the house was empty and no-one heard. He forced her into Anne's study, ignoring her slaps and kicks, and pushed her down, face down, against the desk.

'You think you're so damned smart,' Chaney snarled.

'I'll show you ... I'll show you what I know...'

He was going to rape her, and as Kay felt him move behind her, she knew that she could not, dare not resist. Tears streamed down her face. 'Paul...' Kay barely heard the noise, a clatter of something hit the floor, but his hands left her, and Kay turned quickly, tugging her skirt into position. Anne was standing in the dining room. Her newly bought set of paints at her feet.

'Aaaaah!' Kay Chaney sat bolt upright in bed, her breathing wild and out of control. Paul was beside her, his arm around her shoulder.

'O.K.?'

Kay nodded.

'The same dream?'

'Yeah.'

'Don't worry. We'll be away from him soon. You'll never have to look at him again. You will be able to forget it in another country.'

Kay shook her head. 'I'll never be able to forget it.'

Chaney padded silently downstairs. There were two things he needed to do. When he returned he was carrying a glass filled with whisky in his left hand. He entered the bathroom.

Chaney took a drink of the whisky, swilling the liquid round in his mouth and then spitting it into the sink.

There was a knock on the door.

'It's time, Mr. Chaney.'

Chaney straightened his tie and left the room; took his drink with him.

The audience roared their approval and Chaney paused, smiling, looking around him. He was in control. As always. Chaney sat down, the audience hushed. He took another drink, retched, but forced it down. Chaney turned his attention to the figure sitting opposite him. He saw the fear in his eyes and smiled softly. Sometime ago this would have been so difficult, but now... well, everyone has a weakness. Chaney nodded in recognition, felt his heartbeat quicken. The figure tried to change its shape, to escape, and Chaney laughed out loud at its fear. There could be no escape. It was time to begin. The glass slipped from his fingers. The figure was no more than a blur in front of him.

'Facing me tonight...'

Chaney slumped forward, his body falling to the floor beside Katherine. He emitted a long sigh and his right leg jerked once. The empty bottle in his right hand rolled slowly off his palm and onto the carpet, its label hidden from view.

In the gilt-edged mirror the reflection stared at the body as if at an enemy.

* * * * *

There had been no noise in the house for sometime now, and Soul inched cautiously from behind the settee.

A force he did not understand ruffled his fur, and Soul spun nervously to face it. There was an opening in the wall, by the place where he often sat. The man he knew best had made it. Soul had watched him from his hiding place.

The wind blew again, and this time Soul sniffed at it and moved towards the open window. The curtains danced wildly in the wind and Soul hesitated, waiting until he was sure they posed no threat. Then he leapt onto the sill and out into the grass beyond.

The ground was cold and soft, and Soul crouched low, letting the snow settle on him. A flake landed on his nose and Soul playfully attacked the next one that came near, grabbing at it with his paws. He continued the game for some time, leaping and twisting in the air, and then his sense of fun disappeared and was replaced by an inquisitiveness. Soul began to explore further.

He jumped onto the brick wall that surrounded the garden, and padded stealthily along it. In a house to his left, a downstairs light was switched on, and Soul immediately moved towards it, knowing that it represented warmth and shelter. In the silence he heard another noise, below to his right, as a rodent that had been scavenging around bins, scurried home. Soul sank low, possessed of an instinct he had never felt before. For a second he remained still. His body quivering. The light he had originally sought was only yards away.

And then he jumped.